ARROW'S
REST

ARROW'S REST

Joel Scott

Purchase the print edition
and receive the eBook free.
For details, go to ecwpress.com/eBook.

Published by ECW Press
665 Gerrard Street East
Toronto, Ontario, Canada M4M 1Y2
416-694-3348 / info@ecwpress.com

Cover design: Michel Vrana

This is a work of fiction. Names, characters,
places, and incidents either are the product of the
author's imagination or are used fictitiously, and
any resemblance to actual persons, living or dead,
business establishments, events, or locales is entirely
coincidental.

LIBRARY AND ARCHIVES CANADA CATALOGUING IN
PUBLICATION

Title: Arrow's rest / Joel Scott.

Names: Scott, Joel (Novelist), author.

Identifiers: Canadiana (print) 20200383345 |
Canadiana (ebook) 20200383388

ISBN 9781770415720 (softcover)
ISBN 9781773056968 (ePUB)
ISBN 9781773056975 (PDF)
ISBN 9781773056982 (Kindle)

Classification: LCC PS8637.C68617 A77 2021 | DDC
C813/.6—dc23

The publication of *Arrow's Rest* has been funded in part by the Government of Canada. *Ce livre est financé en partie par
le gouvernement du Canada.* We acknowledge the support of the Canada Council for the Arts. *Nous remercions le Conseil
des arts du Canada de son soutien.* We acknowledge the support of the Ontario Arts Council (OAC), an agency of the
Government of Ontario, which last year funded 1,965 individual artists and 1,152 organizations in 197 communities
across Ontario for a total of $51.9 million. We also acknowledge the support of the Government of Ontario through the
Ontario Book Publishing Tax Credit, and through Ontario Creates.

PRINTED AND BOUND IN CANADA

PRINTING: MARQUIS   5   4   3   2   1

PROLOGUE

The Prophet sat at his desk sorting through the mail that the girl had just brought in. Amy: thirteen years old and just budding out. She waited nervously by the door, conscious of the old man's gaze.

He opened the hand-addressed envelopes first; they'd hold the monthly tithes. Small amounts, sometime only one or two hundred dollars, but they added up. There were fewer of them every year now, but still enough to keep the commune going. He'd been worried after that last spate of bad publicity following the convictions, but to his surprise it had resulted in a large donation coming in from a fundamentalist group in Utah who believed his sect had been discriminated against. The unexpected windfall had allowed them to enlarge the barn and increase their dairy herd quota. *Mysterious ways*, the old man thought.

He signed some brief thank-you notes for some of the larger tithes, addressed their envelopes, and motioned Amy over. He held onto them for a moment as she took them and their hands touched and he smiled as she attempted to pull away. She'd be a spirited one. Another six months. Some things were worth waiting for. He released his grip on the letters, and the girl bolted for the door.

He turned to the rest of the day's post. There was the usual junk mail filled with false promises and things that no one needed, and the begging letters from people who thought the church was a soft touch, and, at the very bottom of the pile, the quarterly report from his local lawyers. A stiff greeting followed by some housekeeping couched in legalese he didn't fully understand but gathered meant that all was well. And then he saw the handwritten note from Ammon, the lawyer's clerk who'd been raised here in Plentiful.

Dear Jeremiah,

I hope this finds you well. I'm afraid I have some bad news. The firm received a phone call from an Abbotsford lawyer's office yesterday regarding a property that had been forwarding a large annual tithing cheque for deposit to the church account. The payment was cancelled by Elizabeth Kane from Abbotsford immediately prior to her decease and the subject property willed to her grandson, Jared Kane. The firm will be sending you a copy of the new will and associated documents by the end of the month, but I thought you'd want to know immediately.

Yours sincerely,
    Ammon

Jeremiah reread the note, blinking rapidly as his fury mounted. He could barely recall the woman, Betsy, a titmouse, but he remembered her husband well. A righteous true-believer who paid his tithes in good times and bad and had promised him his holding would be left to the church when he passed. Unconditionally. Jeremiah had been notified of his death and knew his widow was in poor health. He had been counting on the sale of their property. One last remaining quarter section of land was still held by an outsider in the heart of the church's holdings here in Plentiful, and the money from the Abbotsford farm was going to get it for him. He had boasted about getting that final piece of land, and his rivals would be quick to attack him if he didn't deliver. There were factions in the commune who resented him, chief among them the younger men who coveted the power and rights which were his due as the prophet. How in God's name had that frail old woman managed to spite him? She hadn't even raised her eyes from the floor of the old house the last time he'd made the rounds of his disciples.

And that reprobate she'd willed the property to? The old man had left his grandson with the commune one summer to school him in the ways, and he vaguely remembered a pale, insignificant youngster who didn't get along with the rest of the class and had required constant discipline. And hadn't one of his wives told him that he'd served time in jail a few years back? He was almost certain of it. And now he was just going to walk in and take the church's rightful property? This was not right. It could not stand!

But what to do? He couldn't risk seeking help from the council; his position could be in jeopardy if word leaked out about difficulties with the Abbotsford farm. They might even call for a leadership vote, and he wasn't a hundred percent sure he could survive that. He didn't have anybody in Vancouver he could call on with confidence. One of his wives thought she had seen Jimmy on TV giving a speech at some do in the city a while back, but he hadn't spoken to his son in decades, not since that East Texas whore had run from the commune with him and those boys of hers. It had been a bad business back then and he might have overreacted. But when Ella — that was her name, he suddenly recalled — had told him Jimmy was twice the man he was in bed, he'd gone crazy. Might have done some serious damage if her two boys hadn't jumped in.

Well, it was all water under the bridge now. At the time he'd thought good riddance to the lot and never tried to contact his son to patch things up. It wasn't what he did. But the boy had shown a lot of promise and could have been a big earner for the church. He had spoken a few times in the tent on the road that last summer and had got people up jumping and crying on their way to pulling out their chequebooks. Some of them had even called him the Preacher. He had the true gift. It sounded like he was doing pretty well for himself now, maybe it was time to give him a call and settle things between the two of them. They'd never gotten along back then, too much alike perhaps, but that was a long time ago and things had changed for both of them. Maybe his son could help him out here. Another possibility was the commune in Arizona that had taken the last two child brides. The cross-border trafficking charges arising from that had eventually been dismissed but there had been some hefty lawyers bills and a lot of bad publicity for Plentiful. His American counterpart Karl, a tall bearded man in a business suit with a cold smile and flinty eyes, had helped out with the legal costs and said he owed Jeremiah. Maybe now was the time to call in that debt.

His thoughts were interrupted as a cup of coffee was brought in and set down on the desk in front of him. It smelled delicious, as did its bearer, Lucy, the saucy young one with the knowing eyes. Perfume was forbidden in the commune, but there was a musky personal scent attached to her that stirred him. Every so often a girl came along who didn't fear him, maybe even looked forward to her initiation, and he felt that she might be one of these. He thought of them as his Delilahs, sent from God to test him. He didn't know which one he was looking forward to more, Amy or Lucy. Sugar or spice.

Jeremiah roused himself and began writing a letter, slowly and carefully printing each word and checking his spelling in the old dog-eared Webster's dictionary that sat on the corner of the desk. One of his many daughters would gladly have sent an email, but he didn't trust any one of them to keep silent. They were relentless gossips. He finished the letter and placed it in an envelope and copied out Karl's address from a business card he took from a drawer. He looked up and Lucy smiled and a thrill ran through him.

"Ask your mother to look up an address for me, will you, sweetheart? Jared Kane is the name, shouldn't be more than one of those. In Vancouver I understand. And fetch me some American postage."

CHAPTER 1

The man in the mask laboured on, his mind detached from his thick body as he toiled in long, swinging thrusts that slammed the woman's head into the teak headboard in a steady hammering rhythm of lust and pain. He had readied himself for her earlier that evening, his phone shut off and the messages all on hold as he punished his body relentlessly, lifting weights, running in place, doing push-ups and chin-ups, gasping and sweating until his veins popped blue and swollen and he had to stop for lack of breath and buildup of lactic acid.

When he was like this he could endure forever, the exercise and the alcohol and the drugs joined in an unholy communion that raised him above and beyond the labouring body that worked and sweated for the elusive orgasm that would release him into that semblance of normality he put on each day like a cloak.

Not yet though. Only a faint glimmering promise at the edge of his consciousness. Perhaps another ten minutes, perhaps another thirty, it made no matter. Like everything else in his life, it had to be struggled for. Nothing came easy. And if he ever even thought about it, that was the way it ought to be. In another place and time he was a respected man, but that person had left after the first bottle, and what remained was mindless appetite.

The woman lay with closed eyes and clenched fists, trembling with fear and exhaustion, hoping only for an end to it all. It seemed to have gone on for an eternity, a mindless mechanical coupling where his cruel, impersonal hands bent her body to grotesque shapes as he hunched and worked over her endlessly. She realized she no longer existed for the man: he was caught up in a private fantasy of which she was only an anonymous part, a receptacle, and any other would have served as well.

She tried once more to scream, but her voice was raw with fatigue and despair, and the unformed wail caught in her throat. She began to pray, long-unused phrases issuing unheard from her bruised lips as the agony compounded to a whole new level and she started to black out with the fierceness and terror of it all. It went on and on, and what remained of her sanity cast frantically about for escape and found it in the memory of a cloudless day, and she caught it to her and shrouded herself in the white glare of sails in the sun and the soft hiss of water sliding past a gleaming wooden hull.

CHAPTER 2

It was one of those perfect sailing days on the west coast of British Columbia, where the late summer winds can be as fickle and inconstant as the promises of its politicians. Cat stood at the rail, head thrown back, savouring the warm breeze as the autopilot guided *Arrow* along her track, beating hard and gaining every second on the chartered Hunter with its crew of novices flogging its sails a quarter mile to windward. They made a clumsy tack, oversteered, and then sailed too fine again, conscious of her swift overtaking.

She played it safe and headed off their stern another ten degrees before going below for a fresh bottle of water and a new layer of suntan oil. She had been on the bright water for five hours now and was nearing her limits. When she swung back up on deck a short minute later, the Hunter had tacked again in defiance of all racing tactics and common sense, and now appeared set to run her down. She swore savagely, punched in a tack and cast off the starboard sheets, hardened up again portside, and sailed away from them, her hands stinging from the sudden burn of lines.

It was another hour and a half to Montague Harbour, and God alone knew how many more idiots she'd meet out here. Most boats were sailed by men, and the sight of a slight redheaded woman single-handing a heavy old forty-six-foot wooden sailboat was guaranteed to send their testosterone into overdrive. Oftentimes the winds were so light that she was forced to ignore them as they passed her by, but every once in a long while there was sufficient breeze for the sweet old girl to spread her wings and fly, and she'd be goddamned if she'd forgo that pleasure because of some drunken morons. She wondered if they realized that *Arrow*'s heavy timbered frame could run their shiny plastic bathtub under her keel and not even require a trip to the boat-yard afterwards. She took an angry sip of her water and glanced behind her again.

The Hunter had lost interest in the uneven contest and was bearing off towards Salt Spring Island. Cat's good temper reasserted itself and she flipped them off as she reached down and clicked in a new course setting on the autopilot that took *Arrow* off the wind another twenty degrees and stood her up on her feet again. In two hours, they'd have the anchor down and the fresh caught salmon on the barbecue. Even this late in the season, Montague Harbour would be busy, but *Arrow* had more than enough chain to anchor out near the middle where they'd be alone. She sometimes wondered why she enjoyed solitude so much, unlike Lauren who was the social butterfly of the family.

Although she never raised the subject with her, Cat worried about her sister sometimes. She'd taken Lauren out on *Arrow* once, and while her sister had seemed to enjoy the grace and beauty of sailing, she'd begun to fret after the second day, already missing the glittering life of the city. She'd have to phone her soon, it had been too long since they'd had a good chat. Cat suspected she was involved with somebody again; her voice had had that excited, breathy, new-man lilt to it the last time they'd spoken.

No doubt she'd find out all about it soon enough, the giggling sexual confidences meant to shock her at the beginning and then, somewhere down the road, the teary post-mortem. Lauren had a knack for picking the wrong kind of man. *At least they had that much in common*, Cat thought with a wry smile.

The radio crackled into life down below, and through the static she thought she heard someone calling *Arrow*. She waited to see if Jared would answer, but he must still have been sleeping. After a final check around for traffic, Cat went down the companionway stairs and picked up the call.

CHAPTER 3

The big detective waited impatiently as the Coast Guard patched him through, scowling at the report lying on the scarred desk in front of him. It wasn't his case and Christ knew he had more than enough on his plate already, but he'd overheard the name of the boat and that was enough to get him involved. Clarke had always felt a little guilty about the two years Jared had spent in jail, as if he should have been able to do something about it at the time. In fact none of it was down to him; he'd only interviewed the witnesses and given his summary of what had taken place during the vicious fight, but still. He'd thought at the time it had been a raw deal for an eighteen-year-old kid.

Anyway, that had all happened a long time ago and they were friends now and he would do what he could. So he'd grabbed the file from Wilson and told him he'd take care of it. Clarke was just months away from retirement and knew enough and was mean enough to pretty much do whatever he bloody well wanted. To prove the point he took out a cigar and lit it with a match dragged ostentatiously across the top of his desk and felt immediately better. He didn't need to inhale; his high was in the white lipped glare of his lieutenant seated across the room beneath the no smoking sign.

"Coast Guard, this is *Arrow*."

A woman's voice, it must be her.

"Is that Caitlin Campbell?"

"Yes."

"This is Detective Clarke from Vancouver. I need to speak with you. Can you call me back on a private line? As soon as possible please." He gave her the station number.

"I didn't bring my cell phone on the boat. It will be at least a couple of hours until I can get to a land line. What is this all about anyway?"

"Extension three please. I'll be waiting. Say hi to Jared for me."

Clarke put the phone down and picked up the report and read it through one more time.

The woman had been found lying on a bench in Stanley Park early Saturday morning. At first glance the patrolman assumed she was a street person sleeping off a high, but then he noticed the expensive clothes and the bloodstains and called in for an ambulance. They rushed her to West Van emergency where she received a transfusion and was treated for shock. She'd lost a significant amount of blood, and there were internal injuries that required immediate attention followed by some hospital time, but the doctor said Ms. Campbell was expected to make a full recovery. She was in intensive care at the moment, sedated, and unable to give a full statement. Maybe in another couple of days.

The doctor said it was one of the more extreme cases of sexual assault she'd dealt with, and the battering the victim received had caused severe internal bruising. She thought that foreign objects might have been inserted into her, although she had found no direct evidence of them. Just her considered opinion that a penis could not have inflicted that much damage.

There was a small hand purse in the pocket of her jacket containing her driver's licence and credit cards, and an organ donor card with her next of kin. Caitlin Campbell's roommate said she was out for the weekend on a sailboat with a friend. The name of the sailboat was *Arrow*, and Clarke knew the friend had to be Jared Kane.

Clarke rolled the cigar around his lips and blew smoke rings across the room and thought about life's coincidences while he waited for the call back from Lauren Campbell's sister. Trust Jared to get caught up in something like this. For a man who tried to keep his life simple, he had an uncanny knack for attracting trouble.

CHAPTER 4

Cat slammed the radiophone down and went across to the main cabin and jerked open the door. As it swung back and resonated against the bulkhead Jared shot bolt upright, blinking the sleep out of his eyes. He glanced at his watch and then at the small woman standing there, glaring at him, arms akimbo.

"Hi. Good nap that, guess I must have needed it."

In retrospect, he thought he might have overserved himself with wine at lunch.

"Who the hell is Clarke, and what does he want with me?"

"Clarke? You mean the detective?"

He'd never told Cat about the big man and their unlikely friendship, it had never come up. There were a few things about him that had never come up between the two of them, he reflected, but then they'd only been going together for a few months. He'd learned over the years to release his confidences sparingly, letting each be absorbed to build up tolerance before progressing to the next one, like increasingly strong doses of medicine.

"Yes. That would be the one. He called *Arrow* on the VHF, wants me to get in touch with him. ASAP. Asked me to say hi to you."

The level grey eyes bored into his. They were one of the first things that had attracted him to her. That and the way she handled herself, the prickly standoff exterior and sardonic tongue that masked her generous nature. She had a strong moral streak at the core of her that Jared was wary of, echoes of the old school Puritanism he himself had been schooled in. In theory he supposed a warm, fun-loving Mediterranean type would suit him better, but in practice he was mostly attracted by the difficult ones. The more Jared got to know Cat, the more he realized just how difficult she was.

"We're friends. Maybe he called up to warn you about me," he said in a feeble attempt at jocularity.

"Whatever it is sounded serious."

Jared said, "I guess you should have brought your cell phone along."

He had finally succumbed to the nagging of his friends and bought one, but rarely turned it on. At the moment it was lying mute in the drawer under the chart table. If he'd been at the helm, the VHF would have been shut off as well, and they wouldn't have been bothered.

"Sod that. This is my getaway time. Those bastards would never leave me alone."

She was, of all things, a fashion photographer. A very successful one, it turned out. It was so at odds with her character, being associated with such a lightweight profession, that Jared had assumed she was joking and made the mistake of laughing when she first told him. He'd have bet money that she was in one of the serving professions; a doctor, a teacher, a feminist lawyer, something along those lines. She'd coloured fiercely, the bright spots glowing above her cheekbones as she snapped back at him about part-time seasonal fishermen criticizing the work of real people with real jobs.

It was at their first meeting, although encounter might have been a better word, and she'd never brought up her career again. She was busy and successful by all accounts, but had no connections with that world outside of her working hours. Jared sometimes wondered if her relationship with him was simply an anti-fashion statement.

He went to the sink, splashed water on his face, and went out on deck. They were nearly across Georgia Strait now. Three miles ahead he saw the break between the islands that was Porlier Pass. The current had set them a little north, and he shut off the autopilot, picked up the tiller, and steered *Arrow* onto her proper course. The wind moved aft of the beam on the new track, and he debated setting the mizzen staysail to pick up a little extra speed but decided it wasn't worth the effort. There were no boats around to contend with at the moment, and *Arrow* had nothing left to prove to him. Cat sailed *Arrow* fiercely when the wind was up, but he preferred to glide easily along. Some people might say their sailing styles kind of summed up their differing philosophies of life, he reflected.

He wondered what Clarke wanted with Cat and felt a twinge of unease. It damn sure wouldn't be good news, of that he was certain.

CHAPTER 5

"Good to see you, Jared. It's been awhile."

The big detective might have been wearing the same clothes he'd been in the first time Jared had seen him in court all those years ago. A wrinkled brown suit hung on his bear-like frame, and a crushed hat was tipped back on the bald head over the creased face with the potato nose. Clarke realized he presented as something of a caricature and cultivated the image to his advantage. He was a lot smarter than he looked. He rose clumsily to his feet and shoved a chair towards Cat while extending a large white hand to Jared.

Shortly after Clarke had hung up on his call to *Arrow*, Cat had been on Jared's phone trying to get hold of her sister. When she kept getting the recorded message, she began calling their mutual friends. With all her connections in the media world, it didn't take Cat long to find out what had happened. She'd had a floatplane chartered and waiting for them when they pulled into Montague Harbour.

"So what can you tell me?" Cat inquired, never one for small talk. "I've been to see Lauren, but she was pretty much out of it with all the painkillers they're giving her. Doesn't remember much about the evening after the public breakup with her boyfriend. She's not even certain which nightclub they had the fight in."

"We've checked out the boyfriend," Clarke said. "His alibi seems to stand up. He took a cab home after the incident and we've got him on video entering his apartment building in the right time frame. Some of the witnesses we've interviewed said your sister was angry and drinking heavily after he left her at the club."

"So then it's probably all her fault," Cat said.

"No, not at all. That's not what I meant," Clarke said. "It's just that her recollections of the evening might not help us much. We think she may have been drugged at some point."

"Drugged!"

"Yes, probably one of the roofies. No way to tell when it was administered, but likely put into her drink at one of the clubs. We've showed her picture around, and some of the staff remembered her." Clarke paused to choose his words. "It seems she was quite noticeable," he said carefully.

Cat's nostrils flared and two bright spots of colour appeared on her cheeks, but she remained silent.

"No doubt you've checked the security videos. Do you have her leaving with anybody?" Jared asked.

"We've had somebody on that. The club that we think was probably her last stop has a video camera above the entrance. We can see her entering with a man, not a great picture, but probably her boyfriend. So far we can't spot her leaving the place. There's a lot of traffic going in and out of the club over the course of an evening, sometimes rowdy groups mixing and jostling in both directions, so it's possible we could have missed her. I've got people taking a second look."

"Maybe we could help, canvass the clubs, talk to some of the regulars," Cat said. "Sometimes people don't feel comfortable with the police. Whereas with us—"

"That's a really bad idea," Clarke interrupted. He was talking to Cat, but looking at Jared. "We don't want to see someone else getting hurt. Leave this to the police."

"Why would anybody get hurt?" Jared said. "You'd think the last thing the clubs would want is to be connected with some asshole that is drugging and assaulting women. They ought to be offering us free drinks for trying to find out who he is."

Clarke looked uncomfortable. "Well, the truth is there have been other cases similar to Ms. Campbell's. We've managed to keep that information under wraps so far, but I've been told there's a story breaking on the news tonight that has most of the details about the previous incidents. Women drugged and brutally attacked before being dumped on West End park benches in the middle of the night. All of the victims are similar types: successful women with good jobs who are fairly well off. High-end, if you will. It's an unusual profile for this category of case and it's going to attract a lot of media attention. It's more the type of thing we see happening with sex workers, or, less often, street people. Basically the more vulnerable members of society." Clarke paused.

"And?" Jared said.

Clarke said, "And one victim's family went out and hired a private investigator. Well known to the department and a decent enough fellow as those types go. The woman in question had also been doing the nightclub scene when she was taken, and he went around to the ones she remembered and made some inquiries. A week into his investigation he was attacked by two men with baseball bats and ended up with cracked ribs and a broken leg. When we interviewed him, he said he didn't recognize his assailants." Clarke shook his head. "But I think he was lying. He spent ten days in hospital and another half dozen in rehab before he left town. Word on the street is he received a payoff and is recovering somewhere down in Mexico at the moment. The carrot and the stick is my guess, and that makes the whole thing that much more unusual. We've contacted the authorities down south to try and find this PI, but I'm not holding my breath."

"What the hell does all that mean?" Cat said.

"My guess," Jared said, "is that it means these aren't isolated incidents, they're being done by some rich asshole for kicks, and they're probably not going to stop."

"Is that what you think, Detective?" Cat asked.

Clarke shrugged. "Maybe. Anything is possible, and we can't rule it out at this stage. On the other hand it could just be your everyday psycho ratcheting things up a notch. It is certainly somebody very dangerous in any case. Definitely not a person you want to mess with, Jared."

"I'll bear that in mind," Jared said. He stood up. "So then, are you going to give me the names of the clubs, or am I going to have to go on a drinking tour to find them out?"

Clarke sighed and reached down onto his desk and threw across a piece of paper with scribbling on it. "Those are the three places that Ms. Campbell and her boyfriend visited that we know about for certain. It's quite possible there could be more. We're still showing her picture around and looking for potential witnesses. The last club they stopped at, to the best of our knowledge, was the Sergeant at Arms."

"I know it well," Jared said.

CHAPTER 6

"What do you mean I'm not coming? I damn well am." Cat stood with hands on hips, head bent towards Jared, her colour up, grey eyes flashing. Sometimes she reminded him of Katharine Hepburn in one of her skirmishes with Spencer Tracy in an old black-and-white movie. Cat's lips a little lusher maybe, although thinned right out at the moment.

The first time he'd seen her she had looked just like this, standing outside the East End food bank where she volunteered one night a week. She was giving it to three tough-looking teenagers who were set to rip off an old homeless guy's groceries. Jared crossed the street and stood alongside her, and the lads decided it wasn't worth the trouble. Cat thanked him when they left but assured him that she could take care of herself; she carried bear spray and took a martial arts class in self-defence. Jared said he was sure of it, but suggested his presence might at least have saved her from scuffing up her clothes. After carefully checking him for irony, she let Jared buy her a drink. One thing led to another, and to their mutual surprise they became a couple.

Arrow proved to be the deal maker. Cat had done some racing on a stripped-out thirty-six-foot Jeanneau at the Vancouver Rowing Club and fell in love with the old wooden sailboat's history and charm the first time she went on board. She found it hard to believe that such a beautiful old boat had been gifted to Jared by an elderly couple, out of the blue and for no good reason whatsoever, from what he'd told her. Sometimes when they were out sailing he caught her studying him sidelong, as if searching for some hidden merit that would warrant such a spectacular legacy.

"I am not worthy," he'd said once, surprising her in her scrutiny, and she'd blushed to her roots.

Now she stood looking at him, a grim expression on her face. "Well, are you going to answer me?" Cat demanded. "You think I can't handle it?"

"Nothing at all to do with that, I just think it's a really bad idea to put yourself out there. This is a vicious man who came damned close to killing your sister by all accounts. It wouldn't be that difficult for him to find out who you are. If Clarke is right, this is not a one-time incident where someone got carried away on an impulse, but a regular happening by a well-organized serial rapist. The police don't appear to have any leads, which suggests he's smart and he's careful." He knew she didn't like what he was saying, but he continued. "On top of that, he's thumbing his nose at them with the park bench thing. So part of the thrill seems to be the risks involved, and that makes him that much more dangerous to you personally. Two victims from the same family would be a real coup for someone who thinks like that. It could even be someone working in one of the clubs who could pick up on you asking questions. Why would you want to take that chance?"

Cat said, "Because Lauren is my sister and I love her and I owe it to her? Deal with it, Jared. This is totally my business. Your detective friend seemed sincere, and I'm sure he has good intentions, but I doubt Lauren is going to be high on the police department's list of priorities. There are a couple of gang wars playing out at the moment, never mind when a woman is out partying on her own there's always that 'Well, what the hell did she expect?' thing."

"That might be true sometimes for the media and defence lawyers, but not for Clarke. He is damned good at his job, and I guarantee he will do everything in his power to find the person responsible for your sister's attack."

"I'm sure you're right. He did seem very decent, and I kind of liked him." Cat paused. "So then, Jared, are you coming with me, or am I going clubbing all by myself?"

"I'll just grab a quick shower," Jared said.

❀

The Sergeant at Arms served two distinct clienteles. The business lunch trade that wanted good food and drink at a reasonable cost in a quiet setting, and the night trade when they ratcheted up the music and the prices, threw in a band or local celebrity to DJ, and blew the doors off. It was one of the nightspots favoured by the local shakers and movers in the Vancouver real estate and stock markets, and even the bouncers wore suits and ties and were polite.

Jared recognized one of them from the marina where *Arrow* was berthed, a gillnet fisherman earning some extra cash between trips, and they exchanged polite nods. Cat nudged him and gestured upwards as they passed under the high entrance canopy, and he saw the camera pointed down at them as they went in. The detectives had been told there was no surveillance inside, but Clarke acknowledged that they had probably been misled on the subject. It would be highly unusual if there was not at least one camera behind the bar, overlooking the servers as they rang up their tallies.

Danny was seated at a table in the far corner, talking with one of the hostesses. He looked up and waved them over. He had a pint waiting for Jared and a bottle of overpriced Pinot Noir for Cat.

"I didn't realize you were joining us," Cat said with a pleased smile as she bumped fists with him before giving him a hug.

"Well, somebody has to watch out for the little guy," Danny said.

"No telling what kind of trouble he might get into on his own." He winked at Cat and raised his pint. "Cheers."

Jared raised his mug in response and studied Danny over the rim. Five years his senior, he was his oldest friend in the city and had changed little in the years since they'd first met in the police van delivering them both to prison. Danny had been released a month before him, and when Jared's time was up Danny was waiting at the gates and took him home to the spare room in his family's house in the East End. Within a month Jared was closer to the First Nations family than to the austere remnants of his own. That was over a dozen years ago now, and he hadn't been in touch with his grandparents since he left their house for the last time on his way to prison. It was the way they all wanted it.

Danny was a little heavier now than when they first met, and had maybe a thread of silver showing here and there in his thick black hair, but he still moved like warm grease and was as dangerous a man as you could hope to find. With a Scots father and First Nations mother he was light complexioned and sometimes taken for Asian in the cosmopolitan city of Vancouver. But his loyalties ran deep, and in some ways he was more traditional than even his Haida brothers. Family was always first in Danny's book.

"How is your sister doing?" he asked Cat.

"Better, I think. She still doesn't remember much of anything though. Not surprising, I guess, given what she's been through. She does remember hearing a constant noise. Like an engine running in the background. And loud music playing the whole time; opera, she thinks, although she's not really sure of anything, she was in and out of consciousness. Maybe from the drugs Clarke mentioned, as well as the viciousness of the assault itself. Bastards. We have to find them. Have you heard anything?"

"Nothing worth mentioning as yet. I've put the word around, but it's still early days," Danny said. "I've spoken with Clarke; it seems damned strange about the drop-offs on the benches around Stanley Park. Why make such an obvious connection between the incidents?

Unless it's just pure arrogance and whoever it is figures he's above it all and can't be touched. That would certainly go along with this crowd. Check out all the high rollers in here. I'm amazed that they even let you through the door, Jared."

"C'mon," Jared said. "They let in Indians, for Christ's sake."

"Jared!" Cat said in a shocked voice. She still didn't get the two of them sometimes . . .

"My bad. I should have said First Nations."

"Well, there is that," Danny said. He turned to Cat. "I need a recent picture of your sister, something I can show around, and maybe a few others to hand out as well. The more information we put out there, the better our chances of finding something out."

"I printed a bunch up," Cat said. She pulled some photos out of her purse and laid them on the table. Danny picked one up and studied it.

"Pretty lady," he said. "Beautiful even. People will remember her. I know the manager here; I'll talk to him and find out who was on duty that night. Maybe he saw something he didn't tell the police. Sometimes people don't want to get involved. Then there's the video from that night to check."

"Clarke told us the police have already done that," Cat said.

"Yes, but I'll lay odds they didn't see the inside surveillance. The video the club will swear on stacked bibles they don't have because that would be an infringement of their patrons' privacy. That lead I mentioned?" Danny leaned towards them and dropped his voice. "Erin's son has a friend who sometimes helps out behind the bar on busy nights and does early cleanup the following morning. She's coming in later on tonight and he says she's okay about talking with us. In the meantime let's have a few drinks, do some crowd watching."

It was a typical midweek bar scene with couples chatting comfortably at tables and most of the singles lined up along the bar and regularly changing places in a shifting complex social pattern. If you watched closely enough, you could see the winners and the losers, the acceptance and rejection, and the studied casualness that overlaid the desperation of it all. The music was loud and catchy, the flash of teeth was everywhere, and none of it seemed much like fun.

"God, it's all so depressing," Cat said after a while.

"Even Jared must look pretty good to you compared to that sad shuffle," Danny said, nodding towards the bar.

"Let's not get carried away," Cat said.

"Screw the pair of you," Jared said amiably.

Cat smiled and put her hand over his. "Never mind, luv, another few drinks and I'm sure you'll look just fine. I might even let you take me home if you get me drunk enough. Oh bugger, here comes some of the studio crowd."

A half dozen overdressed people swept up to the table and grabbed Cat up in a blizzard of hugs and kisses. A small exquisite blonde stood apart from them, frowning at the scrum. She looked slightly familiar, and Jared thought he had seen her picture somewhere. She couldn't possibly be over fifteen years old, and he doubted she weighed ninety pounds. The gamine was dressed in a matelot sweater, white slacks, and a pair of distressed combat boots. Given the company she was with, he didn't doubt her outfit had cost more than his entire wardrobe.

"What the fuck are you staring at, mate," the urchin uttered in a nasal Kiwi accent.

"Sorry," Jared said, startled. "I was wondering how you managed to sneak into the club."

"I'm plenty old enough, sport. You one of those pervs that likes the young ones then, are ya? Not in your wildest dreams, you sick bastard. You fancy a quick kick in the goolies then?" She shuffled her booted feet.

Jesus Christ.

The words coming out of that angelic countenance were so incongruous he was almost speechless. "I'm with Cat," Jared stammered.

"Oh, you're the one with the old wooden sailboat," she said, her expression changing. She grabbed Jared's arm and pulled up a chair beside him. "Sorry about that, mate. Since that last photo shoot every weirdo in the fucking universe wants a piece of me. You wouldn't believe the stuff

I hear from some of the assholes out there. I've even got a minder now. Me, Sally Owens for fuck sake. My mates back home would die laughing if they knew."

The big scarred man with the buzz cut who'd been staring at Jared winked.

"You race her then? Did a lot of that back home on the Fourteens. I was damn good too. You should take me out on her sometime. I'm a winner." She patted Jared's shoulder, grinned, and looked even younger. "I'll be sure to clear it with Cat first." She downed her drink and stood up and grabbed her bodyguard's arm.

"C'mon, you ugly mother, dance with me. You're making everybody else too scared."

Jared turned back to the table and met Cat's amused look.

"She's something, isn't she?" she said.

"No kidding."

"Just nineteen years old, and if I told you what she makes for a single day's fashion shoot, you wouldn't believe it."

"Oh she's the absolute tops," the man in the plaid vest said. The group accompanying Sally had pulled up a table alongside them and settled in with assorted colourful drinks with miniature umbrellas.

"I'll bet she gets twenty covers this year," the rake-thin purple-haired woman under the beret said to Danny.

"Wow," Danny said, not having a clue.

"Never mind that when the *Vogue* interview comes out she'll be swamped by even more offers," granny glasses uttered solemnly.

"Double wow," Jared said.

The conversation stalled.

"So," Danny said, "the husband comes through the kitchen door, slams it shut behind him, the wife looks up and he's cradling a sheep in his arms. And he says, 'See the pig I'm with when I'm not with you?'"

Cat hung her head.

"And the wife says, 'That's not a pig, you pathetic imbecile, it's a sheep,'" Jared contributed.

"And the husband says, 'I wasn't—'" Cat's glass suddenly tipped and red wine spilled everywhere. Shrieks and scrambling, frantic dabbing and apologies, and the visitors got up and left mumbling about places to go and people to meet.

Cat frowned. "Under the circumstances, I suppose I have to forgive the pair of you," she said. "Now let's try and look like we're having fun."

❀

Two hours later, nothing had changed except the size of the crowd and the level of the noise. The dance floor was packed with gyrating bodies, and you had to shout to be heard above the din. Masked men could have pulled little brown bottles embossed with skulls and crossbones out of their pockets and poured them into glasses and it would have been difficult to detect in the melee. Dancers were bumping into tables, drinks were spilling, and two fights had been broken up by the smoothly efficient bouncers. Cat had been scooped up by another friend from her workplace and was now out on the floor and part of it all.

"Now I remember why I avoid these places," Jared said.

"You have to work at it harder, drink more and get into the spirit of it," Danny said. He was downing two drinks to Jared's one and looked exactly the same as always. Drink never affected him the way it did most people.

"I am trying, really, but I'm just getting a headache."

"Uh-oh, brace yourself. Here comes the conga line back again. And this time Cat is leading it."

Jared leapt to his feet, and started for the men's room when he was picked up from behind, turned around, and propelled forward.

"You treacherous bastard," he hissed.

"Reconnaissance, old buddy," Danny said. "Swing those skinny hips, you tight-assed little whitey."

CHAPTER 7

Jared opened his eyes and gazed about the room, disoriented for a moment before the evening came flooding back and he remembered he was at Cat's apartment. It had been a late evening; a pretty good one, considering. He could remember almost all of it. Somehow he'd gotten into drinking shots of tequila one-for-one with Danny, a contest he was never going to win. They'd gone to Chinatown for food after quitting the Sergeant at Arms and arrived back at Cat's flat in the early hours of the morning.

As far as gathering information about the attacks on the West End women, which was the main purpose of their night out, the evening was less successful. Danny had talked to his nephew's friend Raina over the course of the evening, and she told him she thought she might have seen one of the other women who had been assaulted in the club. She hadn't told the police when they showed her the pictures of the other victims at her interview because she wasn't one hundred percent sure. It wasn't much of a lead, given that the Sergeant at Arms was the most popular nightspot in that part of town, but Danny said he'd follow up with Clarke and see if the department had looked at tapes from the Sergeant at Arms for any of the earlier incidents involving the other victims. He promised to keep Raina's name out of it.

Jared considered getting up, but he could hear Cat was still in the shower and decided to grab a few more winks. He closed his eyes and settled in under the blankets. The apartment door slammed and the next moment he was lying naked, scrabbling for covers.

"Up and at 'em, partner. There's work to be done. I've brought coffee."

Danny. The son of a bitch didn't know what a hangover was. Jared sat up cursing and pulled on a pair of sweatpants.

"Keep your voice down, for God's sake," Cat growled, emerging from the bathroom in a robe with a towel wrapped around her hair. Among the many things that endeared Cat to Jared was the fact that her morning-afters were almost as rough as his.

"Ah, the lovebirds are a little tetchy this morning, huh? Here, coffee for you as well, my dear. I've got some video for us to watch."

He took a flash drive from his pocket and set it down beside the laptop on the coffee table.

"Easiest thing in the world. Raina goes in at six this morning to clean up and run the glasses through the dishwasher; she's by herself for the first couple of hours before the regular staff checks in. Turns out the manager runs a hidden cam behind the bar panning the crowd during open hours. Nothing sinister about it, just insurance if someone gets naughty and accuses the bouncers of being overzealous, or the wrong ass gets pinched and the word *sue* is mentioned. Plus it also helps to keep the bartenders and waitresses honest. The club keeps the files for thirty days and then deletes them."

Cat said, "Not the sort of thing you want your patrons hearing about, I should imagine. Nobody likes to learn there's a record out there of them being overserved, so to speak."

Danny nodded in agreement. "When Raina went in this morning the first thing she did was copy the files and phone me, and I dropped by and picked them up. Easy peasy."

"I've got a shoot downtown in an hour, I'll have to take a rain check," Cat said.

"Fifteen minutes," Jared said, grabbing his coffee and heading for the shower.

When he emerged a few minutes later, Danny was sprawled on the couch watching the news. He switched off the TV as Jared sat down beside him and plugged the flash drive into the laptop. They watched in silence as the evening unfolded before them.

✼

"I'm glad Cat isn't here," Jared said a few minutes later. "This would have been tough for her to see."

"Yes."

It had been surprisingly easy to find. Each night was in a separate file organized by date. Fast-forwarding in one hour on the night in question, there she was in high definition and colour. She was unmistakeable, both for her beauty and the rage that consumed her. It was eerie; you'd see her for a few seconds and then the camera would pan away across the room before it swung back across. You saw the hand drawn back for the slap, and then the boyfriend leaning across the table snarling at her, and then the thrown drink. And then a steady series of drinks and men coming and going in jerky frames. Self-pity merging into self-hatred in abbreviated three-second vignettes. After a couple of hours she was drunk, pirouetting around the dance floor, bumping into people, rubbing herself against other dancers. And then back to the table for more drinks and more men. They were coarser and bolder now. Assholes she wouldn't have let within twenty feet of her sober were cozying up and trying their luck.

"Hard to watch, all right," Danny said. "Whoa. Right there."

Two men, middle-aged, dressed in windbreakers and slacks. One holding her hands and talking while the other one reached into his pocket.

"There. Something put into her drink for sure. You can see him tear the packet and then it's back in his pocket." They backed it up and played it again in slow motion.

Jared said, "You notice anything unusual about those guys? Apart from their clothes?"

"They don't have any drinks on the table. Guys always bring their drinks with them when they're hustling. It's like they just came in and haven't ordered yet."

"You're right, but apart from that. They're out of place, a little too old, not dressed for the club scene. And look at those haircuts. They were out of style twenty years ago. I'll put it up on the TV, get a better look."

Jared pointed at the big screen. "See those tan lines? They look like the farm kids I grew up with in Abbotsford. White forehead and back of the neck, forearms brown as leather. The town kids called it farmer's tan when they were joshing the hicks. It comes from being out in the sun all the time with a wide-brimmed hat. With ball caps, the back of the neck gets tanned."

"Could be that. Could be a lot of other things, Sherlock," Danny said. "Loggers, fishermen, there's a dozen different trades that fit."

"The thing is their foreheads and the back of their necks were so white because they all wore fedoras. Usually grey or brown. Brims all the way around. You know, Frank Sinatra hats."

"I know what a fedora is," Danny said.

"Damnedest thing you ever saw, all those churchgoers coming down the steps in their fedoras and brown and black suits. Probably ball caps were too homeboy for them, now that I think about it. Cowboy hats might have been too racy."

They watched the cam for another few minutes, and Jared winced as Lauren's head began to sag and she was clearly on the verge of passing out. The two men bent towards her and grabbed her under the arms and moved off, threading their way through the crowded dance floor, disappearing and reappearing in three-second fragments.

"Okay, one fifteen," Jared said. "Put on the canopy tape."

They ran the second tape forward and stopped.

"There."

Two men supporting a woman with a flowered kerchief over her hair moving out from under the canopy towards the curb. They were clearly aware of the overhead surveillance camera, their heads under the hats bowed right down.

Danny said, "You might be right about the hats, Jared. Could also be Stetsons, though, it's hard to tell from this angle. But there was nothing cowboy about the windbreakers, so I'm going to grant you the fedoras. And then there are the clunky black boots they're wearing. If you wear the cowboy hat, you wear the cowboy boots, guaranteed. One hundred percent. The shirts with the little arrows stitched over the pockets are more optional, in my opinion. And that would be your babushka covering Lauren's head."

"Yes. Not something Lauren would ever wear. By all accounts she's a high-fashion lady. So we can assume the men brought it with them to get cover from the outdoor cam on their way back out with a woman."

"Probably not your spur-of-the-moment psychos then."

"No. That would make them more like professional collectors."

The exterior video showed a cab pulling up to the curb, Cat's sister getting into the back seat with the two men, and driving off. A cartoonish picture of a smiling man with arm outstretched for a handshake on the door — the Courtesy Cabs logo.

"Can't see the licence plate, but it should be easy enough to find out where it dropped them off. Good thing it wasn't an Uber." Jared pulled out the yellow pages and ran his hand down the columns. "Here we go, Courtesy has their office on East Hastings just past Main. A brisk fifteen-minute walk from here."

"First let's see if we can spot them entering the club."

They spent a half hour searching back and forth through the video, but couldn't pick out the two men on their way in.

"The hell with it. Let's hit the taxicab company." Danny stood up to leave.

"Perhaps a quick Caesar to dull the sunshine before we head out." Jared said.

CHAPTER 8

It was a beautiful late autumn day with a perfect fifteen-knot sailing breeze out of the west and Jared wondered why in the hell he didn't just phone Clarke and pass on what they'd learned from the videos. Let the big detective handle it from here on in. That was what the police were paid for, and Clarke was very good at his job. Jared figured he and Danny could have *Arrow* out and sailing in Georgia Strait in under an hour if they hustled. But he knew his friend would never let the matter drop, no matter what he might say. He would absolutely agree with every reason produced for non-involvement, solemnly swear to Jared on a stack of bibles to stay clear of the matter, and then he would press on regardless. That was who Danny was. He'd never met Lauren, but her relationship to Jared through Cat made her family. In Danny's world, family took care of family. Period. End of discussion.

Jared sighed and followed Danny along the street until they came to the underground parking station and adjacent office that housed the taxi operation. The premises were bright and clean, and a smiling secretary ushered them through to the back office where a harassed man was giving and receiving instruction over the phone. Dots were moving slowly across a grid map on the screen in front of him. It seemed safe to assume the lit ones were carrying fares.

The dispatcher was not helpful. He said that the taxi logs were private and they would need a warrant in order to see them. He was sorry, he would really like to help them out, but surely they could understand it was impossible. It was an issue of trust and confidentiality between the business and the client. Their request was highly improper and perhaps even against the law.

The dispatcher was a big man of Middle Eastern heritage, and clearly relishing this opportunity to exert his authority. Jared pulled a fifty-dollar bill out of his wallet and laid it on the desktop.

The man brushed it onto the floor and said, "I'm not bought that easily."

Jared flushed and was halfway around the desk before Danny collared him and dragged him back. The dispatcher reached down and pressed a button under the desk and two more men appeared from the back. Large men. They came and stood on each side of the desk, arms folded across their chests.

Danny held up his hands. "No need to get excited here," he said. He reached into his pocket and brought out a card and handed it to the dispatcher.

"That's Detective Clarke. Feel free to phone him and ask about the two of us. Danny MacLean and Jared Kane. He'll vouch for me and my partner, and he'll want to come down here with a warrant and a subpoena for the records and then you'll be on his radar."

"Maybe not the best idea," Jared added.

Danny said, "On the other hand, I could give you another fifty dollars and you could show us the driver's log for the night in question. We just want to check the one entry, we have the date and time of the pick-up already, no big deal. We just need to see where the cab dropped its passengers off. A couple of guys were a little rough with my sister, and we'd like to have a chat with them."

One of the men leaned down and whispered into the dispatcher's ear and he nodded his head.

"Family is important," the dispatcher said. "Fifty for each of us."

❋

Jared said, "I was hoping for a house, or even an apartment at worst."

The two men were standing in front of the locked steel gate of the Queens Own Yacht Club gazing at the hundreds of boats moored inside along the fingers.

"Looking on the bright side," Jared continued, "at least we know they must have gone in here. There are no other buildings within three hundred yards in either direction, and they wouldn't have wanted to drag a woman along the waterfront at that time of night. They'd want to get her off the street as quickly as possible before they were seen. Plus, we're in the heart of the West End, and Lauren was laid out on that park bench not half a mile from where we are standing. So the attack in all likelihood happened on the other side of this gate. Inside the yacht club." Jared paused. "You know, Lauren told Cat she thought she heard an engine running steadily in the background. That could have been a boat engine or even an onboard generator, which would make sense if she was on a big boat. Some of the larger ones can't tap enough power from the shore hook-ups and have to generate their own."

Danny said, "I'm just a poor fisherman, you're the guy with the yacht, so what's the deal here? Are any live-aboards allowed?"

"I don't know for sure, but I'd guess there are probably a few allowed for security reasons. It helps to cut down on the casual theft. Thieves will come into the marina in small boats or inflatables, cruise the docks, pick a boat, pop the companionway padlock, and do a quick in-and-out. It's hard to stop that kind of crime altogether, but people living and sleeping inside the marina certainly helps. They would know who belongs there and who doesn't." Jared looked up at the gate entrance. "I don't see any surveillance cameras here. I'm sure there will be some out on the docks to catch the incoming boats, but given that our lot came by taxi, they won't help us."

Jared paused and pulled out his wallet and began flicking through cards as an elderly man in cargo shorts and a Tilley cap strode briskly down the docks towards the gate.

"Thanks, mate," Jared said, catching the gate on its backswing and holding it for Danny as they passed through. "I know the damn card is in here somewhere. Seen Alfie around today?"

"Haven't spotted him," the man replied.

"Who's Alfie?" Danny asked as they moved along the walkway past the first finger of moored boats.

"Damned if I know. It's a big club and the geezers don't like to admit they can't remember. The visitors dock is down at the far end. Small chance our guys are tied up there, but seeing as we're here we might as well have a walkabout. You never know."

"If I see anybody in a fedora, I'll crouch down and track them," Danny said. "I should have brought along moccasins."

The marina had five main docks running from the street side out to the deeper water where the overnight moorage for visiting boats was located. Smaller fingers extended out from the main docks, ranging from twenty-five-foot slips in the shoal end up to sixty-foot slips out where the larger boats were located. Jared knew the club had a five-year waiting list for the smaller berths and a considerably longer period of time for the larger slips and boathouses. When he'd brought *Arrow* back home to Vancouver he'd inquired about moorage at the various yacht clubs in the lower mainland. They were all booked for the foreseeable future and he'd ended up in the commercial basin with the fishing boats in one of the slips they allotted for live-aboards. In retrospect it was a more suitable location for *Arrow*. Jared knew some of the fishermen and nobody ever objected to a noisy gathering aboard a boat in the basin.

"Hey, how you doing, long time no see. You're looking great," Danny said, as he enthusiastically pumped the hand of a codger who was carefully polishing the large stainless-steel anchor on the bow of his boat.

"Don't overdo it," Jared said as they moved along.

"You've got reciprocal privileges here, right?"

"As a matter of fact I believe I do."

Danny said, "So we could moor *Arrow* here for a couple of days if we wanted to?"

"Yep. We might even be able to stay for a week or two if we pushed a little. They'd probably put us in one of the vacant slips where the member's off cruising."

"That could be worth considering. It would give us time to check things out," Danny said, as they made their way down the main dock. "You never know, we might get lucky. At the very least we'd be doing something. And I hear yacht club bars serve cheap drinks."

The visitors dock was bustling with boats, most of them American flagged. Dinghies were heading out into the bay towards the downtown Vancouver shopping district, while others were returning loaded to the gunwales with goods.

"Welcome to the Third World," Danny said. "Not bad enough that my country gets taken over by your lot, now it's the American dollar taking it over all over again."

"How do you think us white guys feel?" Jared said.

Halfway down the visitors dock a long gangway ran back into the sheds where the larger powerboats were tied up. Some of the sheds were well over a hundred feet long.

"What are the rules about staying aboard overnight for members?"

"Most places it's allowed if you're getting ready to go away on a trip, more than a night or two would be frowned upon out on the docks. But here, inside these mega boathouses, how the hell would they even know if anyone is on board? For that matter why would they care? The boats are self-sufficient; any power they do use is metered, and they have their own holding tanks. There are no real costs to the club involved. It's more the smaller outside boats they patrol. In here with the fat cats, no problem. You can bet that a good number of these powerboats belong to past and present officers of the club. People with money and influence in any case."

The boat sheds were divided into two equal-sized sections. The first was a large open unit with a corrugated roof and a six-foot walkway running down the middle with numbered slips on each side. Each berth was capable of holding a powerboat up to eighty feet in size. The second section consisted of individual boathouses partitioned off from their neighbours, each unit under separate lock and key. These slips were even larger than the ones in the open area and had nameplates of the boat and its owner prominently displayed on engraved brass plates. Some of the boathouse slips were vacant and the doors left open. Danny and Jared entered one of these and walked down the narrow catwalk that ran the full length of the berth. The back of the slip exited onto a wide channel. Access to the channel from the boathouse was through two large garage doors that rolled up and stored against the roof at the click of a remote.

"Pretty slick," Danny said.

"All you need is money. Probably twenty grand a year moorage, and that's still less than they would pay at a commercial marina. If our guys from the Sergeant at Arms came off one of these boats, you'd think they would have been better dressed. A lot of these are million-dollar-plus yachts."

Danny said, "So I guess we should copy down all the owner's names, give them to Clarke for what that's worth?"

"I may have a better idea," Jared said.

CHAPTER 9

"A couple more, gents?"

"Absolutely."

They had arrived at the lounge door at the same time as the bartender and were now his new best friends. Big tippers at eleven in the morning are rare birds in yacht clubs, where a word or two of senior advice in the young person's ear is often considered reward enough. The bartender, Darren, was returning to campus in the fall, needed the tips, and was more than happy to gossip about the members he served. So far they had learned little of interest, but the day was young and the beer was cheap.

"Busy this summer?"

"About the same as always for the locals, visitors dock's a lot busier with the Americans. Even fuel is cheaper here for them with the exchange rate, and that hasn't happened for a long time from what I hear. And then of course there's the politics down there. People tell me they just need a break from all that noise."

"A friend of mine used to keep his boat here a few years ago. In one of the big sheds. Dale Selden," Jared said, fashioning a name out of thin air.

"Don't know him, but that doesn't mean anything. It's a big club and I've only worked here since early summer. Check out the moorage allocation charts around the corner. They redid them last month, so they're pretty much up to date."

There were three separate listings posted on the board: sailboats, powerboats in open moorage, and powerboats in the sheds. Each entry had the boat's name, the owner's name, and the slip number. The revisions were thumbtacked over the previous editions and it was the work of moments for Jared to pull out the earlier copies from underneath and slip them into his pocket. The sailboats were the least likely suspects in Jared's opinion for a couple of reasons. First, he thought it unlikely that sailors would be dressed like the men who took Lauren. Those hats! Second, he felt that people who owned sailboats were, by and large, morally superior to powerboaters, although he did allow there might be rare exceptions. By the time Jared returned, Danny had been joined at the bar by a member.

"I'm a guest, actually. Here's my sponsor now. Mind you, he's moored with the commercial fleet down at the Basin, so his status is likely second rate at best. Never mind that I'm First Nations." Danny gazed blandly at the questioner, a stout red-faced man in a Queens Own Yacht Club blazer whose face blanched.

"Jesus. No, no, not at all. It's just that we've had some trouble with non-members the last while. People just walking in off the street for the cheap drinks. You're more than welcome, more than welcome," the man spluttered.

"I'm just messing with you," Danny said.

"Ah. Very amusing I'm sure. Give these chaps another pint, Darren. On my tab, if you please."

Over the next few hours the lounge gradually filled with a mixed crowd of boat people and club members who stopped by for a drink on their way home from work. Jared and Danny were introduced around by their new friend Basil, who turned out to be the fleet captain, whatever the hell that was. It entitled him to wear a beribboned club blazer and spiffy white officer's cap in any event. He was a pleasant, friendly chap, a drinker, and seemed well liked by the gathered assembly. After three hours of going drink for drink with Danny, Basil might have given them the combination to the yacht club safe if they'd asked.

"This is going to seem like a stupid question," Jared began.

"Fire away. If I couldn't handle stupid questions I couldn't hold down my position here," Basil said in his plummy British accent that was only the least bit slurred.

"Have you seen anybody in a fedora around here recently?"

Basil's eyebrows raised. "A fedora? No. Not sure I've seen one of those in years outside of the business district. It might be the only silly hat I haven't seen on these docks. I should talk," he said, pulling off his white officer's cap and setting it down on the table in front of him. "My father was a destroyer captain in the British navy in World War Two with two confirmed sinkings and he didn't have half the scrambled eggs I've got on this. If his ghost were to stride through that door, I'd have to crawl under the table and hide."

"To the British Navy," Danny said, raising his glass.

"Why do you ask? About the fedora?"

"We're looking for a couple of men who got out of a taxi around two in the morning a few nights back. According to the driver, he let them off in front of the club gate. He didn't see where they went, but it seems logical that they came in here. I mean where else would they go? It's the only place along here. But there's no video camera at the gate so we can't be one hundred percent sure."

Basil regarded them thoughtfully, and Jared thought he'd pushed it too far. But the drinks had done their work. Basil ploughed on.

"No camera, that's true. Never felt we needed one out there. But if they came in through the gate, they would have needed a key card. And we have a record of every card used to unlock the gate. Both the time of its use and the identity of the member it belongs to are automatically recorded on the computer every time the gate's opened. Pretty efficient system really. If someone falls behind on their dues or for whatever reason we're having trouble contacting them, we just cancel their key card. They can't get through the gate until they're sorted out."

"That would work for us," Danny said.

"Mind you, those records are confidential and not available to the general membership. For a club officer such as myself, of course, there's no problem." Basil smiled genially and took a sip of his gin and tonic.

"I suppose a bribe is out of the question," Danny said.

"I'm afraid so."

So they told him. All of it from the beginning.

Basil sat quietly, sipping his drink and listening without comment. When they had finished, he stared into space for a long time.

"I would hate to think that anybody at the club had anything to do with something like that," he said finally. "I'm going to the caretaker's office to pull up the records for that night. I'll be back in a few minutes and then we'll decide what to do."

They watched him walk away.

"Not a bad guy," Danny said.

"He told me he owns a forty-two-foot Hunter sailboat," Jared said.

"So I guess he's in the clear then?"

"Well, the Hunter thing is a little suspect, but yeah, pretty much," Jared said.

Basil was away for a good half hour, and when he returned he had another man with him.

"This is Arnie, our club caretaker. I think he might be able to help us. The card used at the time you referred to was reported missing a few months ago. March tenth to be precise. The chap who lost it is a friend of mine, an elderly retired investment banker. Not a likely candidate for any of this I would think. The thing is, he reported the loss to the office immediately, and the card was cancelled that very same day and shouldn't have worked at the gate after that. Except it seems that somehow it did."

"It was cancelled all right," Arnie said. "I keep a daily log of my activities in an annual diary. I put all the important dates on it ahead of time: boat safety inspections, regattas, special events, things like that. I add or check off items from one day to the next. It helps keep me on track."

He laid a beat-up journal on the table and pointed to an entry. "See, it's right there in black and white. March tenth — cancelled nine-nine-two-six. Hubert Rainer. His card wouldn't have worked after that. I issued him a new one."

"Someone must have reinstated it," Basil said.

"Yes. It looks like it."

"How hard would that be?" Danny asked.

"Simple enough," Basil said. "Just get onto the club computer and call up the file. Enter the password and the card number and there you are. Three options: suspend, cancel, reinstate. Check the box, confirm, bingo! It's done."

"How many people would know that password?"

"Probably every club officer for the last ten years give or take. Or maybe even longer. Not to mention all the secretaries, volunteers, committee heads, and who knows who else? I doubt anything has been changed in the program since it was installed a dozen or so years back. It never seemed necessary. Apart from that, any member can walk in and use the office computer at will, and it wouldn't surprise me in the least if the password was written down in the office somewhere for reference. We're not exactly the secret service here."

Basil paused and laid a printout on the table. "Here are the times that card was used since March tenth. Four dates, all of them late night or early morning. Spaced out from a month to six weeks apart."

Jared glanced at the list. "Not a huge leap to think that they might correspond with the assaults on the women."

"I hate to say this," Basil began, "but I'll have to get the police involved and it's going to be an absolute straight-out nightmare for our club when word of this gets out. And you can bet your bottom dollar that it will leak out if our members are interviewed. I can almost hear the other yacht clubs licking their chops already." Basil closed his eyes and took a long drink.

"About the guys in the hats Basil told me about," Arnie said. "I think maybe I might have seen them once. It wasn't much really. Two men in a nice old mahogany Chris-Craft Launch. It was windy and they had their hands raised up clamping their hats on their heads. Why I remember is it was kind of funny because they looked such lubbers. Who goes out in a blow wearing a hat like that on his head?"

"How were they dressed?" Jared asked.

"Street clothes. Not boaty, just jackets and pants. Not jeans I don't think. Khaki pants and windbreakers maybe? I think they were both dressed the same. Not a hundred percent sure really. Just the hats were a little weird, stuck in my mind. They were so out of place."

Danny said, "Do you have any idea where they might have been coming from?"

"It had to be from the main shed or one of the boathouses housing the bigger yachts. There's nothing else down that channel. C dock blocks off the other end."

"Well over a hundred yachts to choose from then," Basil said. "Thanks, Arnie. Talk to you later. Keep this quiet for the time being, okay?"

"Under your fedora, so to speak," Jared said.

CHAPTER 10

"So what do you think?" Danny asked.

"We don't have enough. Basil is obliged to go to the police now that he knows what has been going on. I'm surprised he's giving us any time at all."

"Well, we did say we'd talk to Clarke," Danny said. "And Basil doesn't want the notoriety for the club, so there's that. But you know he'll do the right thing sooner rather than later. This might be one of those times where the police can do a better job. Do the interviews with club members, you never know, they might just get lucky. Someone could have seen something. They'll go through the printouts and match the times the card was used with what they've got on the other assaults, see if any other cards correlate with those times, all that kind of boring detecting stuff. What do you think?"

Jared stared up at the ceiling. "My inclination," he said after a long pause, "would be to purchase fedoras, put on some windbreakers, and motor up and down the channel behind the boathouse in *Arrow*'s dinghy for a spell."

Danny stared at him, amazed. "I've known you for a long time, Jared, and you have had some odd ideas on occasion, but that is undoubtedly, by a multiple of ten, the dumbest single thing you've ever said."

❀

Three hours later, tucked under brand-new fedoras and wrapped in thrift-store old-man windbreakers and slacks, they were putting along the club backwaters in *Arrow*'s little Avon dinghy with the 2 HP Seagull on the back.

"I hope we don't have to make a run for it," Jared said.

"If we come across somebody I know while I'm dressed like this, I'll kill you myself, you won't have to worry about anybody else."

They'd told Arnie that if anyone asked they were doing a survey for an American production company that was shooting a movie on the West Coast and needed a yacht club for some background scenes. With the weak Canadian dollar the American film trade was flourishing in the province, and it was a reasonable premise. To flesh out their pathetic ruse Danny had brought along a complicated-looking old camera he'd bought for an additional twenty dollars when they purchased the clothes at the Sally Ann. He pointed and clicked it thoughtfully at regular intervals.

The boat channel was open at both ends, and a full circuit at dead slow took about ten minutes. Some of the boathouse garage doors were open and they stopped occasionally in front of these while Danny pretended to take pictures of the boats tied up inside. Occasionally a person would appear and wave to them, and they waved enthusiastically back. On the third go-round, a slightly weathered older woman on the stern deck of an enormous old mahogany powerboat waved them aboard. She was sipping a drink and it probably wasn't her first. Stretched out in a teak chaise lounge, she looked bored and expensive from close up. Her grey-streaked blond hair was fashionably cut and dyed, and the rangy body gym-toned. The boat didn't fare nearly as well under close scrutiny, the planked decks scarred and worn, and all the varnish a few seasons past redoing, with green brass and bird shit omnipresent. It looked like it hadn't left its berth in years.

"Just how big is this thing?" Jared inquired as he stepped aboard.

"*Legalese* is somewhere in the neighbourhood of eighty-five feet, I do believe."

Danny said, "Must be a nightmare getting her in and out of the slip."

"It used to be. Hasn't been moved since my husband died three years ago. It's basically my seaside cabin now. For another year or so anyway. Then God alone knows. Insurance survey is due in eighteen months and it probably won't pass without spending fifty grand or more on her. That might be more than she's worth in today's market. Pity. Nobody wants the old ones anymore."

She mused on the personal injustice of this for a few moments.

"Want to buy a boat cheap? Might even be free if you wait another couple of years. Nice kit by the way. I'd offer you a drink but I guess your lot doesn't go in for that."

"Our lot?"

"Yeah. You know, Bible thumpers, snake whisperers, water walkers, whatever. No judgment here." She raised her glass and saluted them with a sardonic toast.

Danny said, "Actually we're checking out the marina for a film company."

"Really? You mean you don't have to dress like that? Wow. Too bad Ralph isn't still around. All that old crap of his I gave to the Goodwill must be coming back into fashion."

She handed Jared the empty jug. "In that case you might be able to mix a decent martini. Booze and glasses in the saloon back there. Very dry, fuck the olives. Beer in the fridge if you'd prefer."

She waved vaguely in the general direction, and Jared took the jug and disappeared.

"My name's Merlynn, like the wizard, only spelled differently. My parents were flakes. You're a handsome devil, aren't you? If I was twenty years younger and not such a lush, I might set my cap for you. If you're even old enough to know what that means."

Danny smiled. "I am, and I do. Speaking of hats, what's with the religious stuff?"

The blue eyes peered owlishly at him from behind the horn-rims. Danny waited patiently for the penny to drop.

"Oh, that. The weirdoes from the end slip. Came in a while back. Big boat, newer I think. Didn't stay for very long. Don't know anything about them other than when I trotted down to see them with my martini pitcher that first evening. Just doing the usual yacht club welcoming thing, you know. Two guys stopped me before I got within ten feet of the boat. Dressed sort of like you two with the hats and khaki and all." She made a vague gesture. "Not boaty. Tall, skinny pair, unwelcoming and tough-looking to boot. Some music blaring inside with a big chorus. I thought it sounded kind of religious so I figured them for maybe church freaks. And then a big good-looking guy came out on the upper deck and said he was sorry, but they were very busy at the moment and had no time to socialize. He was polite but I got the message loud and clear. PFO."

Jared returned with the martini jug and she took it from him and refilled her glass.

"PFO?" he asked.

"Please fuck off." Merlynn tested her drink. "Not terrible," she said.

"Merlynn was just telling me about her neighbours," Danny said.

"Unfriendly bunch," she said. "Not neighbours for very long, either, for that matter. Only saw them for a couple of days that one time. I might have seen them coming in late once or twice after that, although I'm not sure. Another big boat coming into that slip at any rate. My night vision isn't all that great anymore."

Or maybe it's the martinis, Danny thought.

"Or maybe it's the martinis," Merlynn said.

Jared passed Danny a beer and sat down. "Do you remember the name of the boat?"

"No idea. I don't think it was on the bow. That's the sharp end," she added by way of clarification. "It was in the oversize slip on the end, so you could probably find out easily enough, although there have been a few different boats coming and going in there the last couple of months. What is this all about anyway? If you two are working for a movie company, then I'm Jane Fonda and I want a part in your next film."

"Actually you do remind me of her a bit," Danny said.

"Ten years ago I might have taken that for a compliment, but thanks for the effort."

Nobody said anything for a while.

"It's likely nothing," Jared said finally. "Just a stupid hunch."

"Now that's bullshit," Merlynn said. "I was a crown prosecutor for thirty years and I can recognize the odour a mile off. Tell me what's going on here."

"You might know Detective Clarke then. He's working the case we're looking at. He's a friend of ours."

"Don't tell me that ugly old bugger is still around? I would have thought he'd be retired by now. I had him on the stand a few times over the years. Good witness for the Crown, always knew his stuff. Smart, although you would never have guessed it to look at him. I think he might have had a bit of a thing for me once back in the day. A long time ago now."

Jared said, "He has less than a year to go until mandatory retirement. That's assuming he's not kicked out for insubordination first. We met up with him a few days ago after a friend of ours got into some trouble. The latest of the 'girls on the park bench,' to quote the tabloids."

"I saw that story on the evening news. Sounded grim. How's she doing?"

"She should be out of hospital soon. Still pretty messed up."

"What's that got to do with the boat in the end slip?"

"There's security video of the woman inside a West End nightclub on the night she was assaulted. It looks like two guys in windbreakers and fedoras put something in her drink and then took her away in a taxi. The cab company says they were dropped off in front of the yacht club gate. A member's card was used to gain entrance around that time. A lost or stolen card, according to the club's records." Jared shrugged. "What the hell. We decided to buy some windbreakers and hats and troll up and down awhile on the off chance."

Merlynn clapped her hands in delight. "That is absolutely the hands-down dumbest plan I've ever heard in all of my thirty years in criminal justice," she said admiringly.

"That's what I told him," Danny said.

CHAPTER 11

"That is without question, and beyond the shadow of a doubt, the dumbest plan I've heard in my thirty-six years on the force," Clarke said when he joined them at the yacht club. The martini glass looked ridiculously small in his hand.

"Except it sort of worked," Jared said, a bit stiffly. "It led us here, didn't it?"

"It did, but you just got stupid lucky," Clarke said. "You're looking well, Merlynn. Sorry to hear about your husband."

When they'd phoned Clarke and told him they might have gathered some information about the abductions, he said that if they weren't down at the station inside of thirty minutes, he would dispatch a squad car with large patrolmen and multiple sets of handcuffs. When he learned they were at the Queens Own Yacht Club having drinks on a boat belonging to Merlynn Saunders, he reconsidered and instructed them to stay there pending his arrival. Merlynn went out to the gate to let him in and by the time they arrived at *Legalese*, Clarke was almost calm.

When he concluded his lecture on the penalties available to private citizens interfering in an ongoing criminal investigation, Jared and

Danny told him what they'd learned from the videos and their interview with the cab driver that had led them to the yacht club. And then the chat with Basil that led to a dead end, followed by the clothes and the hats and the cruise in the dinghy.

"Talk about blind squirrels," Clarke said, shaking his head in disbelief. "I've told you two before about rushing thoughtlessly ahead without any sort of plan! It's going to catch up with you one of these days, and the two of you are going to end up in serious trouble. If not with the other side, then certainly with me." He glared at them and they remained silent.

"Okay then," Clarke said, mollified. "Let me think about this. I guess the first thing to do is get a list of all the boats and owners and find out where they're moored. I suppose the best way is to get in touch with one of the club officers and—"

Jared reached into his pocket and pulled out the moorage chart and handed it across to him.

Clarke put on a pair of glasses, unfolded the paper, and read it over. "Okay, well, this is good," he said. "Very useful." He sat in silence, his brow furrowed. The others waited patiently.

"Okay then. I think the next step would be to get a list of the times and dates the card was used and see if that links up to the other—"

Danny pulled the computer printout from his pocket and reached over and slapped Clarke on the wrist with it.

"Okay, good," Clarke growled, his face reddening as he looked it over. "Is there anything else you two smartasses haven't told me? I should haul you down to the station right now and charge you with interfering in the course of an investigation."

"I'm not sure that would stick," Merlynn said.

"Probably not," Clarke said, "but at least I'd have the pleasure of putting their dumb asses in the holding tank overnight. So Merlynn, that boat with the two guys you met would have been in slip one-ninety-eight on the end, right? And the winner is . . ." He ran his finger down the list.

"Are you kidding me?" he howled. "The fucking Progressive Conservative Party?" He took his hat off and hurled it across the deck, then lurched across to retrieve it. "Sorry, Merlynn," he muttered sheepishly.

"No need to apologize. I often refer to them that way."

"That can't be right," Clarke said.

"I didn't know that, but it kind of makes sense." Merlynn said. "There are quite a few corporations that lease slips from the club. For PR work mainly. An out-of-town group of clients fly in, they bring them down here for drinks and dinner, and follow up with a tour around the harbour. It's something different and a nice treat for them, especially those people from Eastern Canada or the Prairies who've never been out here. Most of the companies have a specific boat attached to the slip, but that's not always the case. This could be one of those instances where it's just a slip lease and not attached to any one particular boat. The party pays the rent and slots different boats into it at different times." She nodded her head, excited now, and continued.

"I'll bet you that's it. I've seen other yachts in there over the past month, smaller and with the types aboard you'd expect to find. You know, cargo shorts and deck shoes, drinks in hand. Just your typical boat crowd out for a good time. Slip is paid for by the party, tax deductible goodies for the faithful. As long as the club knows about it and the moorage is paid up, why would they care? It's good business for them, not to mention the political influence they earn. Always nice to have friends in high places when you're renegotiating the foreshore leases and that sort of thing."

"I'm not looking forward to interviewing all those people who had access to the computer files," Clarke said glumly. "Goddam bunch of yuppies, I can just imagine the looks on their faces when they see me."

He gestured at his rumpled brown suit and wrinkled tie. The crushed hat sat low on his forehead. They gazed at him without comment. He flushed. "And this is a porkpie for your information, not a fedora. Been around forever and worn by Hackman in *The French Connection*, the movie about the great Popeye Doyle."

"Did we say anything?" Jared asked.

"No, but I know what you were thinking," Clarke growled.

"It suits you," Merlynn said. "And you do kind of remind me of Gene, a little bit. As for the research and interviews, I can help with that," she continued. "Ralph was elected commodore a few years back, and as the commodore's wife I was given full access to all the records. Probably still have the password for that matter, I doubt anything has changed. Most of the files are still on my computer, and we can work here in private. You can be sure the club won't object. They'll want to keep a low profile, the less fuss the better as far as they're concerned. I'm sure I can eliminate a lot of people right off the bat. A fair number of them will be dead or in rest homes by now for starters."

"Sounds like a plan," Clarke said. "I'll mix the martinis."

CHAPTER 12

"I have to go up to the house and see Annie first off," Danny said. "You want to come along?"

"That depends. What's second off?" Jared asked.

"Oh, you know, go out for a few drinks at some of the clubs, ask a few questions perhaps, that sort of thing."

Jared said, "You mean stumble around in the dark until we piss someone off and get our legs broken or worse like that private investigator?"

"You think my plan isn't subtle enough?"

Jared threw up his hands. "Why don't we just take out an ad in the newspaper? Get the police sketch artist to do up composite drawings of the two guys from the club video and say we're looking for them regarding a series of sexual assaults. We could highlight our names and addresses and offer a hand-delivered reward for any useful information."

"That's a great idea, but I'm not a hundred percent sure Clarke would approve," Danny said.

"I was being sarcastic," Jared said.

"You're just too subtle for me sometimes," Danny said.

Annie's house was in the heart of East End Vancouver where even the humblest property was now worth a small fortune. Realtors kept coming by and offering to list it for silly amounts of money. For a time Danny's mother entertained herself by agreeing to sell on condition that they changed absolutely nothing about the house or lot for thirty years or until she passed, as the property had great sentimental value for her. When Annie grew bored with this her father, Joseph, cut a hole in the fence through to the backyard where the dog resided and spoke to him. Nobody knew what was said, but after that Sinbad considered it part of his duties to greet strangers at the front gate. Word spread and visits from realtors ceased.

Sinbad was the dog Joseph had picked up from a pound during a stopover in Santa Barbara a few years earlier when Jared's boat, *Arrow*, was being harried down the West Coast by lethal men in a motor yacht. Sinbad had been raised as a village dog in the Tuamotus and adopted by an offshore cruiser who took him aboard his sailboat when he departed the island. When the sailor's trip was over and he returned stateside, he left the dog at a charity pound in Santa Barbara with money to support him for a few months in the hope that during that time he might find another owner. Given Sinbad's looks and temperament the odds for that were slim, until Danny's grandfather showed up and rescued him.

Sinbad was a hundred and sixty-five pounds of "muscle and ugly," as Danny liked to say, and his appearance alone was enough to caution any sane person. His scarred face was wolflike and his mouth filled with large teeth, usually on display. Above them were staring yellow goatish eyes. His muzzle was foreshortened, as if he had run full tilt into a wall, and most of his weight was in his oversized head, thick neck, and powerful muscled forequarters. His scarred back sloped down to an undersized hind end and a ratlike, shark-docked tail.

If his looks didn't deter you, then the eager, longing whine as he regarded your groin with lifted head and trembling hindquarters would probably do the job. Sinbad tolerated Jared, liked Danny, and loved Joseph. It was Jared's habit to cuff Sinbad on the ear in greeting when they met, whereupon the beast would growl and slaver and snap his teeth just short of finding him.

"One of these times he's going to get you," Danny said.

"Naw, he loves me. He just can't help himself," Jared said. Sinbad was crouched in front of him, growling and snapping at the encroaching fingers, missing by millimetres. Joseph watched, shaking his head.

Nobody knew exactly how old Joseph was, maybe not even him. Probably close to a hundred years, although he looked in his seventies, still showing vestiges of the powerful man he'd been. He understood English perfectly but chose not to speak it, a sore point with Jared, who loved him. Danny said it was to do with Joseph being a Shaman of sorts, and not subjecting himself to the language of the conquerors. It was an absurd concept to Jared, and one which so enraged him he couldn't even let himself think about it. He had heard Joseph utter the sum total of fifteen words in English on two separate occasions, both of which were life-threatening. It was reasonable to assume that Joseph thought they would be his final words at the time.

Joseph watched them, his bright black eyes expressionless. As usual, he was dressed in woollen fisherman pants and a chequered flannel shirt, with fishermen's deck slippers on his feet. Jared went over and threw his arms around him, inhaling the faint scent of smoke and cedar that always defined Joseph to him.

"Hey, you old buzzard. How are the English lessons going? Learned how to say hi yet?"

Joseph smiled and tolerated the hug for a few moments before a pinch on the ribs signalled enough. He turned and led them up the porch into the kitchen where his daughter Annie was pouring coffee into large china mugs.

"Hey boys," she said, a soft-spoken stout, smiling woman with greying hair who'd already garnered more than her share of sadness. "You staying for supper?" She motioned to the old woodstove in the corner where a large cast iron pot was simmering. "Crab and salmon chowder. Jaimie and Erin dropped by earlier. I'll make cornbread to go with it."

Erin and Jaimie were Annie's sons by her first marriage. First Nation Haidas descended from the northern warriors, they were big easy-going men who earned a decent living for their families with their little salmon trollers, and bolstered it by an occasional halibut trip in early spring or late fall. Their boats were tied up in the commercial basin near *Arrow*, and they often came aboard for cards and drinks and stayed late into the night, their soft, sibilant voices scarcely carrying beyond *Arrow*'s decks.

Danny was Annie's last born, conceived of an ill-gotten union with a troubled Scotsman who died of alcoholism and exposure under an East End bridge long before Jared knew the family. Behind the easy smile and casual good looks was a complex man with codes of conduct that would shame a Samurai. He could still surprise Jared, who probably knew him better than anyone.

"What are you two up to these days?" Annie asked.

"We're looking for some people," Jared said. "Not having much luck so far. We think they're connected to the park bench assaults in the West End. The last victim was Cat's sister."

Jared had brought Cat over early on in their relationship to meet the family and give her some idea of who he was and where he was coming from. Or maybe as a caution. In any event, Cat and Annie had bonded and become friends almost immediately.

"I'm sorry, Jared. I saw the story on that news channel that does all the crime stuff. It's awful." Annie reached across and gripped his hand.

"They say she's going to be all right," Jared said. "Physically speaking anyway. Cat is trying to get her to take counselling."

"It will take a long time," Annie said. "I have friends who were attacked on the Highway of Tears. Some of them never get past it."

Joseph leaned across to Danny and began talking in a low whisper. Danny nodded and then the two of them got up and went into the living room.

"You can join us if you like," Danny said.

"Why the hell would I want to join you?" Jared said. "I wouldn't understand a single fucking word you say. Sorry, Annie."

"That's okay. Let me tell you about the Sea Festival. We're entering a war canoe into the dragon boat races next year. All First Nations women and most of them are my age or older. We've been going out twice a week and practising."

Jared nodded politely and took a sip of coffee.

"It's supposed to be all women, but they've allowed Joseph to be our drummer. I guess they figure he adds character." Annie grinned. "He brings Sinbad along with him. He stands back there with his forefeet on the transom, and if another boat gets too close he puffs up and growls and snaps at them. It's hilarious."

Jared picked up his mug and drained it.

"I'm just going to check on them," he said.

Annie sighed.

They were sitting in comfortable silence, Joseph with his pipe, Danny mug in hand. They looked up as he entered the room.

"Well?" Jared said.

Danny might have looked a little uncomfortable.

"Joseph is going to come with us," he said.

Joseph smiled and nodded.

"Come with us where?"

"To the clubs."

"Seriously?"

Joseph nodded again and got up and left the room.

"He's gone to change," Danny said.

"Well, that's a relief. Is he bringing his dog along?"

"Don't be ridiculous, Jared," Danny said.

They sat in silence for the next few minutes while Joseph got dressed.

CHAPTER 13

"We'll start with the Lamplight," Danny said.

According to Cat it was the first club Lauren had visited on the night of her assault. While it was unlikely that they would learn anything of value, there was a remote possibility that her attackers had singled her out there and followed her on to the Sergeant at Arms. It was the roughest and least upscale of the three locations Clarke had told them about, and was situated in the East End adjacent to the commercial docks. In spite of this location, or perhaps even because of it, it was a popular spot for the in-crowd. It wasn't unusual to see fashionable women in the latest runway dresses out on the floor bumping loins with stevedores from the port while their overdressed escorts looked uncomfortably on.

"I've always liked this place," Danny said when their drinks arrived. "Even got myself barred for a week once. Not easy to do."

Joseph nodded in agreement. He was dressed in a beautifully cut herringbone suit with a matching vest and colour-coordinated grey tie. An expensive felt homburg with a tiny raven feather in the band rested on the table in front of him. The outfit minus the feather had belonged to a top-end Vancouver fence, and Joseph had acquired it through criminal circumstances, although you could debate that. Under his blue silk shirt would be the century-old lava knife in a scabbard suspended by a leather thong around his neck. While it was never visible, he was never without it. The last time Jared had seen the lava knife up close, it had been buried to the hilt in a man's back.

Feeling Jared's gaze, Joseph turned and winked at him before emptying his glass and signalling the waitress for another. No money changed hands during the subsequent transaction, and Jared knew the drinks were going on the tab. It didn't surprise him. In all the years he'd known Joseph, he had never seen him pay for anything, from drinks in bars to an unscheduled plane charter in the South Pacific that had set Jared back in excess of a thousand dollars. Not only that, he cheated at cards, although Jared had never been able to catch him at it. The family issued Joseph a free pass on all of this because his Clan was Raven, the trickster. His grandson Danny, on the other hand, was the complete opposite. Generous to a fault. If you didn't pay attention, he would cheerfully pick up every tab and pay every bill with never a second thought. Go figure.

Jared ceased his brooding and turned his attention to the dance floor. Things were slow, but it was still early. Most of the tables were occupied by after-work drinkers who were beginning to wind down and would be replaced by clubbers as the evening wore on. Women were starting to trickle in, singly and in groups, and the bar music had been switched from country to rock. A drunken longshoreman got up and began a slow, lugubrious dance until one of his workmates corralled him and herded him out the door. It looked like being a long evening. There were worse places to spend your time than in a bar, though, and Jared leaned back and settled in with his drink, watching the crowd.

Joseph reached across and pinched him and motioned towards the corner.

The man sitting there alone at the table was someone Jared had never seen before. He was pretty sure of that. Average size, glasses, not one of the after-work crowd from the docks at first glance. He was dressed more for night work in a blue blazer and grey slacks. Jared studied him, but got nothing. Seemed like just another ordinary guy out for the evening. He had his cell phone out on the table in front of him and was busily texting. The man looked around the room, his gaze resting on them for a moment before it slid past and he went back to his phone and resumed tapping.

"Looks to me like someone checking the talent out," Danny said. "Probably his buddies are in other bars doing the exact same thing and then they'll meet up at the one with the best prospects. The marvels of the social-networking age. No doubt some of the women in here are doing likewise. Sit up straighter, Jared, and try not to scowl, they may be texting pictures."

"Go fuck yourself," Jared said amiably.

Joseph leaned forward and said something to Danny.

"I'm not sure," Danny said after a pause. "Could be."

"What?"

"Joseph thinks the guy in the corner has the Queens Own Yacht Club emblem on his blazer. He says he's watching us."

Jared squinted. The guy had a patch on his blazer all right. Could possibly be an anchor on it. Hard to tell. Joseph stared at him and nodded.

"Maybe," Jared said. "But so what? Doesn't have to mean anything. It's a big club with hundreds of members. Bound to be a few of them scattered around in different places."

Joseph stared at him and inclined his head towards the corner.

"All right, all right," Jared said. "Jesus. I'm going, I'm going."

He stood up and headed towards the restrooms located on the far side of the room just beyond the lone man sitting at the corner table. He passed him, did a double-take, and moved in.

"Well, I'll be damned. A fellow member. Good to see someone flying the old flag here. Jared Kane." He held his hand out. "Been waiting for a long time to get in, but the day has finally come. Don't even have my blazer and patch yet. Pleasure to meet you." He grabbed the man's hand and shook it fervently.

The man jerked his hand away.

"Likewise," he muttered. "John Newcombe."

"I'll just give the old weed a shake, John," Jared said. "Be back in no time, and we can have a nice little chat." He headed off into the restroom. When he returned the man was gone.

"You must have scared him," Danny said. "He's on the move."

"I introduced myself and said I was a fellow member. Suggested we shoot the breeze. He could just be a guilty husband out for a night on the town."

"Maybe. Kind of dumb in that case to wear a blazer with your club's logo on it. Why not just print out your phone number and attach it to your collar? Pretty much the same thing as far as tracking you goes these days. The blazer and logo might make you seem safer though. Less of a threat." Danny shrugged.

"That's awfully damned thin," Jared said.

"True. But then what else do we have?" Danny threw money down on the table, and they followed out the door in the man's wake. When they arrived at the curb, he was heading off down Powell Street in a taxi. The three of them climbed into the next one in the queue.

Danny turned to Jared.

"Be my guest," Jared said.

Danny smiled. "Follow that cab," he said to the driver.

❈

The cab turned onto Hastings Street, then out and over the Second Narrows Bridge before climbing up into the lower reaches of the North Shore. Just as it seemed they were going all the way out to the Vancouver Island ferry, the cab veered off and up into the high-rent area of the British Properties. With the recent surge in property values, the average home here was now in the two- to three-million-dollar range. Many were worth more.

The taxi pulled into a private driveway and stopped in front of a high steel gate with a keypad lock. The man who called himself Newcombe got out and paid the driver and the taxi drove off. He went over to the gate and pressed an intercom button and spoke briefly. After a moment the gate slid silently open on greased tracks and he walked through. It closed behind him and he disappeared from view.

"That was really helpful," Jared said.

"Well, we learned that he doesn't live here anyway," Danny said. "If he did, he would have known the gate combination."

"And that helps us how?"

"Just saying. You didn't scare him home. Maybe to someone further up the chain."

They sat in silence for a few minutes, the only sound the ticking over of the meter.

"Well, we've got the address and the name of the guy in the Lamplight for what that's worth. Likely an alias if he's connected to the women. Merlynn can check out the name in her computer records and the club yearbooks. I think it might be time to head out to the next place on the list." Danny glanced at his watch. "The night is still young."

"Hang on," Jared said.

The gate opened and a black Cadillac limo with tinted windows peeled out and headed back in towards the city.

"Follow that Cad," Jared said to their driver.

CHAPTER 14

The limo led them back along the upper Narrows, then swung over the Lions Gate Bridge and into the West End. It paused by the Queens Own Yacht Club gate and a man got out and the limo pulled away. It had begun to rain heavily and it was impossible to tell if it was the same man they had followed from the nightclub. He was wearing a dark green rain jacket with the hood pulled up and could have been anybody. He held his wallet up to the reader, and the gate opened. The man passed through and headed up the main finger and disappeared in the gusty rain.

"We'll have to stay with the Caddy," Jared said. "I don't have a gate card yet." He glanced at his watch. "Eight forty-one. We'll tell Clarke, and he can pull the log from the club computer and find out whose card was used at that time. This could all be just a coincidence and perfectly innocent. If the Caddy heads back to the Properties, we'll leave it."

But after dropping the man off, the limo did an illegal U-turn and drove back past them towards the city. With the rain and the tinted windows, it was impossible to see anything inside. They gave it a couple of hundred yards' head start and then followed.

"Are you guys cops?" the cabbie inquired.

"Yeah," Danny said. "We're undercover. Him especially." He pointed to Joseph who regarded the man gravely and nodded.

"Sorry I asked," the driver said.

They followed the limo for another twenty blocks before it pulled up in front of the club they'd been at the night before. Two men got out and entered the Sergeant at Arms. Neither of them was the man from the Lamplight who had given his name as John Newcombe.

"The coincidences are beginning to stack up," Danny said. He reached for his wallet and Jared brushed him aside and paid the driver.

"It could still be just that though. Coincidence. This isn't the pair that grabbed Lauren."

The men might have been a little older than most of the club goers but not by very much. With their casual sport coats and upscale blue jeans, they fit right in with the crowd. They seemed to be known to the bouncers who spoke to them briefly as they passed by.

"Maybe we should wait a couple of minutes," Jared said. "We don't want to be too obvious." Joseph looked at him without expression, gazed up at the falling rain, and then headed off across the street towards the club.

"Or not," Danny said, and the two of them hurried after him.

The Sergeant at Arms was twice as busy and three times as loud as the Lamplight. Most of the tables were taken, and people were lined up two deep at the bar. Joseph headed to one of the last unoccupied booths along the wall, and they sat back and checked the room out. A harried waitress scurried up and took their orders. She said it might be a few minutes. Joseph pulled out a silver flask and held it out as she moved away.

"That is against the law you know," Jared said to him.

Joseph looked puzzled and shook his head.

"He doesn't speak English," Danny said.

"Right." Jared took a quick drink.

"Check the table over in the corner," Danny said.

Jared glanced across and saw the men from the limo sitting with two others. They were all about the same age and similarly dressed in club casual. They were deep in conversation and one of the men met his eyes and smiled. Jared nodded and looked away.

"You know him?" Danny asked.

"No. Never seen him before tonight."

"Maybe just being friendly then."

They sat quietly as they waited for their drink order, checking out the room as they passed the flask from hand to hand.

Joseph leaned across and murmured to Danny.

"He says the men from the limo are watching us," Danny said. "They could have spotted us in the taxi following them. There's not all that much traffic this time of night. Maybe I'll just pop over there and ask them about it."

He started to rise and Jared grabbed his arm and pulled him back down.

"No. Jesus. We haven't even been served yet for God's sake. Give it some time. Maybe they're just checking Joseph out. You don't get all that many Indigenous centenarians in places like this."

Joseph stared impassively at Jared as the waitress arrived with drinks and apologies.

"Busy night," Danny said, handing her a pair of twenties.

"It'll get worse later on when the shows start getting out." She began to make change, and he held a hand up and stopped her.

"Keep it. Just a quick question. Don't look now, but those four guys off in the corner. Do you know them?"

She looked past them, checking the tables, and waved to a woman with her arm in the air. "With you in a minute, honey," she called, and turned back to them. "I don't know their names, but the two that just came in are regulars. I might have seen the other two once or twice. Thanks for the tip." She smiled and bustled off.

"So what do you think?" Danny said.

Jared shrugged. "I don't know. We should probably get hold of

Clarke, tell him about the guy who went through the gates earlier. Merlynn could likely get the name on the card tonight. I don't imagine there's a pay phone in here anywhere. Probably not one within a mile these days."

Jared had left his cell phone on the boat and knew that Danny was a fellow Luddite in this respect. There were times like the present when it would have been a boon, but he felt the annoyance generally outweighed the convenience. He'd managed just fine before they came along and took over the world. He would slash his wrists before he joined the Social Revolution.

He was roused from his thoughts by a pinch on his arm. In his other hand Joseph held a sleek silver iPhone.

"Of course. I don't suppose you have Clarke's number?"

Joseph scanned his contacts, punched in a number, and handed the phone across.

Jared put the phone to his ear.

"Joseph? How the hell did you get my number? You actually going to talk to me in a language that's been spoken within the last century?" Clarke sounded shitfaced. He and Joseph had a long and chequered history. Jared didn't even bother to wonder why Joseph would have his number.

"It's me. Jared."

"My God. *Quelle surprise.* Aren't you afraid of cancer of the brain? Or is it the ear? I forget which."

"Ha. Listen, are you still in touch with Merlynn?"

A giggle and then a crash in the background and the sound of ice cubes in a blender.

"Can I take that as a yes?"

"I might be able to get hold of her."

A falling chair, more laughter, and then silence.

"Listen, Clarke, this could be important. A man went through the club gate at around eight forty this evening, and we think there's a good chance he's tied into the park bench assaults. We need to find out who he is. We thought Merlynn could get onto the club computers and check the gate log. We'll need his address as well."

"All right. Let me get back to you. In the meantime, stay out of trouble. And tell that old bastard to keep his weapon in its sheath. Speaking of which." Clarke giggled insanely and the phone went dead.

Danny raised his eyebrows.

"He's on top of it," Jared said. "It might take awhile."

Joseph raised his hand and signalled for another round.

Jared reached for his wallet.

CHAPTER 15

"I'm positive it was the same two I saw messing about in the old Avon down at the docks and in the club asking all the questions. A small white guy and the big Indian. There was another Indian with them as well. Well dressed, expensive suit, fucking ancient." John Newcombe stood in the spotless saloon of the converted tugboat, nervously shifting his weight from one foot to the other.

"The white guy came up to me and said his name was Jared Kane. Told me he was a new member and had noticed my crest. It didn't feel right to me, so as soon as he went to the john I left and called the man up and he said for me to meet him at a place up in the Properties. He gave me the address and I went up there and told him about what happened. He said I should come down here and tell you about it right away. So that's what I did."

"Well, let's just check the membership list, shall we? Only take a minute." The accountant crossed the lounge and seated himself at the desk with the silver laptop sitting on it.

"Sit down and take the weight off your feet. You did exactly the right thing. Well, maybe not the giving him your real name part. That was unfortunate. And you're absolutely certain that you weren't followed here? Excellent. You should probably stay out of sight for a while now; we can't have them spotting you again. I can help you out with that. Go ahead and pour yourself a drink."

The accountant opened the laptop, tapped away at the keyboard, paused and tapped again.

"Okay. So, Jared Kane, you say? Let's see. This yacht club program has got to be the slowest in the civilized world. My old Commodore 64 could pull up information faster. Okay, here we go. Hmm. No mention of a Jared Kane anywhere in the club database. Not a member, not up for initiation, not on the waiting list. So he's lying about all of that. Not to worry. I'll find him somewhere, if that's really his name. It's a small world these days and getting smaller by the hour."

He tapped out another entry and checked the screen again. "Not on Facebook, no surprise there, but you never know, be stupid not to check. And I'm not stupid. Well, not about most things anyways."

He half turned and winked at the man. He opened a desk drawer and pulled out a notebook and flicked through it. "Here we go, just need the right password and Bob's your uncle." He hit some keys. "And, wait, wait, and wait, and . . . bingo. I'm in like Flynn. Just put in the name, check the old arrest sheets and court records. Oopsy, here we are. Oh, the sweet boy. So young back then. A little skinny for my taste though. Uh-oh, he's been baaad."

He shook his head in disapproval and scrolled through the report. He stopped and frowned at the screen, then picked up the cell phone that sat on the desk alongside the laptop and made a call.

"Hi. It's me." He paused and listened. "Yes, he's here now. I checked the records, it's like you figured. Yep, both of them. Okay, sure, I can take care of that. Half an hour then. Not a problem. Yep. He did real good."

John Newcombe poured himself a drink and stood by the bar, glancing back at the accountant. The fat little homosexual gave him the creeps. Maybe even scared him a bit sometimes.

"Here, take off your jacket. It's dripping on the carpet. Clint and Travis are on their way over to give you a hand with those naughty boys. Hang it up in the wet locker by the cabin door, there's a good fellow."

He trailed Newcombe back towards the entrance. "Here, let me help you."

He took the drink from him and set it on the counter. As Newcombe took off his anorak and turned to open the locker door, the accountant pulled a small .22 calibre pistol out of his vest and shot him twice, carefully, in the base of the skull.

"Dumb cluck. Why does he think they put wet lockers and drains on boats, for gosh sakes?" Grunting with effort, he dragged Newcombe forward another couple of feet and centred him over the drain. Panting heavily he picked up the freshwater hose that hung in the locker and rinsed away the traces of blood. He curled the man's legs tight up against his body and with some difficulty was able to close the locker door on him.

"There we go now, Bob's your uncle. No fuss, no muss, no bother."

His good humour restored, he picked up the man's drink, drained it, and dropped the glass into the garbage container under the sink. He paused, sighed, slapped his wrist in mock disapproval, then took the glass out again, double-bagged it in Ziplocs, and used the cleaver from the galley to smash it into small pieces. Then he went out on deck and poured the fragments over the side and into the water before returning to his desk and tapping away on his laptop, nodding and muttering to himself as the information rolled across the screen.

"Okay, so here we are. Hello again, Jared. Bit of a bad boy early on, two years in the slammer for assault, couple more incidents on the sheet, nothing too, too serious. Hmm. Not really my type, though I might be persuaded." He licked his lips. "Now I could go for the big fellow, though. He looks dangerous. Probably need the brothers to give me a hand with that one. Speaking of which."

He glanced around the cabin though he knew he was alone and spat on his hand and reached down under the desk. His eyes switched from the computer screen to the wet locker and back and forth again, and his breath grew raspy and uneven.

※

Twenty minutes later there was a knock on the hull and the brothers came aboard. They brought industrial-strength garbage bags with them, and the three of them put on disposable rubber gloves. Within half an hour they had lowered the mahogany launch into the water, and John Newcombe was on his way out of the harbour and under the Lions Gate Bridge, triple-bagged and trussed in old anchor chain. A mile out in a hundred fathoms of water the brothers shut off the engine and slipped him quietly over the side into the dark water. They lit cigarettes and waited in silence for a few minutes, though neither of them could have said exactly why. They hadn't even liked him, and he sure as hell wasn't coming back up.

A freighter herded up with a pair of tugs moved past a half mile out and rocked them with its wake. Clint threw his cigarette butt over the side, then flipped the engine into gear and headed back to the club. When they arrived back at his berth, the accountant was waiting with the slings and helped them crane the boat up out of the water and onto the upper deck. They went into the cabin for drinks and he told them about his latest conversation with the man. The brothers listened, shaking their heads in disapproval.

"I told him we should have gotten rid of them afterwards," Travis said. "Made them disappear. Lots of women vanish and are never heard of again. Happens all the time in the big city. Putting them out on park benches like that afterwards is like a big flashing neon fuck you sign. Does he even use condoms? I doubt it. DNA and all that CSI shit you see on TV, sometimes I think it's like he wants to get caught. Or even worse, maybe he thinks he's invincible and can't be caught, Jesus H. Christ."

"Careful now," the accountant said. "You wouldn't want him to hear you talking like that."

"Who's going to tell him? You, you fat old faggot? I don't think so. Not if you know what's good for you. Now get over here and do your other job." Travis reached down and unzipped himself.

The accountant licked his lips nervously. "I don't think—" he began.

"We don't need you to think. Better get your strap out again, Clint, I guess he must have liked it last time."

His brother grinned and pulled off his belt and undid his pants. They dropped to the floor and he kicked them to one side as he stepped out of them. He tripped the fat man and pulled down his trousers and shorts and moved up close behind him.

"Your turn to set the pace, Travis," he said. "I'll just ride along double back here. Woo-hoo. Giddy up, old hoss."

The belt cracked.

The fat man shrieked.

The brothers giggled.

CHAPTER 16

James Albright stood on the balcony high up in the Properties, his eyes closed in rapture, his arms outstretched as the Götterdämmerung soared to its magnificent finale. A pair of glasses wrapped in paper and an unopened bottle of single malt Scotch sat on a small metal table beside him. He let out his breath and turned and spoke to the lawyer who had been standing by the door in silence watching him conduct for the last few minutes, not daring to interrupt.

"I can give you ten minutes. I have to be at a dinner downtown in under an hour. At five thousand dollars a plate, I can't afford to be late. The party needs that money right now, our war chest is getting low. We can't afford any more screw-ups. Is that understood?"

Richard Sullivan nodded. "Understood."

The lawyer was a tall, well-built silver-haired man who looked like everybody's favourite uncle. If you were ever accused of anything serious, he was exactly the type of man you would want pleading your case, Albright thought. In other words, a lying, cheating weasel. He opened the Scotch and poured out two drinks and handed one across to Sullivan.

"I think we're good," Sullivan said. "Clint and Travis are at his place now, going through his things and making sure there's nothing lying around that could tie him to us. He lived alone in a one-room apartment and had no real friends that we're aware of. We're still checking, but it seems clear that he was a bit of a loner. I doubt he spoke to anybody before he ran. I can't imagine why he insisted on wearing that stupid jacket with the crest. Did he think it gave him a bit of class? And then to give them his real name? How dumb was that?"

"Anyway," Albright said.

"Right. The other two. Jared Kane and Daniel MacLean. Not to be taken lightly it would seem. It turns out that Kane is hooked up with the sister of one of the women."

"One of the women?"

"One of the women on the park benches," the lawyer said, and immediately regretted it. Why the hell had he even brought them up? A slight sheen was visible on his forehead now.

"And just how does that concern us?"

Sullivan stared at him. James Albright regarded him impassively, his eyebrows raised in question. Sullivan was famed for his quick wit and ability to think on his feet in courtroom battles, but at the moment his mind was a blank slate. He felt hypnotized. Like a rabbit in front of a fucking mongoose or whatever the fuck it was. The translucent hazel eyes watched him. The seconds ticked by and the silence grew.

"Well," he began cautiously, searching for a way out of the quagmire.

Albright smiled. "You were saying about the two men, MacLean and Kane?"

Was that Albright's idea of a joke? Was the man playing with him? Sullivan realized he had absolutely no idea. For about the hundredth time he wished he had never become involved in any of this. But really, how could he possibly have known? And by the time he began to suspect, it was already too late, he was enmeshed from the soles of his thousand-dollar English shoes to the feathered tips of his two-hundred-dollar Robson Street haircut. There was no deal to be cut, no plea bargain to be had that would not destroy him and everything he had so carefully built up over twenty-five years of long hours and personal sacrifice.

It would absolutely be jail time for him; he had no illusions about it. Hard time even, and he knew he couldn't handle that. The only sure escape left open to him now was a full-blown slash-and-burn scorched-earth retreat to a no deportation jurisdiction in South America, and he wasn't ready for that yet. It might be sooner than later though. But he thought there was still a good chance for him here if he played it right. Albright stared at him and he wondered for a moment if the mad bastard could read minds. It might not have completely surprised him. He refocused and took a deep breath and continued.

"We're still gathering information. Kane is dating the sister of the last girl. Both he and MacLean have criminal records; they met when they were in prison. Assault for Kane, a bit of burglary for MacLean. Two years for each of them. They've been friends ever since and went sailing offshore together for a few years on an old wooden sailboat Kane inherited. He lives aboard in the downtown fishermen's marina now. We've been told that MacLean sleeps aboard some nights."

"Wooden. Good to know," Albright said.

"Kane has been clean since his release, a couple of minor assault charges resulting from bar fights a few years back that were dropped. His partner, the First Nations guy, MacLean, was knifed during a jewellery store robbery shortly after leaving prison, but charges were stayed when it turned out he was stabbed by his accomplices. They were notorious gangsters from Quebec and there were some questions about whether MacLean even knew what was really going on. He was badly injured and the doctors thought he would never walk again. There was a lot of sympathy for him at the time. It was a big story back then, you probably heard about it. Made all the cable news stations."

"I never watch TV," Albright said. He rose smoothly to his feet signalling an end to the meeting. He rotated his hips, loosening his shoulders, and slipped on his suit jacket and walked over to the side-board mirror and adjusted his tie.

"How do I look?" It was the rhetorical question of a practised politician. He knew he looked good. He was a big man and had to stoop slightly to check his hair. It was, as always, perfect. Maybe he'd accentuate the swept back thing a little more; it couldn't hurt with his base. He'd speak to his barber.

"Have to be at my best tonight. A lot of important people going to be there, a lot of money going to be raised. I'm having a small do afterwards for some of the guests in a private suite at the hotel. Would you care to join us? You'll meet some interesting people. I can guarantee it."

"I'd love to, but I'm afraid I'm booked up for this evening." Sullivan hoped he sounded sincere.

"Ah well. Perhaps next time."

"Absolutely. I look forward to it. I should leave now. I'll be in touch."

The lawyer turned and headed for the door, trying not to hurry. It seemed now that every time he met Albright it was incrementally worse. They seldom met in the same place twice nowadays, and that in itself was concerning. He had a permanent suite in the hotel where he did most of his party business, and a string of different properties where he held those meetings he wanted to remain private. Did he even own any of them? Richard Sullivan realized that Albright knew a hell of a lot more about him than he did about Albright. Maybe it was time that changed.

❀

James Albright watched Sullivan scuttling off, an amused smile on his face. That had been exquisite, letting that tiny glimpse of his new self slip out into the open and seeing the smooth-polished lawyer break into a slimy sweat as the silence stretched. Since the red flags had popped up on his check-up a year back, it was becoming harder to behave as if nothing had changed when everything had. They'd done all the tests, given him all the referrals, the names of the top specialists, the whole nine yards. When the last doctor he'd seen, an earnest grizzled veteran with a wall of fancy diplomas behind him, had begun lecturing him on philosophical positivity, Stephen Hawking, and the quality of life still available to him, it was all he could do to refrain from grabbing the man by the neck and crotch and heaving him out of his office window onto 5th Avenue sixteen floors down.

His whole life had been about being in control, and to think that at this late stage he would hand over his care and governance to an individual or an institution was beyond laughable. Not going to happen. He had chosen instead to take off the gloves, shed the veneers, and become the man he was meant to be. Rather than sinking into morbid depression, he had become liberated, spreading his wings and learning to fly. The rules no longer applied.

"Yippee!" he suddenly whooped at the mirror, and the man in the mirror grinned and winked right back at him.

He finished his drink, pulled out his cell phone, and called for Malcolm. Five minutes later he was seated in the back seat of the Mercedes limousine reading over his speech for the evening ahead as Wagner blared from the Blaupunkt.

His driver smiled at him in the mirror.

"You're looking good this evening, sir."

"I feel good, Malcolm. Going to break the bank tonight."

"God's will, sir."

"God's will, Malcolm." His response was automatic. Religion was just another cloak to be put on or taken off as the situation called for, and what with his early days back in the boonies, he could Jesus right up there with the best of them. Albright leaned back and closed his eyes for a moment and thought about the evening that lay ahead. If he did really well tonight, mightn't he deserve a reward? But he mustn't think about that right now. He crossed his legs against the stirring and went back to his notes for the speech.

CHAPTER 17

Cat snatched up her rucksack and resisted the urge to fire it across the room. She probably would have if it hadn't contained a good ten grand's worth of camera equipment. That little Welsh bastard Reese owed her big time for this. She didn't shoot this kind of crap; they all knew that, and especially him. She'd worked for him for almost a decade, dozens upon dozens of shoots over the years, at all sorts of events and never ever at one of these. She didn't give a fat rat's ass how many fashionistas might be attending or how much coverage the event would attract. She was well enough known in her field to be able to pick and choose her assignments. She'd agreed to shoot the Toronto International Film Festival twice, and God knew what a pain those prima donnas could be, but you had to draw the line somewhere, and she didn't do political. Not ever.

But Reese had pleaded and begged. He'd paid a small fortune for the exclusive lobby shoot. There was no one else available who could do the job. David was sick, Ellie suddenly called away to L.A., and Matt, well, who knew. Probably lying in a gutter somewhere stoned out of his mind, and, greater sin, with his cell phone turned off. Reese had even manufactured a small sob near the end. She stopped him just as the little weasel was set to drop to his knees and said she'd do the shoot for double her usual rate.

If you were going to sell out, sell high.

She'd done some research for the evening ahead, she always did. Even though she only took pictures and never wrote a single line of copy, she felt that knowing something about her subjects made for better photographs. Her research never affected her shots — well, maybe that one time when she'd intentionally shot that fascist French bitch from her bad side — but she felt unprepared when she didn't do it. And there was no doubt that James Albright was an interesting study.

Cat had come across a clip from one of his rallies on the late news one night and found herself vaguely disturbed by the event, from that first fist-pumping entrance down the red carpet surrounded by his uniformed security team to the applause-punctuated speech that followed it. What bothered her most was not the populist speech — although it was a bit unsettling hearing that on this side of the border — but the reactions of the crowd receiving it. Many of them were wearing the arm bands his team handed out — "Albright, he's all right" — and they shouted out the slogan at regular intervals. Sometimes they just screamed out "all right, all right" in a broad wink to their political leanings. Albright's rallies attracted a lot of protesters and there had been several incidents where people had been injured, sometimes by the crowd and sometimes by security. Albright always deplored these incidents when they occurred, but he never actually stood up and condemned them outright.

Definitely not her cup of tea, Cat thought.

She checked her bag for lenses, flash, batteries, chargers, and all the other assorted crap you thought you'd never need until you suddenly did. She kept her kit ready to go at a moment's notice, but it was always a comfort to have the time to make sure. The political rally (for that's what it was — Reese could call it an exclusive dinner for the city's finest all he wanted, but it was a goddamned political rally) started at eight.

So the grand entrances would probably begin around seven thirty. That gave her an hour to get there and get organized. Reese had paid out a large bribe so she could set up early inside the spacious lobby and not have to stand outside in the weather with the rest of the rabble waiting around to shoot the city's celebrities. Ordinarily she might have felt a little guilty about this.

She pulled on a pair of tailored jeans and blood-red ox-hide boots that sort of matched the colour of the leather jacket that was her trademark. Unruly hair twisted into pigtails and a beret over the top and she was done. She could do all this and be out the door in under ten minutes from the bunk in an emergency. The first time she'd done her quick-change call-out in front of Jared, she'd made the mistake of asking how she looked on her rush out the door.

"No worries, Pippi, you look great," he'd said as he ducked back under the covers.

She smiled. Jared. What a jerk. She tucked her phone in her jacket pocket, grabbed her rucksack, and headed out the door.

Cat handed her card to the doorman standing by the hotel entrance and he passed her through to the good-natured jeers of the gaggle of journalists and photographers who were huddled under the canopy outside trying to stay dry. Cat threw them the good-natured finger they expected as the lobby doors closed behind her. She walked around checking the lighting and talked to the manager to make sure it wouldn't be changed when the luminaries began to arrive. It wasn't his first rodeo, and he took her around and made some good suggestions for entrance shots. For some reason that Cat had never understood, editors and readers always wanted pictures of the power couples sweeping into the building. Never mind that most if not all of them would have been more than happy to stand and pose for the camera. Sweeping was what was required. She refocused her attention on the manager at her side.

"So, the banquet begins at eight, there will be a brief welcome from the Party Chairman, say eight thirty for meal start. Some minor speakers while they're being served, an informal break afterwards, and then the real dog and pony show gets going. If you've never heard this guy, you're in for a treat. A real old-fashioned spellbinder. He isn't nicknamed the Preacher for nothing. He'll get them right up out of their chairs. The women will be throwing their knickers and the men will be throwing their wallets. Figuratively speaking of course. They say Albright considered the ministry when he was a young man, before he got into politics."

"Great," Cat said. "My two favourite things: religion and politics."

"Well, it's just politics now. I guess things didn't work out on the religious end, although they say he gave great fire-and-brimstone back in the day. That's when he caught the eye of the party brass, the story goes."

Cat said, "I appreciate the background, but I just take the pictures. Greater minds than mine and all that. I'm Cat, by the way." She reached out and shook his hand.

"Gerald. I've seen your work, it's very good. That little New Zealand model you shot for the *Sun*? She looked positively angelic. Like there should have been some white clouds and a halo around her. Outstanding. Well, time for me to go to work. Have fun."

The couples were beginning to trickle through the lobby, and the manager went and stood immobile by the doors with his hands clasped behind his back in the time-honoured tradition. Off to the side and out of the way, but immediately available should anything be required of him. The flashes began popping outside, and Cat went to her marks and started shooting. She recognized most of the people but took shots of them all, even the ones she couldn't identify. Nothing would be worse than to miss one that Reese wanted. She suspected the little rat wasn't above asking for one he didn't want just to show her up and keep her in her place. A slender man with glasses being pushed in a wheelchair by a very large man came through the lobby doors, and Cat thought that he was someone she should know but couldn't recall his name. She took a couple of quick shots of the unusual pair just in case.

The lobby was beginning to get crowded now; no one was going through to the banquet room. People were dropping off their coats and hats with the cloakroom attendants and then circling back and forming small groups. Drinks were being served and a crackling expectant buzz filled the room. Some cheers, a sudden light storm of flashes outside, and then the doors opened and Albright stepped through. His mild gaze swept the room and conversation all but stopped.

An awkward, hesitant moment of silence, and then someone started clapping and applause broke out. He grinned and gave a slight mocking bow as he moved forward, greeting people right and left as the crowd parted for him, pausing to shake hands and exchange a few words every few feet. Cat had moved up to the doors as he approached, and now she stood off to one side, moving backwards in step as he moved forward, shooting steadily all the time. Cat clicked off another half-dozen shots; thought, *Screw it, that's enough for now*; and faded back into the crowd to observe.

The throng was thick around him and he was constantly stopped in his progress towards the hall. Many of his admirers were women and that didn't surprise Cat. With his swept back hair and deep uniform tan, he had a sleek complacent look of sated appetite about him that vaguely reminded her of some actor in the old black-and-white movies she loved to watch. Victor Mature? His dark navy suit had been cut to show off his athletic physique and he wore it well. Good-looking, probably attractive to a certain type of woman, Cat concluded with some disdain, and then he looked up and his eyes caught and held hers and she felt the impact and she thought, *Whoa!* He stared at her for perhaps three seconds and the mild hazel eyes glowed and Cat knew she was blushing, but she wouldn't look away. And then he turned and moved past her and the moment was gone. Cat stared after him in mild shock.

"Well, what did you think?" the manager asked, moving up beside her.

"I almost took my panties off and threw them at him," Cat said, "and he never uttered a single syllable."

"I know what you mean," Gerald said. "He has that effect on people."

A few feet ahead of them, James Albright leaned down and murmured into the ear of one of his aides. "The photographer. The one with the red hair. I want to know who she is."

The man nodded and slipped back into the crowd. James Albright turned his attention back to his acolytes and smiled and shook the offered hands and continued his stately procession towards the dining room.

CHAPTER 18

"It feels like we're not making any progress. Doing nothing useful, just sitting around waiting for something bad to happen. And if past is prologue, it will," Danny said.

He finished his beer, absent-mindedly crushed the can and set it carefully down on top of the small but growing pile in *Arrow*'s cockpit. It was late afternoon and the shadows were just beginning to creep across the foredeck. The mainsheet swayed back and forth as a seiner rocked *Arrow* in passing, its crew sitting bare-backed on the hatch cover in the warm sun, fids in hand, as they worked on the nets and gossiped.

"I agree, but I don't see that there's anything else we can do right now except wait around for something to break," Jared said. "Clarke cross-referenced all the dates on the computer against the attacks on the women and hasn't found any other links apart from that one stolen gate card which connects to all of them. No other cards used around the time of the attacks that connects to more than one of them. Those were all checked out and eliminated as suspects."

Danny said, "How about the house up in the Properties where the guy from the Lamplight led us?"

Jared shook his head. "No joy there either. It's owned by an offshore shell company, and the name of the real owner is untraceable without the warrants that Clarke says there isn't a snowball's chance in hell of obtaining. We can forget about the private investigator who took off for Mexico, if the locals haven't located him by now they're not going to. Besides which, he wouldn't say anything before he took off, so why would he now?"

Danny shrugged. "Well, maybe sometimes there really is nothing you can do. You just have to sit back and wait for developments."

"To hell with it. Let's go sailing."

Fifteen minutes later *Arrow* was on her way out of the marina, Jared at the tiller, Danny folding back the mainsail cover and hooking up the halyard. The head of the bungeed sail shivered as they motored out into the main channel towards the bridge against a sluggish tide.

"Not much wind."

"No. Maybe find some when we get out past the bridge. Supposed to be a change in the weather tonight, low coming in later this afternoon. Could pick up some breeze ahead of the front if we're lucky."

There were two sailboats further out and they looked to be struggling in light air. A pair of fifty-foot American powerboats blew by at full throttle rocking *Arrow* violently in their wake as their captains waved from the bridge decks. Jared cursed under his breath as he steadied the boom before hooking up the autopilot and seating himself beside Danny on the rail. The two of them stared intently forward into the wind's quadrant as if their combined focus might make it suddenly increase.

The cat's paws disappeared and a sluggish oily sheen appeared on the water as they passed under the bridge and moved out among the anchored freighters. A crewman in soiled galley whites threw scraps over the rail to a dozen gulls and waved insipidly as they went by. Half an hour later they motored past a stalled-out dinghy race off English Bay and threw in the towel.

"Never even got the sails up," Danny grouched. "Talk about nothing happening, this is getting ridiculous."

"Maybe a change of scenery is what we need. How about we head over to the yacht club, tie up at the visitors dock for a couple of nights? We could check in with Merlynn, have a couple of martinis, see how Clarke is making out. It sounded like he was spending a lot of time there last time we spoke."

"Sounds like a plan." Danny went forward and pulled the cover back over the mainsail and tied everything off while Jared unhooked the autopilot and headed *Arrow* back under the bridge.

The visitors docks were busy and they had to stand off and idle in slow circles for half an hour until a space large enough to accommodate *Arrow* opened up. After tying up they headed for the bar where they were greeted warmly by Darren, their well-tipped new best friend who was on duty behind the counter. He drew two cold pints and brought them up to speed on club gossip.

"Everyone's talking about it. All the club officers and staff have had interviews. I had mine with some big old ugly dude. He never really said what it was about. Wanted to know if any strangers had been around, had gone into the office unaccompanied, that sort of thing. Ha! Look around you. There are probably thirty people in here right now and I might be able to tell you who ten of them are. It's high season, man. Anyone can tie up and come in here for drinks. They sign in at the door, or are supposed to, but the guest list is really just an honourary thing. Nobody polices it because nobody really gives a damn either way. It's just there to satisfy the legal requirements of a private club. What's all this about anyway?"

"Not really sure," Danny said. "Is there a John Newcombe registered with the club?"

"The name sounds vaguely familiar." Darren reached under the counter and handed over a club yearbook. "This is up to date, apart from a few new members."

Jared picked up the book and thumbed through it with little hope.

"I'll be damned. There he is. John Newcombe. They've even got an address for him. And a cell phone number. Let's just give him a call, shall we?"

He moved down to the end of the bar and picked up the club phone and dialled. The number rang three times and then clicked over and was picked up.

"Good afternoon. Where may I direct your call?"

A bored receptionist. Answering service would be his guess.

"John Newcombe, please."

"Just a moment, sir."

More clicks as the call was transferred, a half-dozen rings and then a pickup.

"Yeah?" A loud angry voice.

"Mr. Newcombe?"

A pause and then a throat clearing and change of tone.

"Yes, this is he. Who is calling, please?"

Jared knew that voice. Clarke.

"Wrong number," he said, and hung up and moved back down to the end of the bar.

Danny raised his eyebrows.

Jared said, "Wrong number."

The bar phone rang and Darren picked it up.

"Yes, sir, he's here. Just a moment, please." He handed the phone across to Jared.

"Hello, Clarke. What can I do for you?" He held the phone away from his ear and slid a twenty over to Darren.

"Bring us another round, will you? We might be here for a while. Have one yourself."

Danny smiled and flipped through the yearbook pages. He paused and turned back a page and studied it.

"We were getting bored," Jared said into the phone, and then held it away from his ear again.

Danny was looking at a picture of a group of men in wigs and Hawaiian hula skirts holding drinks with umbrellas in their hands. They were standing on a dock and had goofy smiles on their faces. The caption read "Newcastle Island party 2018." One of the men was John Newcombe. He called the bartender back over.

"Sure, I know him," Darren said. "John. Not a bad guy. In here quite a bit. Trying to hustle women a lot of the time. Doesn't do very well at it, though. That would be William Lacey standing beside him, or 'Queer Bill' as he sometimes calls himself when he's had a few. I've seen them together a few times. He's a bookkeeper or accountant, something like that. Does the books for the club."

The bartender told them Bill was one of the long-time live-aboards with a converted tugboat in one of the big sheds. A beautiful old Foss that he kept in pristine working condition. "It's a showpiece, absolutely immaculate, won the Summer Regatta honours this year. He was an officer of the club back in the day, so you'll find his picture with all the rest of the officers for that year in their caps and blazers somewhere on the walls in the boardroom."

"And these two?" Jared asked, indicating the other men in the picture.

"Regulars; they're in here most weekends. One's a lawyer, the other one works in the city. Something to do with banking maybe." He shrugged. "I'm working the bar, people are across from me chatting. I'm not deaf, I hear things."

"Have another one on me," Danny said.

CHAPTER 19

"I'm not going to tell you again," Clarke roared.

If only that were true, Jared thought, but remained silent. Danny and Merlynn gazed off down the channel, their faces grave.

They were seated on the afterdeck of *Legalese* doing the happy hour thing. Except Clarke was definitely not happy. He'd been lying on his back changing oil in one of the diesels in *Legalese's* engine room when the police phone with Newcombe's call forwarding rang and had cracked his skull in his rush to answer it. He'd taken off his greasy overalls, but oil and blood still covered the side of his head. "Medicine first," he'd snarled at Merlynn when she had attempted to clean him up. He was on his third drink in ten minutes. The first two had barely touched the sides of his throat. He was so mad he could hardly speak. Jared debated whether he should tell him about the Bill Lacey lead.

"They were just trying to help," Merlynn offered in their defence.

Clarke looked at her and swelled up once again, and they waited for the explosion. He downed his drink and picked up the jug. "I'm going for a shower. Don't anybody even think about moving from here while I'm gone."

"Does that include me?" Merlynn asked.

"No. You can come with me. Please," Clarke added.

Merlynn winked at Jared and followed him out of the room.

"She's enjoying this," Danny said. "Said it's the most fun she's had since she retired. She'll chill Clarke out if anyone can."

When the two of them returned half an hour later, Clarke was scrubbed clean with a large bandage on his forehead and approaching mellow.

"Newcombe has vanished," he said. "We put an APB out on him but no reports of sightings so far. Early days, though, he's only been missing for forty-eight hours. We'll check the airports and border crossings next. We took out a search warrant on his apartment but it was all pretty sterile — no personal touches, hard to tell that anyone actually lived there; no pictures of family or friends, laptop gone, desk empty, furniture from a rental company."

"Someone beat you to it," Jared said.

"Probably," Clarke agreed.

He continued. "Newcombe doesn't appear to have a steady job — he's an independent public relations contractor who hires out for political campaigns and does some work for the city now and again. Last job was with Citizens United about a month ago. He's unmarried and has no girlfriends that we know of. From everything we've learned so far, his closest friends might be the bartenders at the yacht club. Seems like an under-the-radar kind of a guy." Clarke paused. "Didn't leave much of a wake," he added nautically.

"Did he ever work for the Conservative Party?" Merlynn asked.

"As a matter of fact, he did work for them. And for the Liberals and the NDP and the Green Party as well. So no joy there."

"Still, it is a connection," Merlynn said.

"Yep. And so far it's all we've got until we locate him and bring him in for questioning." Clarke shrugged. "We'll keep looking, he's out there somewhere. It's possible he might just have taken some time off, gone away for a bit. Somebody somewhere will have an idea where he is. It's just a matter of talking to enough people. It nearly always comes down to legwork in the end. I've got a couple of good men on it."

Jared realized now was the moment to speak out about the accountant William Lacey. He looked to Danny who gazed impassively back at him and gave a noncommittal shrug of his shoulders. Leaving it up to him, the bastard.

"I think Danny and I might have—" Jared began in an appeasing tone.

"Don't say another word," Clarke interrupted. "Apology accepted. And I have to admit the pair of you did shake out Newcombe for the department. We wouldn't have that without you two. Not to mention finding Merlynn and all the help she's been." Clarke beamed genially at the three of them and the moment for confession had passed.

"Steaks are marinating. One more round and I'll fire up the Weber. Merlynn's fixed the crab salad, we're ready to rock. Tonight we party, tomorrow we find Newcombe. Or rather, tomorrow I find Newcombe. You boys are officially retired. On behalf of the department, I salute you for your service. No medals, but I do have a tub of iced beer in the galley. Cheers."

Clarke raised his glass and clinked theirs and Jared made a phone call and a little while later Cat showed up with Danny's latest and the evening descended into a blur of good food and alcohol and laughter.

❀

"What?" Jared mumbled, shaking his head as he struggled up from deep unconsciousness. Cat's arm was thrown over his chest and she was snoring softly.

"Shh, be quiet. We don't want to wake anybody up."

It was Danny, crouched at the side of the bed with a penlight.

"It will be light in less than an hour."

"And?"

"And we want to get a look at *Rainbow* before everyone's awake."

Rainbow? What the hell was rainbow? Jared wondered.

"It was your idea. The tugboat. Queer Bill, remember? We're just going to have a quick peek before the docks get busy."

"I'm never going to drink again," Jared muttered as he pulled on his shorts and runners. "And I'm not buying that this was my idea either."

"Well, maybe not entirely," Danny conceded as they crept out of the cabin.

The party had broken up late and everyone had chosen to stay on board *Legalese* for the night. Nobody was fit to drive, and even the short walk along the docks to *Arrow* might have proven unsafe. The old Monk McQueen yacht had plenty of accommodation: four cabins plus the master that Clarke and Merlynn occupied. They had been given the grand tour sometime around midnight, nautical phrases pouring out of Clarke in a steady stream as he showed them over the boat. He had taken some holidays and now appeared to be working nearly full-time on *Legalese*. The results were visible everywhere, from the gleaming engine room to the scrubbed decks and polished brass doorknobs and fixtures. He'd managed to get the long dormant genset up and running and had serviced the main engines.

It turned out the issues with the twin diesels were minor ones of neglect and delayed maintenance and not beyond Clarke's limited skills. Armed with a grease gun and new filters, belts, and hoses, he'd achieved wonders. Clarke's enthusiasm was infectious, and Jared had a dim uncomfortable memory of volunteering to help scrape and recaulk *Legalese's* decks sometime over the course of the evening. That was a serious commitment even if the plywood underlay was not rotten. Which it most likely was. And in more than just a few spots.

"It's right along here according to the chart," Danny whispered. "Number eighty-nine. The door to the shed should be unlocked as he's living aboard."

"Tell me again why we're going to look at this boat, in the dark, in the middle of the night," Jared said. "What exactly are we hoping to find?"

"We'll know it when we see it," Danny whispered. "Keep your voice down, we're here."

Under the dim glow of the dock lights could be seen a piece of multihued cedar carved in the shape of a rainbow fastened to the door of a boat shed. They opened it and passed through.

Inside was another LED light, this one outlining the dim profile of a large ocean-going tug. The carvel planked hull was painted black, with green topsides and a white funnel smokestack with brass trim. Portlights were framed in gleaming brass, and the cabin doors had been redone in heavy carved teak. A massive upswept bow was covered with tires cut in half and fastened outboard down to the water line. The anchor winch was enormous, and another even bigger towing winch rose up from the shadows on her rear deck. As they crept down the dock towards the stern, they could see fresh grease gleaming from its fittings. *Rainbow* looked ready to be back plying her trade at a moment's notice. A white painted crane overhung a tarped runabout on her bridge deck.

"We need to have a quick peek under that canvas," Danny whispered. "Only take a minute. Keep an eye out."

Before Jared could form a protest Danny was up over *Rainbow*'s rail and soundlessly rising up the ladder to the top deck. He lay in the shadows alongside the tender and unhooked the bungees and slowly raised the tarp. He slid his head underneath and then crawled the length of the boat. After a minute he lowered the cover again and refastened the ties. He glided down the ladder and over the rail and grabbed Jared's arm and they left the shed.

"And is it there?" Jared asked in a low whisper.

"Yep," Danny said. "Nice old mahogany Chris-Craft runabout."

"Probably be more than one of those in the club," Jared said.

"There could well be. But you know that's the one."

"Yeah," Jared said. "That'll be the one all right. No doubt about it."

CHAPTER 20

The lawyer leaned against the railing on his West End apartment balcony and sipped from a glass of thirty-year-old single malt as he stared out over the city and thought it all through one last time. The more Sullivan analyzed his interactions with Albright over the last two years, the more he realized just how difficult it was going to be to extricate himself from their consequences. That was if he wanted to take his profits with him at any rate, and goddammit, he was entitled to that money. He'd worked like a dog for it, cut corners for it, even taken a chance of disbarment for it. He wasn't desperate for the money, he'd made some good investments years ago and the penthouse apartment he'd bought for eight hundred K after the divorce was worth three times that now. Hell, maybe even five times what he'd paid for it — the Asians and Americans were jacking up prices every week. Some of those realtor assholes were pulling in over a million a year in commissions for Christ's sake. Driving around in their shiny new Mercs and Bimmers. He'd planned carefully and done all his homework, put in all those late nights and weekends, and those bastards just fell into it.

It wasn't right. If he didn't get his payout on this last deal, he'd be just another guy amongst the well-to-do crowd, and he knew himself well enough to suspect that he couldn't live with that. Especially when he knew that the golden prize was hanging out there now, just within his grasp. He wanted, no, he *needed* to be rich, private island fuck you rich, and by God he would be. He deserved it. It had seemed so easy at the beginning. He came from a blue collar working family, but had made a few connections at varsity and knew some influential people from his frat days. He'd graduated first in his law class, was the editor of the school paper his final year, and a star athlete. Not in hockey or football, but boxing, of all things. He'd gone out for it on a drunken frat night bet, and it turned out he was a natural with fast hands and a deceptive knockout punch. He was the first student from his alma mater to have a shot at the national college title. Doing pretty damn well, too, until he met that Black guy from Halifax in the semis and got his ass kicked. His nose was flattened and still a bit crooked to this day. He was going to get it fixed right afterwards until the campus queen told him it made him look hot just before she gave him the best blow job he'd ever had.

The boxing was a long time ago now, but people still remembered and came up to him wanting to talk about it. The fight game as they liked to call it. He tried to make it to his old club two or three times a month for light sparring sessions. Nothing serious, it just gave him a bit of a workout and let him casually bring up in conversation that he'd just come from a training session at the City Gym, yada yada. Whatever worked. Even Albright was fascinated. Always asking him questions about his old fights down to the smallest detail. Did he even feel the hits at the time, or was it just all swallowed up in the rage and excitement of the contest? Weird.

He'd met James Albright over a decade ago at one of the political fundraisers he sometimes attended and they'd gotten to know each other over the next couple of years. Albright was an up-and-coming star in the party and eventually asked Sullivan if he would consider coming to work for him. It meant increased status with a decent retainer and the promise of an inside track in some big money deals. He'd been flattered — okay and maybe a little greedy as well, if he was being honest — and walked away from the law firm that would have offered him a full partnership in a few more years.

Back then he still had a few ideals, and the legal paperwork on that first questionable rezoning flip might have left a bit of a bad taste in his mouth, but that hadn't lasted for very long. The money started coming in, real money, and he'd dumped the hometown sweetheart who was holding him back socially and was off to the races. In hindsight, the move to the political world had been an error of judgment. He enjoyed the minor celebrity and the high-end women that came with the new job, but then he'd become involved in a real estate venture with Albright and Albright's accountant two years ago. He'd put in three million, it had seriously stretched his resources, and by the time he realized that the reluctant sellers had been pressured by Albright's hillbillies, perhaps even to the point of criminality, it was too late for him to withdraw.

If the complaints led to an investigation, the whole thing could come crashing down like a house of cards. It was going to take at least another six months for the deal to complete and for him to get his initial investment back, let alone the five million from the proposed subdivision that was projected to be his share of the profit over the following years. He'd insisted the deal be structured so that he could sell his interest in it at any time, and he thought he could find a buyer and still take a reasonable profit, but he knew Albright wouldn't like it. That part of it worried him more than he cared to admit. That last scene up at the Properties where he'd stood by the door for ten minutes watching the man waltzing around the room conducting the music that blared from the speakers was disturbing, to say the least.

Recently conversations between them were strained and it felt like Albright was mocking him a lot of the time. The man had changed over the last year. It seemed like he was becoming more reckless with every passing month and blowing off many of those political allies he'd previously courted. His rallies had become more strident and his politics had swung even further to the right. Most people now considered him a fringe member of the party with no real chance of ever becoming the leader. But he was well funded and still a person of influence within the inner circles of the party with a devoted base, and his committee controlled a large block of votes. You offended him at your own political peril.

None of that stuff concerned Sullivan. He was not a political animal and had always been more concerned about profits than politics. What really worried him were Albright's personal soldiers, the brothers Clint and Travis. They had been breezier than usual with him lately, mocking almost, as if they knew something that he didn't. It occurred to him, and not for the first time, that Newcombe's disappearance might not have been entirely voluntary. He didn't think it was paranoid delusion to suspect that he might be next.

If he were to have any chance of getting out with his skin and his money intact, he'd have to think carefully about who to bring on board with him. He needed an ally. The accountant was the obvious choice but apart from the fact he didn't know if he could trust him when it came right down to it, the man gave him the creeps. Not because Bill was queer, the lawyer wasn't prejudiced. He had several gay friends. Hell, truth be known, he'd woken up with a sore ass himself once or twice after doing too many lines. It wasn't that. There was just something about the man that gave him the willies. *Bad word choice*, he thought. Still, Lacey was the main architect of the deal, and Sullivan didn't think it would be possible to get his money out without involving him.

He thought about the last time the three of them had met. Albright had been rough and irritable with bloodshot eyes and a raspy voice, the accountant skittish and nervous. The two brothers had come in at the end of the meeting, and one of them had slammed a newspaper down on the table in front of Albright. It was a curiously aggressive gesture. One of the headlines was about the latest "girl on a park bench."

Albright had looked at the paper and grinned. It was at that point that Sullivan fully understood what he had gotten himself into. Albright might actually be certifiably crazy. The lawyer had mumbled something about being late for another meeting and got up and left the room, stifling the impulse to break into a sprint.

Later that evening he'd dropped into the yacht club for a drink and seen Bill sitting with Albright's lieutenants at the bar. He wondered what in the hell they found in common to talk about. The brothers had been around since the very beginning, when there were still a lot of rough edges on the young politician. But Albright had the pure fire, even back then. The first time Sullivan heard him speak was long before he met him, at the old football stadium, in front of twenty thousand people, and he'd been stunned by his power and charisma. It was what he imagined an old-fashioned gospel revival meeting would have been like, spell-binding, almost hypnotic, the air around Albright crackling and so charged with electricity that even a hardened cynic like himself was caught up in it all. He'd almost stood up and *hallelujah*ed with the rest of them.

And the women. Christ, it seemed like he could have had any woman he wanted, any woman there. They seemed mesmerized by him. It was as if the sweat that flew off him when he was on fire and prancing the stage was full of pheromones and the air around him was sexually charged. The lawyer knew how crazy that sounded. What sounded even crazier was if a guy with that kind of sex appeal was abducting women, assaulting, and discarding them half dead on West End park benches.

If Albright was doing that, then he was as crazy as a shithouse rat, and the lawyer was now damn near certain that was exactly what was going on. He finished his drink and considered having another one, but decided he'd better wait until after he'd made the call. These were tricky waters he was about to navigate, and he'd best have his wits about him. He sat there thinking everything through for another few minutes, then he picked up his cell phone, took a deep breath, and dialled.

"It's me," he said. "Richard Sullivan. Can we meet? It's urgent."

CHAPTER 21

The note card was embossed gold script on a charcoal backing with a simple border. Classy. *The Right Honourable James Albright M.P.* With a phone number and email address. On the back, in an upright flowing script, written in ballpoint, no doubt, but using gold ink, the message:

> I was very impressed by your work at last week's event. Would you
> care to meet for a drink? I think our organization could find work
> for someone with your talents.
>
> Regards,
> James.

Cat held the card in her hand and studied it. Points for the card, in good taste although the gold script might be a bit much. The *James* signature definitely subtracted points. Jameses tended to be stuffy twits in Cat's limited experience, whereas men she'd come across called Jim were, by and large, regular guys. And they all had a choice of which name to go by. Or did they? Maybe they didn't. Now that she thought about it, Cat wasn't really sure.

Anyway.

If it was just a straight-out invitation for a drink, she would probably have had to decline. Although she and Jared were not — what? In a monogamous relationship? Jesus, how old-fashioned did that sound? — they were sort of a couple. A thousand years ago, or so it seemed, they might have said they were going steady, although Cat wasn't sure if anyone used that expression anymore. Maybe nowadays the equivalent was some kind of special friending announcement on Facebook or something like that. She should ask Jared about it. Cat smiled at the thought and took another satisfied sip of her grande latte.

Anyway.

It wasn't social, there was kind of a tentative job offer in there. So definitely not a date then, and she could accept the invitation with a clear conscience if she so wished. The fact that the man was hot as a firecracker was irrelevant; she owed it to herself to explore the possibilities of a gig. Cat picked up the phone and then set it back down again. No. Too soon. Mustn't appear eager. She'd let him wait a few days.

Smiling to herself, she picked up a brush and began to work the frizz out of her hair in preparation for the evening ahead. Reese had been positively ecstatic about her shoot at the political rally and had given her the first choice of upcoming assignments for the next fortnight. She'd picked Sally Owens's latest catwalk show for starters and had two hours to kill before it got underway. Afterwards maybe she would head out for a few drinks with Rob and Sally. Cat was becoming very fond of the girl. Once you got past the salty language and rough edges, there was a pretty nice kid hiding inside there. Given her childhood and the overwhelming success that had suddenly appeared out of nowhere, it was something of a miracle that she wasn't completely screwed up. Never mind that pretty much every man she met hit on her, regardless of their age. She'd idly asked Jared if he found Sally attractive, and he'd been deeply offended. "Do I look like a pedophile?" he'd huffed.

Rob had told Cat that night at the club that Sally was nowhere as tough and experienced as she'd like to seem. In fact, when she was out of the lights with her defences down, she was almost shy. Cat would not be at all surprised if Rob himself wasn't more than a little taken with her. She picked up James Albright's card again and studied it once more before returning to her brushing.

She'd give it three days, she decided.

CHAPTER 22

A bright blue sky, thin cirrus clouds lightly screening the sun, and far below, *Arrow,* hull down and pounding westward under full sail, Jared steering and Danny searching the horizon with the Steiners.

"She can't be all that far ahead," Danny said. "They only left two hours ago, and Clarke said he wasn't going to run the engines over fourteen hundred RPM on the way across."

Legalese had left the Queens Own Yacht Club at ten a.m. with Clarke at the wheel perspiring heavily and trying to appear nonchalant with Merlynn dazzling in whites standing alongside him and attempting to look unconcerned. Danny and Jared had stood alongside in the Avon for the departure, ready to offer it up as a buffer should the need arise. Clarke surprised everyone by exiting the slip without incident and navigating the tight corner into the channel on his first attempt. He'd previously confided to Danny that he'd spent a few days out on the harbour police launch with an old friend and had been given some lessons on boat handling. Clarke had also taken the boating licence exam online, which showed a certain level of commitment even if it was probably more about Merlynn than boating.

"There she is," Danny said, "tight off the starboard bow, maybe five miles ahead of us. Just jogging along, we should catch up before we get into the harbour if they keep that pace."

"Or you chickenshits could fly the spinnaker, and we'd catch them for sure," Sally said, unrecognizable under thick white sunscreen, a Fly Emirates cap, and a black NZ racing jacket. She'd been on their case since they left the harbour and began the long downhill run across the Strait. Jared turned and glared at her and received a wink from Rob, who, as always, was never far from his charge.

"You might as well give up," he said. "She's not going to stop."

Danny shrugged and looked at Jared. "Why not?"

Jared knew he didn't have a reason not to fly the big sail other than the fact that he was the captain, and the decision to do so should have been his. But that battle was already lost. He realized he was in danger of becoming churlish.

"Let her fly," he said.

Danny went below and passed the spinnaker up through the forward hatch where Sally grabbed it and clipped on the sheets and halyard as Rob raised the pole and set it. In under a minute the big red sail was hoisted up and billowing out and they'd picked up a knot and a half.

"I'll trim," Sally said. "Another ten degrees to port and we should be good."

Jared hardened up and *Arrow* picked up another half knot. In spite of himself, he was impressed. He had never gone in for racing much as the local weather conditions were generally too light for *Arrow* to show well, and the go-fast boat crews' condescension in the yacht clubs afterwards rankled him.

"Told you I was good," Sally said, giving him a sharp elbow to the ribs along with a huge grin. Jared was lost.

"I surrender to your superior skills," he said, smiling down upon the urchin.

"Pay fucking attention," she said. "You just fell off five degrees."

They caught up to *Legalese* three miles out of Nanaimo Harbour and reduced sail to follow her in. Once inside Clarke dropped anchor and backed down hard and when the old Monk McQueen had sprung back and rested comfortably on her rode, Jared brought *Arrow* alongside her and tied on.

"Permission to come aboard, Captain?" Danny said as Clarke appeared from the wheelhouse. Clarke flushed and mumbled something which contained the word *asshole*, but he might not have been entirely displeased.

"I can see how you could get used to this kind of thing," Clarke said later as they sat under the shade of the stern deck bridge with their drinks, the bustling harbour spread out before them like a postcard from a dream vacation. "The problem is, I likely spent a good day's wages on fuel just getting *Legalese* across the Strait."

"Short cruises and long lay-ups," Merlynn said. "That was always Ralph's motto."

"What time does the club close?" Sally asked. "Skippers meeting will be at ten tomorrow morning, and we'll have to go in and confirm our registration this evening if we're going to attend."

Jared was starting to regret the whole thing. When Clarke had talked about taking *Legalese* on a "shakedown cruise" — amazing how quickly people picked up on the nautical crap — Jared had casually mentioned there was a regatta upcoming in Nanaimo. Sally had been within earshot and had the race details from her phone in less than five minutes. Danny and Merlynn had piled on and it was settled. Cat was supposed to join them for the trip across but had cancelled at the last minute due to a job interview. She would come over on the ferry Sunday night after the race and stay over for the return sail on Monday.

"What say we all head into the club this evening when I sign *Arrow* up," Sally said. "They're having a barbecue for the race crews that should be fun. I'm buying."

"I'll drop the tender in the water," Clarke said nautically. He glared at Jared. "What?"

"Nothing, Cap'n. We'll take the Avon, meet you there in an hour."

The club was rocking. A lot of brawny, fit-looking young men milled about, most of them in sweaters or blazers with a boat name stitched elegantly on the front. Jared's spirits sank as he realized that this was not going to be one of those casual good-natured yacht races that he'd crewed in back in the day. Had he known, he would never have come. He wondered if it was too late to cancel out. Or chicken out as Sally was sure to consider it. They pushed through the crowd to the bar and put in their order. "Martinis?" the harassed barman said. "You're bloody joking, right?" He passed them their jugs of beer, and Danny reached for his wallet.

"I've got this," Sally said, shoving past them. "Two more jugs of beer and a dozen shots of tequila. Pour them all in a jug as well and give us some limes and six shot glasses." The bartender smiled and shook his head and was about to speak when Rob reached across with her passport.

"Here," he said, "she's legal." He turned towards Danny. "I've been wondering. What did the husband say? When Cat spilled the drink at the club."

Danny looked carefully around. "I wasn't talking to you," he whispered.

The bartender filled the order, took the cash from the big scarred man, and moved on down the line. "We're confirmed," Sally said when they were seated at one of the big patio tables out on the deck. "Fourteen boats in our division, and they're going for a harbour start so it's going to be pretty tight for a while. Four of the opposition are pure racers; we likely won't see them after the start. The others are local cruisers; *Arrow* should rate well against most of them. The good news for us is there's a decent low coming in. They're forecasting twenty knots of wind from the southeast and gusting, so we might be in with a chance. We'd be embarrassed in light air."

"Twenty knots and gusting," Jared said.

"Yes."

He reached for the tequila jug, poured a shot, and threw it back.

"Should be fun," he mumbled, his eyes watering as he grabbed for a slice of lime.

CHAPTER 23

It didn't seem so much like fun at seven the following morning when Sally came aboard *Arrow* and pounded on the cabin doors. "Breakfast in half an hour, Merlynn's cooking. One Caesar limit till after the race."

"I thought the race didn't start till ten thirty," Jared groaned.

"We need to get on the water early and check out the conditions, the wind will be all over the place inside here. A couple of boats are out there already. I talked to a lot of those patronizing twats last night. There are some serious racers here. Three of the boats are high-flyers from Seattle."

Jared already had deep misgivings about the coming day, and it hadn't even started yet. Danny and his goddamned sunny disposition didn't help. He was slightly cheered by the sight of Rob's scowling white face when he went aboard *Legalese* for breakfast. Clearly a fellow sufferer.

"All right," Sally said, "here's the thing. We're going to have to be aggressive at times if we're going to stand a chance. I'll call the shots and do the tactics."

They'd gone through it all the previous evening when the drinks were flowing. It had sounded good at the time. In the sober light of day

Jared might have changed his stance, but it was clearly far too late for that. He had no doubt that Sally knew what she was doing, Rob had attested to that, and he'd crewed on some of the Kiwi trial races for the America's Cup back in Auckland.

Sally went on. "Our spinnaker is bigger than I would have liked for the conditions, but it's heavy and it just might hold up. Anything we break I'll pay for, including damage to *Arrow*. Or any of the other boats for that matter." Jared jerked upright in protest and she shushed him down and continued on.

"I'm not saying that anything is likely to happen, only that on the off chance something should happen, I'm covering it. I've got more money already than I can spend in a lifetime, and this is going to be the most fun I've had in forever, so that's settled. Besides, *Arrow* could run over any three of these shite plastic racers and come away with barely a scratch, so what's to worry?"

Jared closed his eyes and clutched his Caesar.

❁

Sally was right about the wind. It was all over the place inside the harbour. There was a gap between two of the islands just before the committee boat at one end of the start line, and the Venturi effect cranked the wind up another couple of knots on top of the relatively steady fifteen already present. Boats were running back and forth testing sails, wind, and current, constantly searching for that small advantage. Of all the chutes popping out around them, none were anywhere near as large as *Arrow*'s.

"On the bright side ours is quite a bit heavier," Rob said. "Those others are all half or three-quarter ounce. Mind you their boats are a lot lighter than *Arrow*, less load, so there's that." He slapped Jared on the back. "But hey, no worries, mate."

Jared managed a feeble smile although he secretly felt that *Arrow* seemed a bit like a duck among swans. He was fiercely proud of the old girl, and she was often the prettiest boat in the harbour, but she was out of place here. There was a form and function about the pure racers that was impressive. They were clearly designed for just that one thing: to go really, really fucking fast. As they slipped past *Arrow* on all points of sail in the pre-race jockeying, it was hard not to read condescension, if not outright pity, in the smiles and waves. Most of them had probably never raced against a wooden ketch in their lives. Jared reached for a beer and felt a slow burn beginning.

"Okay," Sally said, "upwind start, first leg out and around Entrance Island on a beam reach, then an eight-mile spinnaker run to the buoy off Gull Island. Back on a hard beat to Entrance, then broad reach back to the outer harbour buoy, and a short downhill back to the start line. Twenty-seven miles in all. I think with *Arrow*'s long waterline we can almost hold our own on a beat, probably lose a fair bit on the beam reaches. Downwind we'll get killed. We've got a big spinnaker but she's a heavy old lady with a narrow ass."

"We have a mizzen staysail," Danny said. "That will keep us closer on a reach."

"I've never flown one," Sally admitted.

"I have," Rob said. "I crewed Sunday races on an old ketch out of Whangarei as a teenager. Kickass when conditions were just right."

"What we want to do," Sally said, "is be ultra conservative pre-start when all the hotshots are crowding and testing. We'll pull away early, give up our position if we're threatened, yield to all right-of-way calls even when they're total bullshit. Miss a couple of tacks, be clumsy. Then maybe later on we can take somebody by surprise."

"The clumsy part should be easy," Clarke muttered. He was still smarting under Sally's earlier instructions. "You're ballast," she'd told him. "Stay out of the fucking way on the high side. I'll tell you if I need you."

The start went better than they could have hoped. Most of the hotter boats were engaged in their own dogfights, and Sally got *Arrow* to the weather end of the line a few seconds after the gun on starboard tack. They were in the middle of the pack and *Arrow*, hull down on a hard beat, had all of her waterline working and surprised one of the high-flyers who'd expected to clear her on the first crossing tack. With right-of-way and hard sheeted in with lines strumming and foam flying, even Clarke was grinning as three of the fleet had to duck her stern.

"Run her in as close into the beach as you dare, Jared," Sally said. "This is the favoured tack and every boat length matters. Your boat, your call."

Jared, crouched in place at the tiller, nodded, his eyes glued to the depth sounder. A slow rise in a muddy bottom according to the chart. A Hunter 42 was half a length back and gaining.

"Throw them a dummy in five, four, three, two . . . Tack!" Jared yelled and brought *Arrow* ten degrees closer to the wind. Danny slipped the sheets and the sails quivered and the Hunter was gone. Jared fell off and *Arrow* heeled hard again and the depth sounder showed forty and then thirty and then —

"Tack!" Jared yelled, and *Arrow* spun and fell off onto port tack and the depth sounder showed fifteen and then Jared couldn't look anymore. He saw the Hunter ahead by six boat lengths but too far downwind to tack back across them.

"Good one," Sally said. "I thought you guys didn't race."

"We don't. That was it, we're a one-trick pony. We're done. It's all up to you now."

Four of the boats were running well ahead of the rest of the fleet, clearly in a league of their own. Of the remaining ten, *Arrow* was a surprising fourth.

"That lot all have sick ratings," Sally said, gesturing forward. "If we finish anywhere within sight of them, we'll beat them out on handicap."

"As long as we beat the Hunters," Jared said.

"Oh, they'll have to give us a good nine minutes," Sally said, waving the race sheet. "I'm sure we can keep well inside of that."

"Fuck nine minutes," Jared said.

For the next hour, *Arrow* continued in the middle of the pack, another two boats slipping past on the close reach to Entrance but the remaining half dozen unable to gain ground. Conditions outside the harbour were blustery, one of the Seattle racers rolling so hard on the downwind leg she dipped her spinnaker pole in the water and snapped it. A sister boat hard on her heels ran over the spinnaker and caught it on the keel and slewed wildly to leeward causing a third boat to jibe frantically and loose her sheets in an unsuccessful attempt to stay clear. When the mess was finally cleared up, two of the boats called it quits and made their way back to the harbour.

"Wimps," Clarke said.

When they made their way around the mark buoy at the end of the spinnaker leg, *Arrow* was in fourth place. She managed to gain two positions in the hard beat back to Entrance Island, the wind now gusting into the low twenties and the tide beginning to ebb against the wind and pushing up the seas. The two Catalinas they passed had reefs in their main, but *Arrow* with her heavier rig still carried full sail.

"Another ten knots of wind and we might actually win this thing," Danny said.

"Be careful what you wish for, mate," Rob said.

In spite of the weather and the mizzen staysail, they were unable to overtake *Kerry*, the Seattle boat that remained in front of them on the broad reach that was the second-last leg. Well sailed with a large crew, she stayed within herself, covered their every move, and luffed up on them each time they attempted to get by.

"If I thought it would do any good, I'd strip off and flash my tits to break their concentration," Sally said after yet another failed attempt to get an overlap. "But I'm so flat-chested they'd probably think I was a boy. Anyway, that was a hell of a race — second place, who'da thunk it?"

"It's not over yet," Jared said. The beers had done their job.

"Yeah, it pretty much is. A half mile to go before the turn into the harbour at the light, no way we're getting past them. They're covering our every move. And they're faster than us. Once they round the light, they're as good as home. No time, no room inside the harbour. We just don't have the speed to get inside after the light. They'll stay on starboard tack around the corner, one jibe to the line. Second place is unbelievable. We'll win easily on corrected time."

"The Gabriola Island ferry should be leaving now," Clarke said. "It's exactly 1400 hours. I was reading the harbour regulations last night," he said defensively in response to the amused looks. "She passes a couple of boat lengths off the light. There's a notice posted to stay outside of her."

"Fuck a notice," Danny said.

"There's her siren, she's leaving," Sally said. "*Kerry* is too far in already — she'll have to pass behind her. If we quick jibe in tight to the Island then jibe back close along the waterfront, we can shave the light buoy, maybe gain a few lengths on them. Let the mule go! Now! Starboard jibe!"

Jared swung the tiller and the boom swung across, crashing into the shrouds, *Arrow* quivering from the shock, Clarke ducking and cursing as he leaped across and tailed for Danny as Rob gathered the staysail and dumped it down into the cockpit. Spray rose up from the starboard rail as *Arrow* took a queer one on board and the salt blinded Jared for long seconds.

"Port jibe in twenty!" Sally screamed from her perch in front of the mast. "Fifteen! Ten! Five — jibe jibe jibe!"

Her yell was drowned out by the ferry, the big ship's siren sounding continuously as she pounded into weather twenty feet away off their port side, a crewman shaking his fist and yelling at them on the bow. Jared swung the tiller away and *Arrow* rounded onto the light, everyone ducking as the main slapped across, her speed slowed momentarily by the quick jibes, then as a gust hit *Arrow* she staggered to leeward momentarily and then stood back up on her feet and picked up speed again.

"Port twenty," Sally yelled, and Jared glimpsed the red marker buoy pass too tight on starboard and heard the clang of contact on *Arrow*'s hull and then they were through and hardening up with right-of-way for the last five hundred yards.

"Here she comes!" Rob yelled.

Kerry, a half-dozen boat lengths away and coming like a train.

"She's going to cross our bows," Sally said. "She's got us."

They watched as *Kerry* flew towards them and then she hit the wake from the ferry and bounced and rolled and the air spilled from her sails. She lost her speed in the last hundred feet and Sally jibed on her bow and led her to the finish line.

They'd won.

"They're sure to protest our going inside on the ferry," Sally said. "Never mind if they check the hull for red streaks from the buoy."

"Nah, they won't protest. They'll be too embarrassed," Rob said.

"Fuck a bunch of protests," Clarke said, and high-fived Sally.

❈

"She's still not answering her phone," Jared said. He'd been calling her steadily since the celebration began three hours earlier, and he was becoming increasingly worried.

"Give her some space," Danny said. "Probably busy with interviews, in meetings, something like that."

"No doubt."

But it's very unlike her, Jared thought. Cat always called to check in when they had something set up, no matter how informal. And this had been pretty definite. She'd planned on coming over for the sail back home on Monday morning, and here it was, seven o'clock on Sunday night, and still no word from her. It wasn't something she would forget, and it was getting awfully damned late for meetings and such. He poured another Scotch, trying to drown his rising sense of unease.

CHAPTER 24

It had been a whirlwind day for Cat. James had insisted on sending a car around for her and meeting up for breakfast in the West End with one of his people. They'd obviously vetted her, and the PR rep talked knowledgeably about her recent work as well as the award-winning series she'd done on the families of the sex workers who'd been murdered on the pig farm in Port Coquitlam, and then the Highway of Tears series that had inevitably followed.

Cat was flattered and a little surprised; that had been a while ago, and much of her work since then had been what she sometimes, if she was being perfectly honest, thought of as pop culture crap. The women and their tragedies had disturbed her, and she had lost heart for heavy lifting. Cat was slightly embarrassed by her current work and had been considering getting back into something more serious for a while now. Not that she thought working with politicians was a giant step up the moral ladder. She didn't ask herself if James Albright himself might be part of the draw of the job because she wasn't sure she wanted to know the answer. He was selling again and she refocused.

"So what we're looking for is a series of pictures to go alongside articles by our people, which will give the general public a more complete idea of what the day-to-day life of a politician is all about. I'm sure a lot of folks assume it's all speeches and rallies because that's what they see on the evening sound bites, but . . ."

"That's only one small piece of the picture," she finished his thought.

"Yes. There are numerous other stories that deserve attention. A hospital visit to a worker who's been injured on site and denied compensation; factory visits to discuss shoddy working conditions; a meeting with a disgruntled caregiver who thinks the system is ignoring or abusing the elderly. It's not the sort of thing that jumps up and grabs the headlines, but it is important work, nonetheless. We want to get more of that story out there, and we think you are exactly the right person to highlight and illustrate our message."

He bent forward across the table, totally focused on her, his eyes almost glowing, and she was reminded again of how compelling he was. The magnetism was palpable, and she caught the amused glance of his aide and flushed. No doubt he'd seen all this before and was familiar with the swoon of adulating women around his boss. She rebuked herself and studied Albright more closely. She knew he was aware of his impact; he was an accomplished politician after all, she reminded herself. *Go slow, girl.*

"It sounds as if it could be interesting. I'll have to think it over," she said.

His eyes narrowed, and she wondered if he was unused to women who didn't bend over backwards at his first request. *Another sexual metaphor*, she thought, and flushed once more. What the hell was up with her anyway, she was acting like a giddy schoolgirl.

"Well, it's still early," he said. "Come on, we're going on a tour."

He stood up and took her arm and they went back outside to the limo. She climbed into the rear seat with him, the aide sat up front with the driver, and they were off once more. A visit to an old folks home, a stop at a legion where he made a short speech of appreciation to a pair of veterans of the Korean War who were being honoured at an early luncheon, and then on to a Boy Scout meeting where he handed out badges to three young men whose names he knew by heart.

Albright was immediately recognized wherever they went, always the centre of attention, and usually welcomed with genuine warmth. Cat had seen it before, on some of her fashion and movie shoots. It was charisma, pure and simple. You either had it or you didn't, and it wasn't something you could fake. In her experience it had little to do with looks or attitude or carriage. It was that indefinable something called presence. As if a current of electricity radiated from certain people, affecting those who came within its circumference.

Cat realized she was becoming absurd when Albright reached out to touch her, drawing her towards a small child in the children's hospital, and she flinched away, fearing a spark.

"This is Cathy," he said. "She's my favourite."

The little girl beamed as he bent down and kissed her bald head before pulling a locket out of his pocket and presenting it to her. Cat would have been more impressed had she not seen the aide whisper in his ear and slip him the gift when they entered the ward. But she knew she was being unfair. He couldn't possibly remember everyone he came into contact with. No person could.

A few words and they moved on down the ward, Albright guiding Cat with his arm lightly around her waist, signalling the stops and starts as they made their slow way along. It made her uncomfortable, but it would have been boorish to object. Another half hour and they were back in the limousine and on their way again.

"Is it always like this?" Cat inquired.

"Some of it is because it's the weekend. More special events, more people around."

"More voters," Cat said.

"Oh absolutely, that's a big part of it. If we don't get the votes, we don't get elected and don't get to do all the good work." James shrugged his shoulders and smiled. "As the man once said, it may not be a great system, it just happens to beat all the alternatives. Now sit back and relax, I've got a little surprise for you."

✸

My God, it has to be well over a hundred feet long, Cat thought as they approached the gleaming yacht tied up at the Port of Vancouver. She'd been on large motor yachts before, but never one so big that it had its own gangway and two guys in white kit standing at attention on each side of it. They saluted as she and Albright stepped up and onto the teak decks.

"I'm a little disappointed," Cat said. "I was expecting to be piped aboard."

"Maybe next time," James said.

He nodded to the men and the gangway was raised and swung in and stowed alongside with quiet efficiency. Less than five minutes later they were heading out towards the Lions Gate Bridge. Cat looked back at the retreating city skyline and thought about phoning Jared. But it was early and they'd still be out on the racecourse. She'd call him when she had a better idea of her timetable. James took her by the elbow.

"This way," he said, as he led her below.

The saloon was huge, with one corner set up as a lounge area complete with leather sofas and recliners and a big-screen TV. A long narrow dining table surrounded by chairs occupied the central area, and off in the far corner was a roped-off square with immaculate white canvas laid over the floor inside it.

"I like to do a little bit of sparring now and then," James said. "Trying to stay in shape, you know how it is. I understand you do a little martial arts yourself."

Now how in the hell could he know about that? Cat wondered. It was not included in the short biography that Reese had required of her for his website and Facebook page. Nor was it mentioned anywhere else as far as she knew.

126

"We did a little background check," Albright said, anticipating her. "I hope you don't mind. You know, in politics you can't be too careful about people."

"Actually," Cat said, "I think that maybe I do mind."

She was beginning to regret her impulsiveness in coming on the trip. Up close there was an aura of macho aggressiveness to the man that she found a bit repulsive. It was a combination of overconfidence and physical bearing, a kind of strutting certainty that he was the pack leader and irresistible to the opposite sex. Suddenly he reminded her a bit of a creepy Stallone in one of his later roles. *He's the type that would be irresistible to Lauren, though,* Cat thought, and was immediately ashamed of her betrayal.

Albright said, "I apologize if I've offended you. It's just that our people looked at your portfolio and were so impressed with you that I asked them to do a little extra digging. I shouldn't have done that without asking you first. You ought to have been told, and I regret that you were not. That was a mistake on my part. Please accept my sincere apologies."

He smiled down at her and there might just have been a little touch of mockery there.

I'm not sure he really gives a damn, Cat thought.

His cell phone rang, and he looked at the screen and turned away from her.

"I have to take this," he said. "Please excuse me."

He listened to the call, unmoving.

"Yes. Well, we can't have that now, can we? Have the boys bring him out for a little conference," he said.

He ended the call and turned back towards her, all charm once more. "Sorry about that, slight change of plans, something has come up that requires my immediate attention. The selfless life of a politician in public service."

Again she saw that slightly mocking smile.

"No problem. I should be getting back soon anyway," Cat said. "I have to catch a ferry to Vancouver Island this evening."

"Listen, how about this?" Albright said. "I just learned that two of my crew are bringing out a guest in a bit. I'll have them run you across the Strait in the tender after they drop him off. Only take an hour or so to get to Nanaimo, the weather's laying down quite nicely now. We can talk some more, get to know each other a little better over a drink. Please. I'd really appreciate it."

Cat hesitated for a moment, and then rebuked herself for her timidity. It was the suddenness of everything, she thought, the whirlwind tour and then the unexpected boat trip that had unbalanced her. She was not the type of woman prone to sudden fits of what used to be called the vapours.

"That's very kind of you," she said. "I'll just call my friends and tell them when to expect me."

Albright caught her arm as she reached into her purse for her cell phone.

"Why don't you just hold on for a bit until my company gets here?" he said. "That way you can be more definite about your time frame. No sense in worrying them unnecessarily."

❄

Two hours later Albright stood watching, still undecided, as Cat climbed into the big Zodiac inflatable, the brothers carefully handing her aboard. He wondered if letting her leave was a mistake and went to call her back at the last second, but then the twin Yamahas screamed and the bow lifted as the stern dug in and the boat sped off and the moment was gone. Things were happening fast now.

He'd learned more about her boyfriend, Kane, and his partner, MacLean, but needed more time to assess any immediate risk they posed and calculate the best way to handle it. Bill Lacey had told him the two men had moved their sailboat to the yacht club docks in recent days and were spending a lot of time hanging out in the bar talking with members and asking questions. He needed to slow them down, focus their attention somewhere else. Taking them out right now would just lead to more questions and increased pressure from that cop Clarke they were friends with. He needed to buy some time.

Cat had mentioned Danny MacLean's mother and grandfather in their chats. They lived in an old house in the East End where Kane had roomed before he inherited his sailboat. It sounded like he was pretty tight with them. Maybe there was room for something to be done there, create a distraction to get some space and slow things down a little. He'd get Travis to make a call to that French bunch he got the roofies from. He'd been considering all of this when the call had come in from the brothers, and that had taken precedence over everything else. So much for slowing things down.

He stared over the rail as the Zodiac disappeared from sight and the wineglass stem snapped in his hand. He stood there unaware and felt the anger building.

A man approached and he turned to face him.

"You've cut yourself," the lawyer said.

"It's nothing. A scratch. Good to see you again, Richard. Listen, I've planned a little surprise for you. I've had the crew set up a boxing ring in the lounge. I thought you and I could have a couple of light rounds of sparring before dinner to build up a bit of an appetite. I've fooled around with some of the men, you know, just for a workout, a little exercise, but I've always wanted to go a couple of rounds with a pro. Get to feel something about what it's really like in the ring. I'm fascinated by the whole business, as you've probably guessed."

"Well, I'm hardly a professional, but I might be able to show you a couple of things," Richard Sullivan said.

"I'm looking forward to it," Albright said with a genial smile, and as the lawyer stared at him it was clear the man was uneasy.

CHAPTER 25

"It's hard to describe," Cat told Jared. "He's clever, charming, and well spoken, and he has this way of making you feel as if you're the only person in the room that matters, even when you're in the midst of a large group."

"It's a politician's trick. Like the eyes in those paintings that always seem to be watching you no matter where you are in the room."

Cat considered this. "That's not bad, you know," she said. "Sometimes you surprise me, Jared."

"Of course it's all complete bullshit. The beguiled eye of the beholder." Jared ducked away as Cat swung the pillow at him. They were lying in bed in *Arrow's* aft cabin, working on their second cups of espresso made on the little Bialetti in the galley. Cat had arrived back aboard *Arrow* the previous evening after an exhilarating forty-five-minute trip across the Straits. The wind had dropped, and they'd flown across on the remains of the southeast swell, cresting the waves with Cat wrapped in a wool blanket tucked tight under the canopy and the two crewmen in rain gear and Sou'westers for the spray.

"Are you going to take the job with Albright?"

"I haven't made up my mind yet, but probably not. The money is excellent, over half again what I'm making now, but there's something about the man that makes me uncomfortable."

"What is it?" Jared asked.

"It's hard to know when he's sincere; or if he ever is, for that matter. I spent over ten hours up close with him yesterday, watching him and listening to him pretty much the whole time, and I still don't have the foggiest idea about what his core beliefs are. He always gives his audience exactly what they want to hear, and I know that's the secret of any successful politician, but he just seems that extra bit slipperier than most. At times it seems he's almost mocking his followers, but maybe that's just me. But the man is goddamned hot, I'll say that much for him. A veritable firecracker. The women were literally fawning over him. I kid you not."

"Hotter even than me? Surely not! You jest!"

"Stop making me laugh, Jared. I'm spilling my coffee. What time do we have to leave?'

"Sometime around noon. Little bit of a northwesterly filling in, it should be a comfortable sail across. We've still got a couple of hours to lay around. Or whatever."

"Whatever sounds pretty good," Cat said.

❄

They heard the news halfway back across Georgia Strait. *Legalese* was a few boat lengths off to port, chugging sedately along, when she suddenly gave two quick blasts on her horn and swung her bow towards them. As she approached, Merlynn appeared on deck and made the universal phone signal. Jared turned on the radiophone and Clarke came on. "Channel seventy-two," he said. "Low power. Put Danny on."

"Hey, Clarke, what's up?"

"It's Annie. She's been taken. The station just contacted me."

Danny and Jared stared at each other in shock. "What do you mean, taken?"

Clarke continued, "She was out shopping with Joseph when they were jumped in the co-op parking lot by three guys in a van. They tried to take Joseph as well, but he knifed one of them. Put him on the ground. They loaded the man up and took off with Annie. A lot of blood — I doubt the guy makes it. Jaimie reported it. He said Joseph called him right after it happened. And now he's gone as well."

"Joseph's gone? Gone where?"

"Jaimie doesn't know. He figures Joseph must have gone back home in the Subaru and collected Sinbad after the attack, because now the dog has gone missing as well."

"This makes no sense at all," Danny said. "What have Joseph and Annie got to do with anything?"

"It has to be connected to everything else," Clarke replied. "It's too much of a coincidence for this to be happening right now."

"They must want something from us. Here's Jared."

"When did this all happen?"

"It's been an hour and a half since the incident in the parking lot. Say an hour since Joseph took off with Sinbad. Where the hell can he be going? Joseph doesn't have any leads, does he? Something you two forgot to tell me?"

British Properties, Danny mouthed.

Jared nodded. "No, of course not. If we had anything, we'd tell you. I imagine he's just driving around looking for the van on the off chance. He probably figures it's better to be doing something rather than just sitting around waiting."

"I guess. Stay on this channel the rest of the way in, and if I hear anything I'll let you know. I'm going to head this up myself the minute I get back. You can be damn sure I'll do everything in my power to find her."

But the VHF remained silent the rest of the way in. Clarke took off in a waiting squad car as soon as they touched the commercial dock and left Jared and Danny to run *Legalese* back to the yacht club.

✿

Joseph parked the Subaru on the side of the road five hundred yards away from the house in the British Properties, stepped out, and slipped on a backpack. He opened the driver's door and put a collar and leash on Sinbad, who growled softly in protest. Joseph walked halfway back towards the house before stopping for a rest. The occasional pedestrian and jogger went by, some of them smiling at the old man with the big ugly dog. He made his slow way along to the driveway with the cement columns that supported the ornate black iron gate and sat down against one of the columns, breathing heavily. A cyclist stopped and offered him water from his flask and Joseph took a small drink and nodded his thanks.

The wrought iron fence was ten feet high with spikes at the top, ornamental but designed to keep intruders out as well. Cameras were positioned on the walls on either side of the gate. The fence that fronted the property ran along the road for three hundred feet before taking a ninety-degree turn and disappearing up and out of sight past the rise of the hill and into the trees. Joseph moved along the road for another two blocks until he came to a vacant lot with a couple of parked cars at the back and a beaten track leading up into the brush. He told Sinbad to stay and walked back to the Subaru and got in and drove it back to where the dog waited and parked it alongside the other vehicles. He removed Sinbad's collar and leash, stowed them in his packsack, and started up the slope. Another dog walker was coming down the path and moved off to the side when they approached.

"Big mother," the man muttered as they passed. Joseph nodded and moved steadily upwards, no hesitation in his gait now. A quarter mile on, the path branched and he took the south fork that swung back along the ridge above the gated house. The trail was heavily treed now, mostly cedar and scrub pine with an occasional scabbed arbutus, and it was difficult to see for any distance down the hill. When Joseph judged he had gone far enough along, he left the path and began moving carefully down the slope with Sinbad ranging ahead of him. It was heavy-going through thick bush for the first two hundred yards and then it abruptly opened out into a clearing that led to a rocky bluff with scrubby arbutus scattered about. In the distance, freighters were anchored in a cluster off Lions Gate Bridge with a cruise ship carefully threading its way through them. Joseph approached the edge of the bluff and crouched down and looked over the drop-off. The house was directly below him, the two lines of fencing that enclosed it running up to the base of the bluff. It would be a simple matter to traverse the shallow slope and enter the grounds.

Joseph moved back a few feet and opened the packsack. He took out a jug of water and a small plastic bowl. He took a drink and then filled the container twice for Sinbad. He put the bowl and bottle back into the packsack and pulled out a pair of binoculars, then crawled to the edge of the bluff and rested on his elbows and began scanning the property. There were no cars visible, but a large garage ran out at right angles from the back of the house. He counted three cameras covering the inside grounds. The windows of the mansion were shuttered and there were no signs of anyone inside. Joseph made himself comfortable and settled back to wait for the dark. Sinbad dozed at his side, his ears twitching occasionally at the sounds of cars going past on the road below.

CHAPTER 26

Annie woke to darkness. She was covered in a sticky substance that she knew was blood. What she didn't know was how much of it was hers and how much belonged to the man they'd thrown on top of her in the van as they tore out of the parking lot. Joseph had got him pretty good. One of the men had been crouched on the floor beside him, trying to stop the bleeding. When the injured man shuddered and went limp, he turned on her, screaming and kicking. She'd curled into a ball and put her arms in front of her face to protect herself, but some of the blows had come through and she had passed out.

Annie rolled over and sat up, moving slowly and carefully as she assessed the damage. Nothing broken except for maybe a cheekbone, she thought, not too bad. Ribs sore, but not the piercing pain that she would have experienced had they been broken. Probably just bruised. Her second husband had beaten her badly that one time before the family sorted him, and she knew the difference. At least she wasn't tied up, and she made slow careful movements trying to stretch out some of the pain. As her eyes adjusted to the darkness, she saw she was lying on a cement floor in a medium-sized room with a ten-foot ceiling and a small window with iron bars set high on a concrete exterior wall. So she was probably in a basement.

Annie crawled over to the door and examined it. She gave it a soft tap with her knuckles. Steel. And sounded thick. She managed to pull herself up to her feet with the aid of the handle, moving slowly, and tried to open it. It was locked, no big surprise there. In the semi-dark she moved a cautious shuffling half step at a time around the perimeter of the room, searching for anything she could use as a weapon. Her foot struck something and she bent down, grunting against the sudden pain in her chest, and picked it up. A plastic water bottle with the seal intact. Annie removed the cap and smelled the contents before taking a slow, careful drink and continuing her circuit of the room. She found nothing else. There was no way for her to reach the window and in any case the glass was thick and she doubted she could break it without a tool, never mind the iron bars on the outside. Calling out for help wasn't going to be an option.

Annie lowered herself back to the floor and rested her back against the wall beside the door. She reached up and removed the long whale-bone pin that bound her topknot and began to scrape the tapered end against the rough concrete floor. After a few minutes' work she was satisfied and settled back to wait. She began to nod, and after a while her eyes closed and she drifted off into a confused sleep.

❁

Joseph stood up and stretched his legs, then moved slowly down the slope towards the darkened building, Sinbad drifting along in front of him. As they reached the base of the bluff, headlights suddenly appeared outside the gate and they ducked into the shadows alongside the garage. The gate slid open and a black pickup drove through. It went past the house and continued up the slope to the garage. Two of the men that had taken Annie were inside. The garage door opened and the pickup entered and the door shuttered back down behind it. Joseph went to the window and looked inside. The white van that had taken Annie was backed into one of the bays. He waited there, listening.

". . . seen him that pissed. Thought he was going to do us right there."

"Not our fault. How the hell were we supposed to know? Hundred-year-old guy carries a knife and knows how to use it, what are the fucking odds?" The fat man had a distinct whine to his voice.

"He says it's too risky to hold onto her now. Too much noise out there after the screw-up in the parking lot. He wants it all cleaned up. Get the woman, dump the bodies, torch the van. He wants it done tonight."

"I'll do her right now."

"Bring her up to the van first. No sense in packing her up the stairs if we don't have to. She's no lightweight."

A trace of a smile appeared on Joseph's face. He watched the man leave the garage and followed him out around the back of the building. A set of concrete steps led down to a steel door. The man opened it, then jumped back, cursing. Blood spurted from under the hand he'd clamped to his neck.

"You bloody bitch," he screamed raising his gun, "I'll fucking—" The scream ended abruptly as Joseph brought the concrete block used as a doorstop down on his head. Joseph turned and moved quietly back up the stairs.

"Ernest? Hello?" The back door of the garage opened slowly and a hand clasping a gun extended out. "Ernie?"

Sinbad took two silent paces and leaped, clamping his teeth onto the man's wrist. The man screamed and fell back into the garage, his howl rising in pitch as Sinbad bore him to the ground. The gun dropped to the concrete and Joseph leaned over and picked it up. Annie appeared beside him, her face masked in blood.

"I'm okay," she said. "I think it's mostly from that guy you knifed." She seized the gun from Joseph and levelled it at the man on the ground. Joseph spoke to her.

"I'm not going to hit the dog," she said in exasperation, "just this fat asshole."

"Please. No. I'll tell you everything I know," the man said.

"Okay. So who do you work for?" Annie asked.

"I don't know."

"Right." Annie raised the gun. There was a loud explosion and a bullet ricocheted off the concrete.

"Damn. I missed. Gun's a piece of shit. Give me your knife."

Joseph nodded and reached under his shirt.

"Wait, wait. I don't know their names. There were two of them. Tall, skinny guys. They met with Louie and gave him your address; we waited outside the house and followed you to the parking lot. They told Louie to bring you here, gave us the codes for the gate and garage, said they'd be in touch. Never seen them before. They knew Louie, and he set it all up. We never went inside the house. We never ever saw anyone else, just those two guys."

"Okay. I think I believe you. What's your name?"

"Albert."

Joseph said, "Bert and Ernie." He took the gun back from Annie and cold-cocked the fat man. He reached into Albert's pants pocket and produced a set of keys and a wallet. He opened the wallet and took out the cash, counted it, handed half to Annie, and returned the wallet to the man's pocket.

"Now what?" Annie said. "I don't want to phone in a tip and get recorded on a tape and they might not come anyway."

Joseph bent down and dragged Albert over to the van. He opened the driver's door and the two of them slid him into the seat and fastened him upright with the safety belt. The body of the dead man was still in the back of the van. They returned to the basement and carried Ernest up the stairs and into the passenger seat.

"Thank God he's not the fat one," Annie gasped.

When they were loaded up, Joseph opened the garage doors and then reached inside the van and started the motor. It was all downhill to the gates. He collected his knapsack and nodded to Annie.

"My pleasure," Annie said.

She reached in and popped the van into gear. It rolled down the hill, gathering speed as it went, and crashed through the gate before skewing crossways and stopping astride the curb. A light began flashing on the side of the house and an alarm sounded in staccato three-second bursts. The engine noise increased to a scream, then stopped abruptly. Steam rose from the fractured radiator and dark red fluid ebbed out from beneath the chassis.

Joseph, Annie, and Sinbad moved quickly down the slope, keeping away from the cameras. They slipped out the side gate and disappeared into the night. Off in the distance a siren sounded and then a second one.

CHAPTER 27

The trail had gone stone cold. Clarke had been to the hospital and grilled the two men who'd been in the van, but learned nothing that he didn't already know. Albert and Ernest were smashed up, surly and uncooperative, and stuck steadfastly to their story that the dead guy, Louie, had contacted them and was the one who had made all the arrangements. They were given Annie's address and told to pick her up and lock her in the basement of the house in the Properties with the key they had been given, and then await further instructions. They had been sitting in the van outside her house for two hours when she finally drove out in the old Subaru and headed to the shopping mall. Surprised to discover that she wasn't alone, they'd made a snap decision to grab the old guy with her so he couldn't give their descriptions to the cops. It had seemed like a good idea at the time. As for what had transpired at the estate, they had no idea. Somebody had ambushed them from behind and knocked them out cold. Hadn't seen who. The unknown person or persons must have loaded the two of them into the van, crashed into the gate on their way out, and then made a run for it. It was probably meth-heads who knew the house was vacant and were looking to rob it. It happened a lot these days.

"That's not a bad try. Except how then do you explain ending up in the driver's seat of the van?" Clarke asked.

Albert's brow wrinkled in thought. "That's a tough one," he said. "No idea. I was unconscious at the time."

"And the dog bite?"

"That's not a dog bite. I injured my arm in the crash. Piece of shit old van doesn't have airbags."

"Okay, fine. So you won't need a rabies shot then. What's a little foaming at the mouth, convulsion, and dementia to a tough guy like you? Not very far to go on that last one anyway, I should think. Good luck." Clarke rose to leave.

Albert came clean.

Clarke was remarkably restrained about the situation. He understood that Joseph followed more medieval rules of engagement where his family was concerned, and was relieved and maybe even a little surprised that only the one man had been killed. He'd realized the second the call came in about an incident up in the Properties involving a white van that it was connected to his case. He'd arrived on the scene well before Jared and Daniel showed up, and was reasonably certain that they had no knowledge of what had transpired there. Nobody was inclined to press charges against Joseph for the dead man in the back of the van; his actions were clearly justifiable self-defence. A passerby's video of the attack in the parking lot had gone viral, and two well-known celebrity lawyers had already offered to represent Joseph for free. The department was happy to let the incident slide.

As for what followed afterwards up in the Properties, the feeling of the department was that the less the general public knew about those events the better. It was never a good thing when private citizens got ahead of the police on a well-publicized case such as this one. The department's press release was a jumbled haze of misinformation that made no mention of an old First Nations man and his dog, and suggested muddled drug-gang warfare as the most probable motive for the incident.

A separate press release stated that the police had found the kidnapped woman and she was in good condition apart from some bruises.

Any fear of contradiction of the events that had occurred at the Properties was put to rest three days later when the two men died in hospital of what was briefly described in the police press handout as complications from the crash.

❀

Clarke summarized it for Merlynn over breakfast on the aft deck of *Legalese*. It was visiting hours when the incident occurred, people were coming and going, and the hospital videos showed nothing conclusive. He said that two tall men wearing hoodies could have been the pair who took Lauren out of the nightclub, but that was just a guess. Same body types, tall and lean, but nothing unusual about them save maybe for the way they kept their heads down when they passed the cameras as if trying to keep their faces hidden. It was also possible that they were just slouching teenagers. Apart from that, Clarke said, not a single damn thing. The officer stationed outside the victims' room, soon to be assigned to traffic, vehemently denied leaving his post. When it was pointed out that two men had been strangled in their beds on his watch and only one door led into the room which was located on the eighth floor of the hospital, he acknowledged he might have gone out to the roof for a quick smoke break with one of the nurses.

"They were never going to tell us anything anyway," Clarke said with a shrug. Thirty-four years of police work had left him relatively indifferent to the fate of miscreants.

"Probably not, but their deaths tell you something," Merlynn said. "To murder two men like that under guard in a hospital is beyond risky, and it implies the stakes are high. And why take Annie in the first place? It had to be to put pressure on Danny and Jared for some reason."

"There's nothing in the house in the Properties," Clarke said, "it's empty apart from some basic furniture. The tax records show it's belonged to the same offshore owner for the last seven years. The company that manages the property says it hasn't been lived in or rented out since they've been in charge of it. They send in a cleaning firm once a month to dust things off, and they cash the cheques. It seems like just another spot for offshore money to sit. The city is full of similar places." Clarke paused for a sip of coffee. "With housing prices rising so fast, renting can be more trouble than it's worth on higher-end properties. Anyway, the upshot is another dead end. Just like Ernest, Louie, and Albert. Dead ends. Our one remaining good lead has vanished, and I'm getting a strong feeling that Newcombe's disappearance is permanent. Whoever these people are, they're careful. They don't leave loose ends. So we're back to square one."

"Except for the park bench women," Merlynn said. "They're flashing-light loose ends. And they are a part of it all, there is no denying that, with the whole yacht club connection. And that bit of it is just pure unadulterated crazy. You go to the trouble of killing two small-time criminals who probably don't know very much of anything and wouldn't tell you even if they did, and leave alive witnesses who could put you away for a very long time? And not only do you leave them alive, you display them in a fashion that positively invites making connections between all of them? It's just nuts. There have to be two different parties involved."

Clarke took a sip of coffee, puckered up his face, and glanced at the ship's clock.

"Still too early," Merlynn said. "Even for on a boat."

"I haven't the slightest notion what you're talking about," Clarke said primly. He finished his coffee, picked up the toolbox that sat on the deck beside him, and retreated down to the engine room and the six-pack cooling in the bilge.

"He does look vaguely familiar." Cat passed the newspaper across the table.

"Don't know him," Jared replied after a quick glance at the photo of the missing lawyer. "He was a well-known 'man about town' it says here. That usually means the guy is banging runway models. You probably met him at one of your fashion things. Or with your guy Albright. Sullivan does legal work for the party, according to this."

"He's not my guy," Cat said pleasantly.

"Whatever," Jared said. The up-in-the-air job offer was still a source of some annoyance to him. He didn't really know why, he hadn't even met Albright, although he was pretty sure that if he did meet him he wouldn't like him. So maybe he was being unreasonable. *Bite me.*

"Did you say something?" Cat asked.

"No."

CHAPTER 28

The detective had been sitting in the boardroom for half an hour. He suspected the wait was deliberate, but wasn't about to complain. He was being paid a thousand dollars a month for an occasional report about what was happening in the department, and he couldn't risk losing the money. Child support for his second divorce was killing him.

There were five TV screens placed on the end wall, all tuned to different programs with the sound muted, and not a remote in sight. He wasn't sure he had the balls to switch channels anyway. One screen showed the stock market, one CNN, one NBC, and another an Asian tickertape channel. The fifth TV was tuned to the wrestling network. It was showing an old Earthquake versus Loch Ness Monster match at the moment, and the ring announcer proudly declared there was over eleven hundred pounds of mayhem in the ring. The detective had heard that Ivery's assistant was an ex-wrestler, and given the size of the man, he was inclined to believe it. How anyone could watch that crap was beyond him. A hot lady with a sweet mouth was reviewing stock prices on the Asian channel, and he gazed at her and daydreamed.

He heard a noise behind him and turned around to see Ivery and his keeper at the conference table. He hadn't heard them enter the room. They must have been in one of the suites adjacent to the boardroom.

"You told Thomas over the phone that the department has no leads on the hospital murders?"

The soft-spoken man with the long grey hair and steel-rimmed glasses seated in the wheelchair at the head of the table looked up from the folder open in front of him and fastened his gaze on the detective.

"Nothing that I've heard about anyway. I'm almost sure."

"Almost is not what you're paid for," the man murmured. He had long ago learned the benefit of having listeners strain to hear what you said. It put them at a disadvantage; they unconsciously lowered their heads and leaned forward in an attitude that was inherently submissive. And that made a difference in the social dynamics. When you were a shade over five feet five inches, a hundred and forty-five pounds soaking wet, and physically handicapped, you needed every advantage you could get. In case this ploy wasn't sufficient, there was Thomas, the personal attendant who never left his side and looked like he could lift a truck off the ground by its front bumper and was fretting for the chance to do so. The big man winked at the detective. It didn't comfort him.

"What I mean, Mr. Ivery, is that the department is at a standstill on the case. We have nothing but a video that shows two men in hoodies who are possible suspects, but we don't have enough to identify them. We can put them on the right floor at the right time, and they didn't visit any of the other patients, so chances are they're the guys. We think there were two persons involved as the men were strangled, and it probably had to have been done simultaneously as both men had regained consciousness and would likely have been awake at that hour. Either one of them could have yelled out for help, but no one heard anything." The detective shrugged and spread his hands. "If you ask me, we're likely never going to find out who the killers were unless we get a tip. We're still looking for Newcombe, but that's no longer a priority. The feeling is that we're not going to find him, he's either dead or long gone. Detective

Clarke is like a dog with a bone on the case, but even he is beginning to slow down a bit. He's been taking a lot of time off lately. I heard he's working on a boat that belongs to some old chick he's hooked up with."

"That old chick would be Merlynn Saunders, Q.C.," Ivery said mildly. "A very sharp lady back in the day. I'm guessing she likely still is."

"Okay. If you say so. Anything else?"

"No. Keep me posted. I want to know immediately if there is any new information on the park bench assaults or the hospital murders. You can leave." The detective went to the open elevator, entered it, and left.

The little man took off his glasses and slowly polished them with a soft green cloth as he stared off into space. He often did this for extended periods of time when he was concentrating on a problem. Thomas stood by in silence, his thick arms folded across his chest. His face was impassive, expressionless. He gave the impression he could remain motionless for hours.

"What do you think, Thomas?"

"I think the past may be intruding on the present, sir," the big man replied in a surprisingly soft voice that came from his long years of service to the man in the wheelchair. "It would be naive to assume that the disappearance of Newcombe and the lawyer aren't connected to the murders in the hospital. I think perhaps I should reach out to some of our old acquaintances and make some inquiries."

Ronald Ivery nodded in agreement. "Once again, Thomas, you foreshadow me. Thank you. And now I think I'll retire to my apartments. It's been a long day."

"Of course, sir."

The big man reached down and took the handles of the wheelchair and pushed it out into a smaller second room with a collection of modern art mounted on panels spaced out along the walls. He pressed a button recessed into the wall and one of the panels slid sideways and they entered the hidden elevator. The panel moved back in place behind them as the door closed and they moved silently upwards. They came to a stop and moved out into a large open room. Thomas threw the switch that disconnected the power from the elevator and they were secure in their private world.

The late afternoon daylight poured in from giant skylights in the roof and the floor-to-ceiling windows spaced along the twenty-foot-high exterior walls. When his father died the building was part of the estate Ronald Ivery inherited, and he'd sold a second smaller building left to him and used the greater part of that money to convert the top floor from a giant warehouse and storage area into a luxurious private penthouse complete with a gym, a therapy pool, and a chef's kitchen where Thomas cooked for the two of them. Ivery had used an offshore construction company signed to a non-disclosure agreement to do all the work, and since its completion he and Thomas were the only men who had set foot inside.

There was the occasional woman, selected now and again by Ivery from an exclusive and discreet website and paid well for her services. Thomas brought these dates into the building late at night, through a rear alley entrance, and none of them could have found their way back there on a bet, nor did they have any idea of who they had met with once inside. But women, as was the case with a lot of things in Ronald Ivery's life, were not very important.

What was important was the pill that Thomas now handed to him. He assisted Ivery with undressing and strapped him securely into the harness that hung down from the gantry that spanned the ceiling. Ivery took the controls and ran himself out over the pool and down into the heated waters. One button turned on the hydro jets and another controlled the music that surged out from the underwater speakers in the pool walls. Ivery closed his eyes and was washed away.

Two hours would pass before he came back to himself and rose up and swung back over his chair, lowered himself down into it, and wheeled into his bedroom. The drug and the pulsing water had taken away his pain, and he manoeuvred himself into his bed and slept like a baby. He would awake refreshed and ready for another busy day.

CHAPTER 29

The weather had turned miserable, and the two men in the little inflatable with the electric motor clamped to the transom were having a hard time of it. The night sky had been clouded over with poor visibility when they'd set out, but at least the water had been calm. Minutes later a sudden squall had come through right on the nose and the seas had instantly kicked up into a small chop. The men swore and took up their paddles to assist the little engine. The electric motor was quiet and you probably couldn't hear it from a hundred feet off and that was a good thing, the downside being it was damn near useless in anything other than flat water. But they figured they only had a little ways to go now until they entered the commercial basin, and they lowered their heads and worked and sweated and cursed until they finally passed between the red and green beacons that marked the entrance and moved into the sheltered water just beyond. One of the men reached back and switched off the motor, and they sat there for a few minutes catching their breath.

They'd looked at a chart of the marina in *Rainbow*'s warm and cozy cabin just before they left and everything seemed pretty straightforward, but that was one thing. It was another thing entirely when you were down at sea level, cold, wet, and facing into a near horizontal, driving rain. The dock lights were practically useless in these conditions, and they couldn't read the letters on the end pilings, but they didn't want to chance a flashlight. Nobody in their right mind would be out in a dinghy, and they didn't want to have to answer any questions. They weren't worried about the elderly watchman, they'd been told his main job was keeping track of the foot traffic entering the marina through the gate alongside his office. The odds of him being out and about on a night like this were somewhere between slim and none, but why take the chance.

"It's the fourth one along. D dock," one of the men said.

"Yeah. Two over, I figure."

They paddled across and into the gap between the fourth and fifth docks. Once they were up close they could make out the sign on the piling with the LED light under it.

"This is the one. Should be the seventh finger in from the end."

They paddled silently along until they reached the big sailboat. The wind was down inside the marina, but the rain was pelting them even harder now, hitting their faces and stinging their eyes.

"Good thing it's wood," one man said.

"I mixed a quart of oil in with the gas, it will burn all right," the second man said. "Like a Christmas tree in January."

They set the jerry cans onto the end of the dock beside the sailboat and climbed carefully out of the dinghy. An old troller a few boats down had a cabin light showing faintly through the rain; apart from that, darkness. The men shivered, the heat worked up during their hard paddle now turned to a cold sweat by wind and nerves.

"I'll spread these two cans up near the front, you spill yours at the back end there. We'll light her up from the dock."

They dumped the fuel, jumped back down onto the dock, lit the gas-soaked rags, and threw them onto the boat. The blaze flashed up instantly, lighting the area for a hundred feet in all directions. They stood there stupidly blinking against the glare for a few seconds.

"Get rid of the cans. We gotta go. Now."

They threw the gas cans onto the foredeck of the sailboat and heard a loud clang.

Huh, the lead man thought as they jumped into their dinghy and began paddling furiously. With the wind at their backs, they were soon beyond the tumult and shouting, and the light from the blaze slowly faded behind them. A mile out into the bay, the brothers were waiting with the Chris-Craft, and the two men climbed aboard, tied the little inflatable behind, and planed off into the night. By the time they arrived back at *Rainbow* and helped Clint and Travis winch the tender aboard, it was midnight. Lacey was sitting in the saloon, watching the late news on TV with a drink in his hand. He didn't turn around to greet them.

"I can smell the gas and smoke on you from here," he said. "Stay on the outside mat, you're not coming inside."

"Yeah, well, she went up like a Roman candle. Whoosh! Fourth of fucking July. Lit up the whole marina. Job done. Omelettes and eggs, old chap." There was a faint mincing sneer in the man's voice. Like many misguided people, he associated being gay with being weak.

Queer Bill swivelled around and regarded him.

"Yes. About that," he said. "Old chap. I've just been watching the late-night news. They covered your 'boat arson.'" He made mocking quotations marks in the air with his fingers, and then spoke briefly.

The arsonists hung their heads.

A long silence ensued.

"How are we fixed for spare anchor chain?" Clint finally asked.

CHAPTER 30

Danny looked up as his brothers walked into the room. Erin and Jaimie had stopped by Annie's for a late breakfast after dropping some gear off at their boat in the commercial basin for the final trip of the season.

"There was a fire in the marina last night," Erin said. He went to the stove and poured coffee for himself and his brother. "Looked like arson, they found some old war surplus jerry cans lying on the deck of the boat."

"Insurance?" Danny asked. It wasn't entirely unknown in the fishing industry. It had been a poor season, and a lot of people were hurting.

Jaimie said, "Probably not. It was a fifty-foot steel Waterline sailboat. Just completed last month and on her maiden cruise. She'll need new sails and a paint job, likely a new boom and furling, too, but that's about it. Owned by a tech guy out of Silicon Valley who's stupid rich by all accounts."

"So what are they saying then? Somebody he pissed off?"

"Guess what slip it was in," Jaimie said.

❈

Jared and Danny huddled far forward in *Arrow*'s cockpit, sheltering under the dodger and drinking mildly doctored coffee. The weather had turned bad, with intermittent rain and a blustery southeaster. It wasn't expected to last very long, but for the time being it was miserable.

"You talk to Clarke about it?" Danny asked.

"Yes. He told his squad that it was likely an attempt on *Arrow*. They've spoken to everybody who was around the docks last night, and nobody saw or heard anything before the fire started. With the crappy weather there weren't many people around."

"Well, they can rule out sailors, we know that much for certain. How could anyone confuse a gorgeous new million-dollar steel sloop with an old wooden ketch?" Danny shook his head in disbelief.

Jared said, "Well, it was raining pretty hard at the time."

"Yes, okay, but my God, even so. They would have to be complete and total idiots. Jaimie said the boat is stunning, beautiful lines, swept back house, all gleaming steel and stainless, a real state-of-the-art modern showpiece, whereas *Arrow* is a dated, old—"

"Careful now," Jared interrupted.

"Yeah. Well, you know what I mean."

They sat and thought about it for a while. They finished their coffee and Jared reached down and took two cans from the box of beer that lay at their feet and popped the tabs. He handed one across.

"We don't have a single damned thing," he said finally.

Danny said, "We have the house in the Properties where Newcombe ran to. The same place they took Annie. So there is definitely something there."

Jared shook his head. "Clarke says they went over the place with a fine-tooth comb. Checked all the cameras and found the pictures of the guys coming in and out with the van, but that's it. They dusted the whole place for fingerprints and did find some in the house that didn't belong to the cleaners, but no hits came up when they checked them out in their databases. There were no prints in the van or garage apart from the three dead guys. Bert, Ernie, and Louie were all small-time criminals, street-level drug dealers well down the chain, so no joy there either."

"All right. So that might be a dead end. So to speak. What else?"

"There's *Rainbow* and Bill Lacey. We saw that picture of him with Newcombe. That could just be a coincidence; they do belong to the same yacht club after all. But he also owns an old wooden launch like the one the caretaker saw those two guys in. There could be similar boats in the Queens Own, but what are the odds of two coincidences like that? Lacey is definitely in the picture."

"I think we should pay him a visit," Danny said. "Maybe we could take him out for a sail and swing him from the boom like you did with Jaeger that time. Weather is perfect right now for that sort of thing. I've always regretted missing the chance of seeing that little snitch flying back and forth over the deck on the quick tacks. Speaking of Jaeger, you don't suppose he knows anything about any of this, do you?"

"He might. Although I doubt that he'd tell us if he did."

They sat in comfortable silence for a while, leaning back tight against the cabin house, sipping their beer and enjoying the sound of the wind and rain in the rigging and the slight hesitant motions of *Arrow* as she chafed at her mooring.

"There *is* the slip down from *Legalese* where Merlynn ran into the two guys with the hats that shooed her off," Danny finally said. "The one owned by the political party."

"That's a little out of the ordinary, perhaps, but we don't have any other connections. Nowhere to go to from there. We need something else."

Danny looked uncomfortable. "Actually, there might be one more thing," he said. "Cat's job offer. The timing of it."

"What about it?"

"Her sister gets attacked, and two weeks later she's offered a job by the same outfit that had a boat moored at the yacht club? The club where someone used a stolen gate card that coincided with the West End assaults? What are the chances of all that being unconnected?"

Jared stared at him. "You're talking about James Albright, a man who has been mentioned as a possible candidate for the leadership of his party. That's crazy."

"Maybe not all that crazy. You said Cat was on Albright's boat last Sunday before she came across to Nanaimo. Could that have been the boat in the end berth that Merlynn saw that time?"

Jared shrugged. "I suppose it's possible. Cat said it was a big boat. Maybe too big to fit in the end slot, although that berth is oversized with a raised roof for the big boys. We could probably find out the name of Albright's boat, the trouble is there's no record of the names of the boats using that end berth or the dates when they come and go."

They sat quietly, lost in thought, and then Jared spoke.

"Cat came across to Nanaimo in a big Zodiac with twin Yamahas on the back. Couple of crew kitted out in wet gear dropped her off. I didn't get a good look at them and wouldn't know them again even if I did see them. But they were tall skinny guys, like Merlynn mentioned seeing that time. I suppose I could talk to Cat about all of this. The trouble is, I have to be careful or she might take the job with Albright just to spite me. She's already implied that I'm jealous of him."

"And are you?"

"Possibly a teeny tiny bit."

"You damn well should be. He's got a lot more going than you have in looks, money, and prospects."

"Up yours," Jared said affably.

Danny raised his beer.

The rain poured down.

They drank and pondered in silence.

CHAPTER 31

Clarke was flummoxed. It was a word he was fond of using with his superiors when a case wasn't going well. It often resulted in terminating communications between the participants, an outcome he usually desired. "I'm sorry, Captain, but I'm completely flummoxed." He thought it captured the tone of great intellectual energy having been spent, every avenue explored, no stone left unturned, etcetera, etcetera.

In the case of the West End attacks, that was an accurate description of the situation. Clarke was at his wits' end. Fucking flummoxed. In spite of all the publicity, the questioning of family members and all known associates of the dead trio from the van, and dozens of interviews with past and present Queens Own Yacht Club members, he'd found nothing solid to proceed with. It was time for something different. Although he didn't have the wide latitude of the old days when he could just round up a bunch of guys he didn't like the looks of and lean on them in the hopes of springing something loose, Clarke was not averse to informal interrogations in off-station locales without lawyers present.

He was on one of these expeditions now, sitting in the corner of the Drake Hotel nursing a beer with three full glasses lined up on the table in front of him as he checked out the latest arrivals. Back in the day he'd had a large group of informants, many of them past offenders he paid or threatened, to keep him up to speed on what was happening in their particular corner of the criminal world. Nowadays there was no budget allocated for that sort of thing, a result of a new squeaky-clean police chief combined with predatory lawyers who were quick to exploit and discredit paid testimony on the stand. But there were still ways for devious old cops to sidestep the rules.

Clarke looked up and smiled. Speaking of which, just coming through the door, Froggy, an addict from Manitoba who'd moved west a few years ago to avoid being frozen to death in a drugged stupor. A raging alcoholic who, it being two days until Welfare Wednesday, would almost certainly be desperate. Clarke waved, and Froggy, after a hopeless, trapped look around the near empty bar, came over and sat down.

"How's it going, Froggy? Here, help yourself."

Froggy reached across and took one of the beers, and spilling only a little, drank it halfway down.

"I needed that," he said. He wiped his mouth with a dirty sleeve and finished it off. Clarke slid another glass over, and Froggy put his hand around it and looked at Clarke. He knew from past experience that while the first one was free, the second one would cost him something. A third glass seemed like a distant dream.

"So what do you hear?"

"About what?" Froggy knew enough not to volunteer information indiscriminately. It was his sole remaining asset, and he couldn't afford to squander it.

"The women on the park benches."

Clarke knew it was a long shot, but what the hell, he had to ask. Froggy had been a smart man once, a successful chartered accountant they said, before a glowing red wood stove exploded and incinerated his family and his life one cold prairie night.

"Don't know anything about that," Froggy said, gripping his second beer tightly and already casting covetous glances at the final one. "Some crazy, everyone says."

Clarke nodded. "They're probably right. What do you know about the three men in the van?"

"I heard Louie Tardif was one of them. They say the other two sold drugs for him."

"Yeah, we already knew that." Clarke had suspected it, now he had another little piece of the puzzle. He finished his own beer and reached out and grasped the remaining glass and drew it towards him.

"Wait," Froggy said. He closed his eyes, frowning in concentration. "I did some work a few years ago for Louie. Off the books. It was early on, I wasn't as sick then. He had a legitimate business going on at the time. Can't remember what it was." He frowned in concentration. "Some kind of building maintenance, maybe. Janitor service? Doesn't matter anyway. Louie was dealing on the side then, he had a couple of guys working for him. Pretty small-time operation, I think."

Clarke slid the last beer across the table towards Froggy and waited.

"This car came by when I was there one day. A big black limo with tinted windows. It had one of those lifts on the back for a wheelchair. Guy in the back seat rolled the window down and talked to Louie. He was all puffed up when he came back. Said it was the man."

"The man." Clarke raised his hand and signalled for another round. He waited until the server left.

"How long ago was this?"

"Not long after I came out here. Three or four years ago? Something like that." Froggy sounded almost normal now, the hunger fed, the desperation gone for another few hours.

"What do you think Louie meant by 'the man'?"

"Somebody important I suppose. I don't know."

"Could you describe him?"

"Not really. Small, I guess, 'cause I remember thinking he looked like a kid except for the grey in his hair. Glasses maybe."

He closed his eyes for a few moments, then opened them again. "Maybe not. But I think the lift was for him. There was that look about him. Or maybe it was something somebody said."

"How about the driver?"

"I remember he got out of the car and went into the office and talked to Louie. Came out with a small package. Pills, I guess. Big guy, I mean really big, maybe like six-six and three hundred pounds plus. Not really fat either. Scared the crap out of everybody." Froggy shrugged. "That's all I can remember." He looked anxiously at Clarke.

"Better than nothing, Froggy." Clarke took a fifty out of his wallet. "I'm going to leave this at the bar, order you a burger, and tell them to drop the change on the table. Take care of yourself."

Froggy nodded and smiled, in the happy place now. He pulled the two beers in close, as if someone might attempt to steal them. The money was an unexpected bonus, another chance to punch a ticket on the fentanyl train. Maybe this time he'd be lucky and get back to Marie and the girls waiting at the end of the line. He sat hunched at the table, his eyes half closed, a scarred man in a tattered coat lost in dreams of the past.

The bartender dropped his order and change on the table, and Froggy carefully wrapped the burger in its napkin and stowed it in his coat pocket for later. He drained the last beer, picked up the money, and floated out the door to find a dealer. It wouldn't be difficult.

CHAPTER 32

"What do you mean she turned me down?" Albright's tone was incredulous.

"She said she was flattered, realized what an honour it was to be asked, and had spent a lot of time thinking about it, but in the end she decided she just wasn't ready for that big a change in her life. She said she still enjoys her present work and wants to continue on with it for a while."

Albright came out from behind his desk and walked towards his aide and halted a foot in front of his face.

"Why didn't you put her through to me immediately?" he shouted.

"I told her you would want to speak to her, sir, but she said she would rather not."

"Rather not speak with me."

"Yes, sir, those were her exact words. And then she hung up before I could say anything else."

Malcolm realized he might have stuttered slightly over the last part of his statement. Albright was glaring at him, and he tried to focus on the space between his eyes like it said in the books he'd read on anger management, receiving end. He thought if he looked away the man might strike him.

"Who the hell does she think she is, turning me down?"

Malcolm took this to be a rhetorical question and remained silent, his face screwing up into what he hoped was a representation of intelligent and obliging agreement.

"Get out of my sight. Now!" Albright screamed.

Malcolm fled, wondering, and not for the first time, why he didn't just up and quit. The money was good, but at times like this it was nowhere near worth it. And times like this were becoming more and more frequent of late. He thought if he didn't make the break soon, he might not be allowed to.

"Send me the brothers," Albright yelled after him, and his aide took out his cell phone and made the call as he escaped back to the sanctuary of his office. He collapsed into his chair in front of the computer, called up his resumé on the screen, and began working feverishly on it.

❀

The Mercedes rolled up in front of the building, and Albright climbed into the back seat and cranked up the Wagner. He'd sat through the whole Ring Cycle on three successive nights on his trip to that specialist in Germany and had been enthralled. It spoke to him now more than ever. The brothers, whose taste ran more to country, closed the partition window and shut off the front speakers after loading Albright's luggage, and the three men headed out on the highway towards Blaine. Albright turned back for a last look as they pulled away and wondered if he would ever return. He wasn't a superstitious man, but he had a strong premonition that he would never see his office or the city again. He found that he was fine with that.

The great thing about knowing the future, inasmuch as it applied to you anyway, was that, as the man said, it concentrated the mind. As the tracks narrowed and the end approached, it was sinful not to focus on what was most important and devil take the rest. No rational person would argue with that, of course, but the real trick was in deciding what the most important thing was. Albright knew one thing for sure. It sure as hell wasn't politics. He leaned back against the leather, working the Gripmasters he had bought the day after the diagnosis, lifted up and carried by the music booming from the speakers. He closed his eyes and was swept away.

They used the express lane at the U.S. border and a short time later arrived at the marina on the American side and climbed into the big Zodiac Albright stored in one of the covered slips. From there it was a quick half-mile run to the little floating dock at the foot of the anchored yacht's gangway. The three of them went aboard and into the great saloon where Clint rang for the steward and ordered drinks.

"Leave the bottle," Albright said. "We won't need you again tonight."

"You two set up the ring." He picked up the intercom and spoke to the captain. Five minutes later he heard the anchor come aboard and settle in its chocks and then the increased revs as the boat tilted and picked up speed as it swung onto its new course and accelerated northward back into Canadian waters.

Albright drained his glass and thought about Cat and his anger grew. He wasn't used to being refused by anyone, let alone by a goddamned woman. He poured himself another drink and considered the situation. Surely it couldn't have anything to do with that sad little dickweed she was going around with?

He'd had the party's detective agency do some background checks on her long before he'd made the offer, and his name had come up as her current boyfriend. Jared Kane, a born loser if ever he'd seen one. A commercial fisherman who made mediocre money six months of the year and worked on and off at odd jobs for the other half. Pathetic really, even discounting the prison history and that Indian family he hung out with in the East End. Any comparison between the two of them was an insult. Well, he supposed there was no accounting for taste. She'd soon enough learn better.

But he had other things on his plate at the moment. First things first. He thought about the man chained up in the engine room and smiled in anticipation. This was exactly what he needed; it had been far too long since he'd had a chance to test himself. Although it was no longer all that much of a test if he was being perfectly honest. Maybe he'd tie one hand behind his back this time.

Although maybe not.

The brothers unrolled the stained canvas and centred it in the ring and fastened the corners to the clips at the base of the four posts. They tightened the tensioners on the ring ropes and measured them to the pound with a spring gauge, conscious of Albright's oversight. Everything had to be done to strict professional standards, right down to the smallest detail. Given what had transpired already in the ring and what was in store, it seemed ridiculous, but they weren't about to question his instructions. They opened the storage room door and removed the stools and the half-filled buckets with their sponges and set them inside the ring in opposing corners with towels carefully aligned over the ropes alongside them. They returned to the closet and reached onto the shelves for the wrapping tape, boxing gloves, and helmets that were lying there.

"We won't be needing any of that this evening, boys," Albright said. "We're going old school tonight. Bare knuckles and whisky, and may the best man win." He raised his glass in a toast.

The brothers glanced at each other and tried not to roll their eyes. They'd seen this show before, and it wasn't pretty.

"Finish your drinks and fetch him up."

❁

Richard Sullivan stumbled through the door wearing only faded old boxing trunks, blinking rapidly as his eyes adjusted to the light. He was unshaven and the grey stubble only partially hid the bruising and swelling that marked his face. His body was covered with purple, red, and blue welts, and his eyes were blackened and hopeless. They wandered the room, avoiding the presence at the bar that dominated it.

"Howdy, partner," Albright called out with a genial smile. "How about a drink before we get started then? As my old daddy used to say, you never know when it might be your last."

CHAPTER 33

Annie leaned forward on her outside knee and dipped the paddle in the water and pulled as she straightened, then leaned forward and repeated the stroke, shaking her head to get the rain out of her eyes and cursing the weather and that Tlingit cow who'd decided not to cancel practice. She cursed Joseph as well, who she suspected was sneakily ramping up the drumbeats. She'd seen the woman speaking to him before the session. She looked familiar, but Annie couldn't place her. She seemed too old for Danny and too young for his grandfather, although she wouldn't absolutely rule anything out in either case.

It was her arthritic knees that bothered her most, and she'd made an arrangement with the paddler across from her to switch sides every thirty minutes so she could alternate on the pressure points. The cow had whined about teamwork, bonding, synchronicity, and some other yuppie bullshit, but she and the other woman, a fellow sufferer, had ignored her. Annie knew they were two of the stronger paddlers on the team and equally competent at either station.

They'd been going for a while now, and she was warming up and almost starting to enjoy it. Or, to be more precise, dislike it less. It was always like this at the beginning, she thought, the questioning of your sanity, the idea of other things you could be enjoying, like coffee and a book in a warm place, but then the endorphins began to release, the stiffness and pain faded as the muscles heated and loosened, and what had begun as misery inched towards pleasure. She turned her head at the end of her stroke and glanced back at Joseph in the stern. He stood with the steering paddle locked under his arm and rapped the rhythm out on the drum fastened to his waist. Behind him was Sinbad, looking aft over the transom and longing for pursuit. The cow had objected to having the dog on board that first time, but Joseph had taken her aside for a word and she'd returned to the boat blushing furiously and the matter was settled. Annie would like to have known what was said.

They passed under the bridge and were out of the inner harbour and into wind and a slight chop now. The occasional bit of spray was added to the rain, but the slap of the waves striking the hull and the surge and roll added spontaneity and freedom to what had previously been mere mechanical exercise, and the women bent forward and pulled and straightened, bent forward and pulled and straightened, and the beat increased and the canoe raced onwards and one of the Elders began to sing and Annie's heart swelled as she joined in the old travelling songs and in that moment she could not imagine being anywhere else as the memories of kidnapping and police interviews faded and disappeared under the soothing rhythms of chant and drum.

Joseph steered in towards the shoreline for a few hundred feet, the big dugout canoe quick and responsive, and then he straightened it out again and they gradually disappeared into the rain and mist and only the distant drumbeats and windswept catches of song remained, and then these too faded and disappeared and the last sign of their passing was a faint trace of wake that thinned and spread and vanished under the hard beat of the rain.

❀

"It's them all right, I can just make out the old guy in the back of the boat," the short slender man with the binoculars said to his companion as he peered out at the water through the window of the beat-up Dodge Ram 4x4 with the Arizona plates. A .308 hunting rifle with a scope lay in the back seat. "I might be able to touch the old guy up if they come back the same way but I can't guarantee it. I'm never going to be able to pick out the woman. They all look the same to me."

His partner said, "This was a dumb idea right from the start. I can't believe we drove all the way out here for this. I know Karl owes Jeremiah for the girls and all, but this is just crazy. Never going to work. And why are we going after these two anyway? Isn't it the grandson who inherits the property?"

They gazed morosely down at the ocean. They were from dry country and not comfortable with any of this maritime vengeance business.

"It seems those two are the closest thing Kane has to a family. If he's made a will, they'd inherit. Jeremiah guaranteed his council that Kane's farm will be coming to the commune and is in trouble if he doesn't deliver. Could even lose his place as Prophet, so he can't afford to take the chance of a will lying around. Karl says we need to help him out or the pipeline could dry up. No telling what his successor will decide. A lot of Plentiful's members are against sending women to us no matter how much we pay for them."

"We'll just have to come up with a different plan then. One that doesn't involve a dozen witnesses in a hollowed-out log," his partner said.

"Travis said they live in a crappy old house in the East End. Not exactly your high-end neighbourhood with security patrols passing by every few minutes. How hard could it be to deal with them there?"

"You know, you're right. Who cares how we get it done? Let's just do it our way and tell them about it afterwards. I need to get back home. I heard a rumour that a new crop might be coming in from Utah next week, and I want to be there in time to get an early pick."

Arrow lay at her berth near the marina entrance, gently rolling and tossing as the wind and currents acted upon her. Occasionally she'd bend to a harder gust and surge up against the dock bumpers before falling back into her irregular restless motion. Traffic was busy in the outside channel and wakes from passing boats added another variable to *Arrow*'s movements. Inside the cabin where Jared and Danny sat brooding over morning coffee there was the soft clink of glasses tapping and the occasional slither of something in a locker, poorly stowed and seeking freedom.

The Waterline was back onto the hard for repair. The berth where she'd been previously tied up had undergone significant fire damage, and upon her return from the yacht club she'd been assigned a transient mooring, which was more subject to the vagaries of wind, tide, and marine traffic. Jared could identify with *Arrow*'s unrest and felt that he and Danny were in similar circumstances, the three of them tossed to-and-fro by unknown and unpredictable forces over which they had no control. He expressed this thought to Danny.

"A sea of troubles," Danny agreed. "If we knew who to oppose, I would be all for taking arms."

Their search for Albright's boat had proved futile. The party office said that any information regarding Albright's private life was exactly that, private, and refused to give them any help. Cat had spent hours on the net looking for some connection between Albright and a specific motor yacht without success, while Danny and Jared had wasted two days walking the docks of every marina in and around the city looking for a boat resembling Cat's meagre description. Cat hadn't seen the name on the stern apart from a brief glimpse from the Zodiac when she was leaving and the yacht had swung back towards Vancouver. With the swirling rain she hadn't been able to make it out. Two words, she thought. Short words, about equal in length, she thought. Dark paint, maybe blue, she thought. *Not helpful*, Jared thought, but knew better than to say so.

"Cat thinks the boat she was on might belong to one of the party faithful," Jared said. "It's possible that one of their donors lends or leases their boat to the party. It would be tax deductible and perfectly legal, but not required to be disclosed to the general public."

She had managed to get a copy of the party donor list and come up with the names of six people with boats on the West Coast that were large enough to be possibilities.

Jared picked up the list, glanced at it briefly, and handed it across to Danny who read them out.

"*Sea Maiden, Sea Dancer, Feelin Nauti, Sea View, Wave Symphony,* and *Blue Harp*. I'm hoping it's *Feelin Nauti* and we get to sink her. With a name like that, she's earned it."

"When was the *Blue Harp* registered?"

Danny glanced down at the sheet. "In 2006. It's the newest one of the bunch."

Jared said, "Isn't that the year Harper became national party leader? Conservative blue."

"That's pretty corny."

"Downright elegant compared to some of the other names," Jared said. "Don't forget we're talking about a political party here. Named to appeal to the old guard blue blood party loyalists. A lot of old money Tories wouldn't be caught dead on boats with some of those other names. Did Cat get the port of registry for it?"

Danny ran his finger down the printout. "Campbell River, B.C. Owned by Ronald Ivery."

"The real estate guy?"

"That's him. Lives in a penthouse suite in an office block he owns in the West End. The 'Ivery Tower' as the press likes to call it."

Cat had sent some press clippings along with the list of boats. Ronald Ivery's parents had been killed in a car accident when they were driving home after picking him up from his private school in Boston twenty-five years ago. An only child, he'd inherited everything. He'd been partially paralyzed in the crash.

"Cat says there are rumours that he's hit rehab a few times because of the drugs he takes for his pain. Gets about in a wheelchair, on his good days he can do crutches for a short time. Something of a recluse, he never married and has no known girlfriends. Keeps a low profile, stays out of the news. Has one manservant who does everything for him. An ex-wrestler who's been with him since the accident. Ivery has given millions to charities and is a big Tory donor, but stays out of the public eye and has never granted an interview."

"I think I saw a picture of them just recently," Danny said. "Huge guy pushing a man in a wheelchair. Had to be the wrestler."

Jared said, "Every so often there's a piece about the 'lonely man in the Ivery Tower,' but Cat says they're mostly speculative according to her friends in the business. He's intensely private. No one knows much about him other than that he's a billionaire or within spitting distance and owns a lot of expensive downtown real estate."

"Doesn't sound like there would be that much to know," Danny said. "We need a break."

A loud roar of "Permission to come aboard" broke the silence and *Arrow* tilted slightly.

"Morning, lads, I've brought breakfast," Clarke said as he deposited a greasy paper bag and a dozen Dos Equis on the chart table. "What's up?"

"Nothing much," Jared said. "We're just running down one more dead end." He selected a sausage roll and motioned to the pile of clippings on the table.

Clarke picked up the top one and skimmed through it as he cracked a beer.

"I've heard about this guy," he said. "A bit crippled, isn't he?"

"I believe the correct term is disabled person," Danny said.

"Right. My heartfelt apologies, Red Man."

Clarke read on and then shook his head and smiled. "I'll go to hell," he said. "You've got to be kidding me. Thomas Rodgers. The Slab. I haven't seen that name for . . . Christ, it must be thirty years. Before your time."

Danny and Jared waited.

"Pro wrestler. He's got to be pushing sixty now. Guy was huge, probably had to bend his head and turn sideways to go through a door. They called him the Slab because he was so wide and had this thing he did where once he had his guy stretched out on the canvas, he climbed up onto the top rope and put his arms down along his sides and just fell forward on top of the poor bugger, stiff as a board."

"That the end of the fight?" Jared asked.

"Usually, but here's the best part. He had this beefy pair of ex-wrestlers, a husband-and-wife tag team, and they'd come jogging down the aisle dressed in hospital whites with their names on the back and a sort of stretcher with wheels on it, and they'd load the guy up and cart him away. The guy was called Otto and his wife was Topsy. Otto Topsy. Get it? Rodgers was British and did this formal schtick with an upper-class accent. It was all pretty funny. He was a damned good wrestler too. Very popular at the time. I haven't heard his name for years."

"Well, that's all good to know," Jared said politely.

"Ah, but here's the thing," Clarke said. "There's this guy Froggy, who dabbled in drugs, and he told me about this huge guy who made a big buy from his dealer a few years back. And the car he was driving had a wheelchair lift on the back."

They sat there in silence.

"Has to be him," Jared said at last.

CHAPTER 34

Jared awoke to black silence, *Arrow* resting motionless in the night, not the least whisper of wind or water, nor the faintest creak of working wood that always accompanied her slightest movement. The clock by the bunk showed two forty, no sign of morning light to disturb the opaque darkness that surrounded Jared as he lay there motionless, seeking the thing that had roused him. But there was nothing save a sense of nervous unease centred in the pit of his stomach. He pulled on a sweater and shorts and went up the companionway stairs searching for what had changed and pulled him up from unconsciousness. It was the sense born of a thousand nights at sea, a tuning of the inner self with *Arrow* so complicit that each one of a hundred different sounds was subconsciously assimilated and weighed and assessed for change, be it the shifting sound of a friendly wave changing to the hard slap of a rising sea, or the ascending pitch of the rigging calibrating a gusting wind.

Jared crouched motionless in the cockpit for long minutes as he searched for the source of the unease that shrouded him like a pall. A damp yellowish predawn inversion hung static in the air and transformed the dock lights into hesitant flickering haloes that only increased the isolation. A distant freighter's foghorn sounded from Roberts Bank far off in the distance, the sound so muted it was scarcely audible. Beads of moisture blossomed and grew on *Arrow*'s rigging and dripped to the decks and the boat turned suddenly cold and unwelcoming. Far distant down the channel a fisherman headed out for the early morning bite, his running lights invisible and only the soft *ka-thunk* of an old Easthope engine giving sign he was there, followed minutes later by the last ripples of his wake dying silently against *Arrow*'s hull. At the end of the slip a heron stood sentinel, its head tucked under its wing in what passed for sleep. Leaving it to oversee the boat in his absence, Jared laced his Pumas and headed out for a solitary run. He knew he owed penance even if it wasn't clear yet what for.

He jogged slowly through the silent marina and came out on the barren city sidewalks, the slap of his soles echoing softly up through the grey concrete corridors. Away from the water the fog thinned as the road tilted up before him, but the cold became more pervasive and he increased his pace in an effort to build up internal heat and overcome the bleak complicit chill rising inside him.

Jared left the deserted canyons of the city and ran towards the park seawall, and then, on a sudden impulse, turned again and moved down Hastings Street towards the East End, past the little park where the transients huddled in their cardboard shelters and a lonely sex worker scuffed the sidewalk, a thick scarf wrapped over her spangled top. She glanced up, dismissing Jared as he passed her by, cupping her hands around her cigarette for warmth. A cab approached, its headlights flickering towards her, and she posed and stuck out her chest as it drew up beside her and the rear window opened. A brief negotiation and she climbed into the back seat where a shrouded passenger sat with lowered head. She closed the door and they moved away and faded into the darkness.

Jared was accelerating now, driving himself towards the unknown thing that summoned him, no understanding yet, caught up in a nightmare where he ran endlessly on, never knowing the reason or reaching the final destination, a human hamster caught up in an eternal mocking treadmill. For a moment he wondered if he was dreaming, then shook his head against the absurdity.

It was coming up on three miles now and still Jared couldn't get warm. It was as if he were labouring in a separate body, one that was subject to an outside set of imperatives, and somebody had turned the thermostat down to zero. He should have been sweating heavily by now, doubled over against the punishing pace and fighting for breath, but still he ran free, his cold breath merging with the cold night, moving silently in the chilled air, the only sound of his passage a slapping echo that trailed behind until it too was swallowed up by blackness.

He concentrated on lengthening his stride, building speed as the road sloped down and away before him, leaning forward in juxtaposition and letting gravity's drag pull him on, extending his arms for balance as his body fought to stay synchronous with his stride. A lonely siren rose up from back in the city and grew louder, a land-locked foghorn splitting the ghostly air before the fire truck whipped past and the icy mist scattered in drifting streams in its wake before reforming once more. The truck's tires screamed in a hard turn down Clark Drive and Jared turned in its wake and pursued the fading flashing lights, willing himself to greater speed for a reason he somehow knew but didn't yet understand. A second fire truck sirened past and then an ambulance pursued by a police car, and then a light rose up brilliant and grew in the east but it wasn't dawn, and the cold knowledge rose up from the pit of Jared's stomach and enveloped him and his body turned to ice and shattered.

It was another two miles to Annie's house, but Jared never doubted for a second what he'd find when he got there. He raced on and the sirens grew louder.

CHAPTER 35

Clarke and Danny stood on the sidewalk among the tangled hoses and smoke-stained men with their grim faces and endless thermoses of coffee. Little remained for the firefighters to do now but gather their equipment and commiserate before leaving the site of yet another defeat.

Inside the yard that had contained Annie and Joseph's home nothing was left standing over three feet high. The concrete blocks that made up the foundation had been blown out into the yard by the force of the explosion, and what remained behind was an undefined pile of steaming black embers interspersed with scorched and blackened objects that had once been appliances. Where the porch had stood, a yellow enameled wood stove was tipped over on its side with empty holes where the lids once sat. Even the detached woodshed off in the corner of the lot had been caught up and incinerated in the inferno. It was already too late when the first crew arrived, and most of their efforts had been spent on hosing down the adjacent houses to prevent them from catching fire as well.

Clarke stood to the side and waited for the chief to finish his string of mild "no comment" and "too early to say" to the aggressive reporter and her cameraman. Her eyes were red and her hasty lipstick crooked, and she was trying her best to disguise how pissed off she was at being dragged from her lover's bed at this ungodly hour of the morning, and into a second-rate neighbourhood to boot. The chief, a man she knew well from previous on-site confrontations (and who, once upon a time, God forgive her, she had let comfort her after a particularly gruesome apartment arson), wasn't helping.

"Assholes," the chief said to Clarke, when the reporters finally packed up their gear and left. He pulled out a pack of cigarettes and offered one to Clarke.

"You'd think I'd know better after all the mattress and sofa fires I've seen," he said as he lit it. He sucked in a lungful of smoke and gazed bleakly out over the charred remains of the house.

"But not this time," Clarke said. He and the chief had attended a lot of fires together over the years, most of them before they'd achieved their current ranks.

"No, not this time. There won't be anything official until the Fire Marshal issues his report in a couple of days, but it was arson beyond a doubt," the chief said. "First responders could still smell the gasoline. Thrown into both ground-level bedrooms in bottles, Molotov cocktail style. One of the boys cut his boot on a shard of its glass. Sorry to say no chance at all for the old guy, he never made it out of his bed. Lady was lucky she was in the bathroom at the time. If you can call any of this luck. What is this all about anyway?"

"Too early to say," Clarke said, mimicking the chief.

"Fuck off, you asshole," the chief said affably, and walked over and crouched down beside one of his new guys, the one who'd spewed his guts out when he discovered the blackened remains of the old man curled up tight on his bed in the fetal position.

Danny put his cell phone back in his pocket as Clarke approached and shook his head.

"Jared says Annie's still in intensive care," he said. Jared had been the first member of the family at the scene and had gone to the hospital with Annie in the ambulance.

"They won't know one way or the other for a few days," Danny went on. "Even if she does pull through, there's going to be some permanent damage to her lungs. It's a miracle she wasn't killed outright."

Like Joseph, Clarke thought. The two men avoided looking over to the far corner of the house where Joseph's bedroom had been. As if by not acknowledging it, it hadn't happened.

A small tent had been erected, and inside it the coroner's team was working over something once human, slowly clearing away small bits of debris and working their way down through the layers of ash and rubble with the care and patience of archeologists. Clarke had spoken with them before Danny returned from the hospital and they'd confirmed it was an average-sized male, but that was all they could say for the moment. The corpse had been near the centre of one explosion, and all the clothing and most of the skin had been incinerated by the blast. Positive identification would have to wait. *Until the Otto Topsy*, sprang unbidden into Clarke's mind and he stifled a snort. Sometimes cop humour shocked even him.

"I was at a friend's," Danny said. "Poker night. Or I might have been here as well. Game ran late and I slept on their couch. Have they found Sinbad yet? He usually sleeps in Joseph's room. Joseph leaves the window open so he can come in and out. I wonder why Sinbad didn't hear them. Maybe he was away. He sometimes hunts at night." Danny spoke disjointedly, without thought. Thinking was too hard just yet.

"They haven't found the dog," Clarke said, "but there's still a lot of debris to search through. It's suspected arson at the moment which makes Joseph's death murder, so they'll go slow and lock everything down. It could be days before we hear anything definite. I'll tell the neighbourhood patrol cars to keep an eye out for Sinbad just in case. There's nothing for you to do here, why don't you head back up to the hospital and join the rest of them? Or try and get some sleep — it's been a long night. I'm heading back to the hospital to interview Jared. Let me give you a lift. As soon as I have any news, I'll be in touch. You have my word on that."

An old experienced cop, Clarke could cheerfully lie bald-faced with the best of them. The last thing he was going to do during the investigation was keep Jared and Danny in the loop. They were his friends, but he knew their innate capacity for violence, and under these circumstances silence was the best policy.

Deep down Clarke felt there wasn't a single member of the family who wasn't capable of committing murder under the right circumstances. In fact, with Joseph incinerated and Annie grievously burned, they might even consider it their solemn duty.

That group of potential assassins included Jared, who Clarke thought might well be the most disordered of them all. He had some serious questions for Jared, the prime one being what in the hell was he doing showing up at Annie's house in the middle of the night. One of the firemen had told him the truck had passed a man running full-speed towards the house a couple of miles out from the blaze. The description fit Jared, so he was likely in the clear, not that Clarke had ever had any doubts about that. But there were questions that still remained unanswered. What had raised him out of bed and sent him flying down the road to Annie's at that unearthly hour? Had he received a phone call, some kind of threat or warning? If so, why hadn't he taken a taxi? Clarke hadn't questioned Jared at the hospital, the call had come in about Joseph's body being discovered before he'd had the chance, and he'd had to head back to the scene. What a horrible bloody night. He'd been fond of the old man and somebody was going to pay dearly for this.

He gathered up Danny and they drove back to the hospital in the squad car, stopping to pick up coffee on the way. Clarke had told Jared to wait for him at the hospital so they could do their interview when he got back and he'd promised he would, but it didn't really surprise him all that much when he arrived at the hospital and found Jared gone.

It did surprise Clarke, though, when he arrived at the vacant slip in the marina and found *Arrow* had disappeared as well. The night watchman said that she had left two hours earlier. Not surprisingly, Jared hadn't bothered to tell anyone where he was going. Clarke dialled Jared's cell phone and the call went straight to message. He then proceeded to the marina office and repeatedly hailed *Arrow* on channel sixteen in as civil a voice as he could manage. There was no reply to his broadcast, and Clarke slammed the handset back down on the cradle so hard he broke it.

"So send the fucking bill to the department, then," he snarled to the cowed watchman, who hadn't said a word.

CHAPTER 36

Jared brought *Arrow* under the Lions Gate Bridge, the engine screaming at 2800 RPM, a blue-tinged white fog rising in protest behind her. The revs were dangerously high but he was in a mad hurry. He knew Clarke would come looking for him sooner rather than later and be onto the harbour patrol the moment he saw the empty berth. He wouldn't begin to feel safe until *Arrow* was a good three hours out from the city, and even then he didn't put it past Clarke to send up a chopper or float plane. *Arrow* was an easy target to spot with her two sticks as Jared couldn't afford the time to drop the mizzenmast. He figured it would probably be a waste of time in any case, there weren't that many old wooden sailboats of her size out on the water and the authorities would certainly check any that they saw, whether they had one mast or two.

Time wasn't something Jared had to spare, the fog that had shrouded the city earlier in the day was beginning to dissipate out on the water, and the tips of *Arrow*'s masts might break out into clear view at any moment. He'd given the barometer a knock on the way by and it dropped sharply, so there was a chance that some wind and weather was on the way. A southeaster would be welcome, push *Arrow* north with maybe some rain as well to help screen her from the search, which would soon be full on if it wasn't already.

He didn't know why he hadn't waited for Clarke at the hospital and given him his statement. Maybe because he didn't really believe his story himself. *You woke up in the middle of the night with a bad feeling? Okay. Got dressed and started running like a madman towards Joseph and Annie's house at three o'clock in the morning? Right. That's it then? That's your story? Okay then. Got it. Hold out your hands for the cuffs, please!*

He'd always been close to Joseph in spite of the fact that the two of them had never carried on a normal conversation. Fifteen lousy words in English spoken by Joseph to him over the years and that was it. Fifteen! And yet they communicated in some unfathomable way. Always had, right from the beginning. And what if he'd told Clarke that what he thought had roused him in the middle of the night and sent him careening through the empty streets was a final contact from Joseph? A message of farewell or a summons to revenge?

He was an atheist, he didn't believe in any of that crap. And yet he'd awakened and dressed and run as if programmed, subject to some deeply coded genetic impulse that had pulled him from his berth and blew his reason and common sense away and sent him sprinting out into the blackness like an automaton. During times like this, when your mind was seared with blame and you had a black hole in your heart that was expanding and consuming you, a little religion would have been a good thing. But he had nothing to cleave to. If he'd ever had an ounce of faith it had been obliterated by his grandfather, that pious monster who emphasized his daily sermons with weekly whippings.

He moved out from behind the anchored freighters into Georgia Strait and set the autopilot. There was no traffic nearby and he laid a course paralleling the coast a couple of miles off, and after a last glance around he went down below. He stripped and stood before the mast support where it came down from the cabin top and grounded on the steel plate that spread the load along the keel. The post was whipped in cotton cord with ornate knots every few turns, the whole covered in multiple layers of thick white paint. Jared closed his eyes and took a deep breath and held it until he centred and his breathing slowed and he could feel every separate beat of his heart. He exhaled and on the ebb of that long, drawn-out sigh he reached out and tapped the mast with his closed fist, his knuckles clenched and extended.

He moved in slow progressive harmony, caressing the pillar with his palm edges and fists as a loved thing known before gradually speeding up and extending his blows until there was a faint fleshy sound as he struck. Every few cycles he balanced on one foot and struck the post with the other, switching back and forth and striking at random heights along the post from the cabin sole to the cabin top. His breathing grew harsh and ragged as his pace increased and he exhaled as he struck, the sobbing hiss of his breath merging with the meaty sound of the blows.

He was sweating now as he worked and he felt the beginnings of the pain and he let it build and brought it inwards from his scourged hands and feet and centred it deep in the hidden place inside. The fog had followed him below into the cabin and in those elusive wraiths Jared summoned long-dead faces from the past: Jennie and Delaney, Laura and Summers, Justine and the man from Scarab; some of them loved and some of them hated and all of them dead now and gone. He squinted through the fog and found the ruddy post and struck harder, searching for the shaded messages patterned there, and saw the first faint suggestions of new outlines and needed more to fill in those unknown taunting visages, and he broke the old scars loose and the blood flowed freer and he saw Annie's face and thought her dead. Another blackened, fire-devoured visage appeared, the flesh all gone and the grinning skull wore a Shaman's headdress and spoke in an old dialect that he seemed to understand for the first time a split second before it changed into a gibbering mocking insanity and Jared struck it savagely and it faded under his blows and ran down the post in long bloody streaks.

The sweat was pouring off him now, merging with the streaked column as he laboured on, etching meaningless patterns of violence and despair with his bloodied fists, searching for that final knowledge that waited just beyond the last escalation of pain. Faster and faster he danced and struck the moving mocking half-seen faces until at last he sank breathless to the floor, his body running in sweat and flecked in blood. He thought he might cry now, but found his tears all vanished, sucked dry at the fire's site, and what remained was a dusty, ashen despair and a white-hot flame of revenge that flickered and burned within him.

He lay gasping until his breath returned and then grasped the bloody pillar and pulled himself to his feet. He looked at his stinging knuckles and discovered them torn and bleeding and he took a pint mug and half filled it with brandy and carried it into the cockpit and plunged each fist into it in turn. The alcohol stung and burned and incarnadined in a blasphemous chalice of fire and blood, which he raised to his lips and drank from greedily.

Ahead of him a quarter mile distant, a flotilla of powerboats emerged from the fog into a sudden patch of sunshine and came proudly down the Strait towards him in a flying wedge, four of them strung out in array across *Arrow*'s course, their pennants flying, their horns sounding in arrogant imperious blasts. Jared stood indifferent, *Arrow* running straight against them with slight ticks of the autopilot holding her true. The cacophony increased as they closed in at twenty knots of combined speed, the central boat suddenly swerving towards his neighbour who juked in turn and flushed out his wingman, all of them standing on their bridge decks with raised fists cursing the red-spattered man who stared straight ahead but did not seem to see them.

CHAPTER 37

"Was his face painted blue?" Danny asked.

Clarke glared at him. "You think this is a joke?" he said.

The report had come in an hour earlier. Clarke had asked the Coast Guard to let him know if there was any word about *Arrow*. Small chance, but he'd covered all the bases just in case, and he'd gotten lucky. The report stated that Jared had tried to run down some powerboats. The complainants said he appeared drunk and was holding a pint mug containing a Bloody Mary or Caesar. "No lime wedge," the boater's blue-haired wife had snarled. Yes, he was that bloody close when they passed she could see.

"Think Mel in *Braveheart*," Danny said. "I've seen this show before. He's out of control and he's going after the *Blue Harp*. He wouldn't be pounding down the middle of the Strait if he was trying to hide. He'd be tight into the shoreline and dodging in behind the islands."

"I checked with the Campbell River detachment," Clarke said, "they say the *Harp*'s not in her berth. The police chief talked to the mayor who called his contacts in the party. They told him the boat is away with Albright for a few days, heading up through Desolation

Sound and some of the northern fjords. He's taking a few days off before the election push starts and will be out of touch, barring some major political catastrophe. They might be able to get hold of him if we give them a good enough reason. What could we say that wouldn't sound crazy? We think there's a man on an old wooden sailboat coming for him because he thinks Albright might be involved in the park bench assaults? There's a fucking lawsuit for you, ready-made. If there's any good news in all of this, it's that the odds of Jared actually finding the boat are slim. Desolation Sound is a big place, and we don't know that Jared even knows enough to look there."

Danny said, "I thought he might be going after Ivery on the off chance."

"I shouldn't tell you two anything," Clarke said. "I don't know what the hell is the matter with me, you'd think I'd know better by now. I must be getting senile. Speaking of Ivery, I think it's time I had a chat with him. That's the second time his name has come up, and I don't believe in coincidences."

"Can I come along?" Danny asked. "I promise not to say a word. I used to watch the WWF with Joseph on Saturday nights back when I was a kid. The Slab was one of our favourites."

Clarke assessed him carefully. "You're lying."

"I remember watching a tag team match on TV where he stood on the top rope and his partner pulled out a lumberjack's toque and put it on, then yelled *Timber!*, and pretended to saw the Slab down. He landed on top of the bad guy."

"Bullshit. I must have told you about that move."

"Scout's honour. I remembered after you left. I even went to the old downtown arena with Joseph a few times. We never saw the Slab in person though."

Clarke gave in. "Come along with me then. Why not, it's not like I have a career to jeopardize. It's unofficial anyway, and I sure as hell won't be reporting it. I'm still supposed to be on my leave of absence. We'll take a taxi."

The Tower was a mid-eighties building, one of many knocked up back in the boom days, differing little from its neighbours before the renovations it had undergone under Ronald Ivery. The article Clarke had found online about the building said the only exterior signs of the remodelled penthouse were the tinted two-story-high windows along the south and east face and a full-length west-facing balcony and garden. A helicopter pad had been incorporated into the new roof.

The commissionaire standing outside the entrance nodded to them as they went in through the revolving door and made their way to a long desk with a styled middle-aged woman standing behind it working a raised keyboard. An armed security guard was seated off to one end in front of a desk computer. He glanced up and Clarke saw the word *cop* forming in the man's mind as he surveyed them. Ex-services guy for sure. Behind him the directory on the wall displayed eighteen stories of company names, with anywhere from three to six offices on a floor. At first glance, none of them were familiar to Clarke. Two elevators stood side by side in the far corner of the lobby.

"How can I help you?" the woman asked.

Her tone was courteous, professional, and disinterested. About what you'd expect, Clarke thought. It was perhaps a little unusual that you had to come right up beside the security guard to read the directory though. Usually they were posted by the entrance. But having it up here meant that any visitors who hadn't received directions would have to approach the counter and come under the scrutiny of the guard. Cameras were placed in every corner of the lobby, and one was above and behind the woman, covering the desk and its environs. Clarke glanced over at the security guard and saw his image on the man's screen in the split second before he reached out and turned it away.

"We'd like to speak with Mr. Ivery," Clarke said, laying his department ID on the desk.

The woman studied it carefully before looking up at him. "Might I ask with regard to what, Detective?"

Clarke smiled. "Police business."

A phone under the counter rang and she answered it.

"Certainly, sir," she said.

Clarke glanced over at the security guard who gave an apologetic shrug.

"Take the farthest elevator to the top floor," the woman said, and went back to her keyboard.

They entered the elevator and pressed the button. The elevator ascended swiftly and then stopped, but the door remained closed. They waited in silence. A phone rang and a light flashed on a small panel above the floor buttons. Clarke opened the flap and picked up the receiver.

"Who is that with you, Detective?" A pleasant voice with an English accent.

"Daniel MacLean. A civilian."

"Just a moment, gentlemen."

A slight humming noise and the elevator ascended briefly and then glided to a halt. The floor readout did not change. The door opened silently and they stepped out into a large room with a long table at the far end with several large TV screens mounted behind it. All of them were dark save for one rolling the numbers for the Nikkei. At the head of the table was a slight man with streaked grey-blond hair and glasses, seated in a wheelchair. Standing behind him with folded arms was a very large man with prominent cauliflower ears and mild blue eyes surrounded by old scar tissue. His head was close shaven and he was dressed in a navy-blue pinstripe suit and vest and regimental tie. The effect on that big body was somewhat incongruous, but Clarke would have bet money that nobody ever laughed. The man was as big as a small forklift.

And that would be your Slab, Danny thought.

"This is my associate Thomas Rodgers, and I'm Ronald Ivery. But you already know that of course. Please be seated. Can I get you gentlemen anything to drink? Tea, coffee, water? Perhaps something stronger?"

"We're fine, thanks," Clarke said.

"As you wish. How can I be of assistance?"

His voice was muted and they had to strain to hear. It was hard to determine his actual size seated in the chair, but he seemed frail and unhealthy. His face was pale and his gestures were hesitant. The eyes behind the glasses were lively, though, and, Clarke thought, perhaps slightly amused. He studied the two of them for a moment before replying. There was something unusual about the duo apart from the glaring contrast in size and strength, and then he realized it was their nearness to each other. Rodgers was standing so close behind Ivery that he was almost touching his employer. Over the years Clarke had spent a lot of time in interview rooms studying body language and this seemed odd to him. Most people would have been uncomfortable with the proximity.

"Your name came up in connection with an old drug case," Clarke said. "Louie Tardif. I wondered if you could tell us anything about him."

"I don't recall that name offhand. How long ago would this have been?"

"Five years, give or take. You had a transaction with him at that time. Perhaps more than one."

"Five years ago I was still a recovering addict. More addict than recovering for most of that period, to be honest. After my accident there was a lot of pain for a long time. Still is for that matter. I got hooked on painkillers, prescription opioids for the most part. I was in and out of a few rehab programs, and I bought a lot of drugs, not always legally." He shrugged. "That part of my life is behind me now, I've been clean for going on three years. It's pretty much public record if you can call those gossipy rags masquerading as news magazines public records. I was a bit of a tabloid sensation for a while. Tragic young millionaire, money can't buy happiness, and all that. If you've done your research, I'm sure you've seen the stories. I was a bit of a mess there for a time."

He spoke calmly, without rancor or emotion.

Danny studied Rodgers. The more he looked at the man the bigger he seemed. Danny had been in a few fights over the years, sometimes against men considerably bigger than him, and had won more than his fair share of them, but he found it hard to imagine going up against the Slab resulting in a good outcome. The man was so outsized there was nothing to grab onto. From the polished head atop the square body down to the thick wrists protruding from the tailored cuffs, it was hard to see how you could get a hold on him. Not hard to understand about the cauliflower ears, they were about the only grips there were. Rodgers, aware of Danny's thoughtful study, gave him a slow wink and Danny looked away.

"Do you remember anyone called Louie Tardif from around that time, Thomas?"

"No sir, I can't say that I do."

The accent was upper class, surprising coming out of that beat-up face, but the toffee-nosed schtick was his thing back in the day, and apparently he'd kept it upon retirement. Or maybe it was how he always spoke. Clarke realized he didn't really know anything about the man apart from his lurid wrestling PR, which would be mostly invention, and reminded himself to check out Rodgers's background when he returned to the office.

"So is there anything else I can help you with, Detective?" Ivery said.

"I understand you're a contributor to the PC party."

"Yes. And how is that relevant to your inquiries?"

"Have you ever chartered your boat out to them?"

Ivery regarded Clarke for a moment. "I think you already know the answer to that question, Detective."

Clarke waited.

"The answer is yes. I'm a registered donor to the party, and I've leased the *Blue Harp* out to them at different times over the past two summers for a nominal fee, for which I receive a tax deduction for making a political donation. I don't use the boat much these days and it makes sense for me. Everything is above board and a matter of public record. If you have any specific questions about the lease, you can contact my attorney. He will have all the details."

Clarke smiled. "And your attorney. Would that be Richard Sullivan by any chance?"

Ivery nodded.

"I'm sorry to have to tell you that he's gone missing. As has John Newcombe, another person with connections to the party. Might you know him as well, by any chance?" Clarke watched him for a tell, but Ivery revealed nothing.

"I think we're done here. Thomas will see you out."

The big man moved out from behind the wheelchair and ushered them to the elevator.

❀

Ivery was annoyed but not particularly surprised. He'd always thought that his minor incursion into crime when he was heavily addicted to the opioids might come back to bite him in the butt. He'd become involved in the wholesale purchases of illegal drugs on a silly and arrogant whim. It went against the grain to be ripped off by such eminently stupid people back in the day when his habit was costing him thousands of dollars a month and he'd decided to move a step up the chain closer to wholesale. Since the day the stoned driver had run a red light and wiped out his family and turned Ivery into a lifelong wheelchair jockey, fine moral distinctions didn't much concern him. Even then, everything would have been fine if his dealer hadn't tried to add blackmail to his cupidities.

Not satisfied with the excessive profits from the opioids, his dealer, a man Ronald knew as Jean-Paul Delveaux — not his real name it turned out — had threatened to reveal Ivery's addiction in a tell-all interview with a local TV station. He and an accomplice had secretly filmed Thomas purchasing the illegal drugs complete with a shot of Ronald seated in the car in the background and obviously complicit in the transaction. They said they'd showed a TV reporter the video, and he'd agreed to run the story with Delveaux's face blocked out.

Unless Ivery paid two hundred grand within the next seventy-two hours, the story would be broadcast on the weekend news. If Ivery handed over the money, the reporter would be paid off, and the video would disappear.

They showed Ivery the tape and he agreed to the terms and set up a meeting with Jean-Paul and his accomplice, Armand. He would bring the payment in cash and wanted the reporter present and all copies of the video in his hands before he would turn over a single dollar. When they met the following day, it was only Delveaux and Armand present.

"I was exaggerating a little about the reporter," Delveaux said, "but I did talk to him and he said he was definitely interested in the video if it was what I said it was. He would have to run it by his legal department first."

"What's the reporter's name?"

Delveaux told him.

Ronald knew of the reporter and the whole enterprise sounded just about his speed. "Okay, good then."

He nodded to Thomas who grabbed Delveaux and broke his arm, and then turned his attention towards Armand.

"Wait, wait. I'll get you the video. There's only the one copy. Please. It wasn't my idea."

"What do you think, Thomas?"

"Maybe just his little finger."

Armand gave them the video, Ivery's lawyers contacted the reporter's editor and delivered the appropriate legal threats, and it had all gone away. He didn't think there were any other copies of the video out there. Armand would have told Thomas if there were.

The big detective still worried him, but that was in reference to something altogether different from his past history with drugs. It was one thing to play around in politics, make some donations and get a few early heads-up on profitable business opportunities; it was something that happened all the time in the real estate game. There might still be idealists in politics, but damn few of them were over the age of thirty, and grey areas were the norm. But he had become involved with Albright and his accountant and lawyer in a land development deal that in retrospect had been reckless. Perhaps even illegal if the rumours he'd heard after the fact, about Albright's men applying pressure to the sellers, were true. There was a thin line between persuasion and coercion, and it sounded as if it might have been crossed.

That was concerning enough on its own, but when Thomas told him what Sullivan suspected about the park bench assaults, Ivery was stunned. Before he could meet with the lawyer to discuss the situation, Sullivan had disappeared. Thomas had made inquiries through his contacts but had run into a brick wall. The man was gone. From their previous dealings, Ivery had a clear picture of the man's tight financial situation and knew he wouldn't just take off when a big payday was on the horizon. Something had happened to him, and it was not difficult to figure out who was the other person involved.

Ivery wasn't sure what to do now. If he had suspected Albright was this out of control, he would never have gone into business with him in the first place. It wasn't as if he needed the money. But how could he have known? Questionable real estate deals involving inside information were one thing, they happened all the time. Brutally assaulting women and leaving them half dead on park benches was something else entirely.

If what the lawyer suspected about Albright was true, sooner or later there would be a criminal investigation of him that was almost certain to branch out and encompass all his financial dealings, and that would end up involving Ivery as well. Pleading ignorance about Albright's methods in the subdivision acquisition was not going to cut it. He was going to have to do something — that was clear. The problem was what.

CHAPTER 38

Cat threw the cell phone at the back of the couch. She wasn't quite mad enough yet to fire it at the wall, but it could happen soon. She had been dialling Jared off and on for six hours now without any response. She'd tried to leave a message but his inbox was full. She knew he would take Joseph's death hard and that his first reaction would be to go off and isolate himself. He was not good at giving or receiving comfort. She thought he might head to *Arrow*, his last refuge, the place he would go to grieve or punish himself, or — God forbid, but way more likely — plan something really bloody stupid.

She'd headed down to the marina from the hospital immediately when she learned that Annie was resting comfortably and out of any immediate danger, but she'd arrived there too late. The manager told her about Clarke's visit earlier on, so she knew that he'd been unsuccessful as well. She considered touching base with Clarke, then decided against it. He would only tell her what he wanted her to hear, and to stay out of it and let him handle everything, and she was never going to do any of that.

She tried to think of what she could do to find Jared before he did something sensationally reckless. Jaimie and Erin would have put the word out to the commercial fleet, so there would be a lot of fishing boats out on the water keeping a watch for the sailboat. Clarke would have all of officialdom on the lookout, marine patrols, forestry boats, police in port towns, the B.C. ferries, hell, maybe even the Navy patrols. Even sending a chopper up was a possibility depending on how mad Clarke was. Nothing she could do to help out there. She could only hope they located Jared soon. She had no clue as to where he was heading or what he had in mind. What she did know was that with Joseph's death he was capable of anything. She had seen him go off the rails before, and he had loved the old man.

No, what she had to do was use her brains and her connections. She was well known in the big city, and had made a lot of friends in the media, many of whom owed her for various intros and tips she had given them over the years she'd been doing celebrity shoots. She'd tell them what she knew or suspected about the suspicious fire and get them to use their contacts to keep her informed.

She drew up a list of possibilities and made some calls. The last one was to a well-connected court reporter she'd once dated, and they chatted for a while about old times. When Cat brought up the East End fire, he told her there were no official statements from the police yet, it was still too early. It was not an unusual story for the big city, a fire in a working-class neighbourhood resulting from a propane explosion. With one fatality and one person severely injured it did move up the newsworthy scale a little. Maybe even a short clip on the evening news, if they could find a family member able to produce leakage on demand. Cat told him that there were suspicious circumstances, remnants of what appeared to be Molotov cocktails had been found, and arson was a distinct possibility. He thanked Cat for the tip and promised to work it with his sources and let her know if he heard anything new.

What else could she do? She was fiercely angry about Joseph's death and would do everything in her power to ensure his murder received top priority. She knew all about pressures on police resources, an under-staffed and overworked detective division, and the political priorities of limited budgets in the real world. Investigating the possible murder of a First Nations centenarian in the East End wouldn't be right up there at the top of the department's to do list. She knew Clarke was all in on it, but there was no guarantee he would be given the resources required to do a full-blown investigation.

Cat thought about it for a while and came up with the perfect solution for applying pressure to the police department. He might be a little ticked off with her, given the circumstances of their last meeting, but she was sure she could jolly him along. He was a man, wasn't he? With a faint smile, Cat picked up her cell phone and dialled the private number he'd given her. It rang on and she was about to give up when James Albright finally picked up.

❁

"Your Thomas Rodgers is an interesting fellow," Merlynn said. "An Oxford graduate, no less. Received his degree in fine arts, and was active in their theatre group. He played Cyrano de Bergerac in a well-reviewed production in his graduation year, if you can believe it." Merlynn had her tablet out and was busily clicking away.

"That must have been before his nose got spread all over his face," Danny said.

Merlynn continued. "Came from a titled family active in British political circles. They disowned Thomas when he took up professional wrestling for a lark. It turned out he had a flair for the game and after a couple of years working in England he moved to America and created the Slab character. He made some serious money over his career and invested heavily with the Ivery family's merchant bank."

Her finger flicked over the screen. "They became close friends over the years, and he was appointed the boy's godfather. After the acci-dent, he retired from the wrestling circuit and took charge of Ronald's care. It was Rodgers who oversaw all the renovations to the building, put in the therapy pool, set up a first-class gym, and badgered Ivery into partial mobility. I'm told they're very close, more like father and son than employer and employee. It's a private company, but word on the street is that Ivery made Rodgers a partner a few years ago. He's an interesting character, there's been a lot written about him over the years." Merlynn took a sip from her drink and went back to her search.

"Give me some scandal," Clarke said. "And another drink if you don't mind."

It had been three long days since the fire and everyone was on edge. There had been no further sightings of *Arrow* in spite of a widespread search, and the waiting was grinding them all down. The world had moved on, new crimes had occurred, and finding Jared was no longer a number one priority of the police.

They were seated at a table in the Queens Own bar drinking martinis served from a chilled glass pitcher. Even Clarke had been converted. *I'll be wearing a straw boater and gathering around the piano to sing Noël Coward ditties before long*, he thought, but obediently held out his glass as Merlynn poured. Damn, they were some good. Merlynn had given strict instructions to the bartender. She continued with her report.

"One dropped assault charge against Rodgers a few years back, apart from that nothing on the official records. The location of the dispute was a little odd, it occurred at a dive in the East End that is well known to the vice and drug squads. You have to wonder what he was doing there, a man with his background and money. Not the kind of place he would normally frequent. He racked up half a dozen fellows; put two of them in hospital. Nothing ever came of it as nobody was willing to press any charges . . . Hang on, one of the men in the brawl was Louie Tardif."

"So that's the second time his name has come up in connection with Rodgers," Clarke said. "What are the odds of that? Unfortunately we can't question Louie as he's no longer with us."

Merlynn said. "There are six names here. Weren't the other two in the van Albert and Ernest? I remember thinking, *Bert and Ernie, Sesame Street, at the time.* Albert Villeneuve and Ernest Gagnon are listed in the court documents. It's the same guys. So the other three involved in the bar fight are probably connected with them. Right?"

Merlynn was excited. Sometimes she missed the old days of court intrigue.

"Sounds about right to me," Danny said.

"I'll call the office," Clarke said. "Meanwhile, whose round is it?"

"I've got this," Danny said.

He went to the bar and pushed in alongside Bill Lacey who had just entered with a pair of tall raw-boned men. Similar to the types who had taken Lauren from the nightclub, Danny observed. No fedoras in sight, but maybe it was God Save the Queen Night or something and hats weren't allowed. You never knew with yacht clubs, there was often a lot of weird shit happening and much of the time it was British related. You'd think they were the only country with maritime traditions. What the hell. Time to stir the pot. Unloading some of the anger consuming him since the fire was an added benefit.

"'Scuse me, gents," Danny slurred, bumping the two men apart as he bellied up to the bar. "First come, first served, as they say."

"We were here first, asshole." One of the men grabbed Danny's shoulder and pulled him back and away from the bar.

"But I've been here since opening," Danny said as he punched him carefully in the nose. The man fell back against Lacey, who staggered back against the bar and then turned and scuttled for the exit.

The man Danny had hit was white faced with rage and coming back hard when his partner stepped in front of him and grabbed his arm.

"Not now," he said. He turned back to Danny and forced a smile. "I'm sorry, friend, why don't you just go ahead and order your drinks and we'll—"

"You cocksucker," Danny roared, kicking him in the crotch. "Nobody calls me that."

The first man reached around and caught Danny a glancing blow on the side of his jaw, and he fell back against the counter and used the leverage it gave him to springboard forward and head-butt the second man under the chin. As he fell, Danny turned and was caught flush on the button by the other combatant and staggered back on top of the first man who was dazedly trying to rise, blood pouring out of his mouth from where he'd bitten his tongue. Danny rolled to avoid a kick and managed to divert it from his balls to his thigh. He caught the foot as the second kick came in and twisted it viciously and the man roared with the pain and staggered and went down. Danny was up and on him, throwing punches as the first man rose and came back towards him. He turned to face the other one and then there was a loud clanging noise and his world went black.

❁

"I'll say this much for you lot, my life has become much more interesting since we met," Merlynn said as she bent over Danny who was spread out on the lounge on the aft deck of *Legalese*. A bucket of pinkish ice water sat in front of her, and she wrung out a cloth and swabbed Danny's face. A red-faced Clarke was puffing furiously on a cigar and saying nothing. He hadn't uttered a single syllable since they were escorted out of the bar.

Clarke finally came over and stood above them.

"I think I might just have contained it," he said through gritted teeth. "You realize if the lieutenant gets word of this, I'll be suspended. Never mind losing my pension. I'll end up standing outside of some lousy office building wearing a jackshit security badge and making twelve bucks an hour. Probably be the Ivery Tower with my luck. Tell me, what in the hell were you thinking?"

"Those are the guys," Danny said. "You know it."

"No, actually I don't know it. But even if they are 'the guys,'" Clarke made elaborate finger quotations in the air, "what in God's name did you hope to accomplish? Other than to let them know that we're onto them, if it is them, and we don't have one iota of proof that it is them in any case."

Danny said, "I've learned that sometimes in life too much thinking can just complicate matters and often the better plan is just to go at them."

"Just go at them? How old are you, anyway? Fourteen? Just go at them?"

"Keep your voice down, dear, people on the other boats are staring."

Clarke snapped his mouth shut, the veins pulsing on his forehead.

"Just go at them?" he seethed. "Who the hell do you think you are? Horatio Lord Nelson?" Clarke had been reading nautically.

"I know their type," Danny said. "They won't be able to help themselves. They'll come for me now. We'd never have flushed them out otherwise."

"And what about Jared — is he going to 'just go at them' too?"

"Seems like it," Danny said. "At least we'll have distracted those two for a bit."

Clarke stared at him and then went over and sat in a chair as far away from the sofa as he could get.

"Just go at them," he muttered, into his glass half empty. Merlynn drew up another chair and sat next to him and patted his hand. His cell phone rang and he pulled it out and stared at the number. The coroner's office. Great. Just what he needed. A mood lightener. He held the phone to his ear and listened without comment before shutting it off and turning back to the others.

"Still no conclusive ID on Joseph," he said.

Danny nodded but didn't speak. Clarke might as well have been commenting on the weather.

The coroner had told Clarke that they'd have to wait for DNA testing and compare the results with a sample from a family member for positive identification. There was enough left to know the remains were those of a male on the medium-to-small side. Even the teeth had been partially melted by the fierce heat. Clarke was not going to tell the others any part of that. They had enough misery to contend with already without him depositing that grim image into their memory banks.

He did tell them one odd thing the coroner had mentioned. Joseph's forearm was crushed and snapped, perhaps not entirely unexpected in an explosion where objects were moving through the air at high speeds and the entire second story had dropped to the ground floor. What was surprising, the coroner said, was that the injury had impacted equally on both sides of the bone. In effect his forearm would have had to have been trapped between a rigid object and the moving force in order to cause the equal damage on both sides.

"The result was like something incurred by putting your forearm in a vise and tightening it to the breaking point," the coroner had said. Odd, but perhaps not entirely impossible in the high-impact explosion when the propane tank went off. It had been up against the outside wall of Joseph's bedroom and sent objects flying about at warp speeds. The coroner had seen stranger things. Or, a second long-shot possibility to consider, he'd been tortured, and the fire destroyed all other signs of external damage to the body. They would probably never know for sure.

"Why in God's name would anyone torture that poor old man?" Merlynn exploded. "For kicks? He didn't even speak English, for Christ's sake. And they brought along a vise? Who the hell does that?"

Clarke shook his head but didn't respond. He'd thought he had seen everything. Danny remained silent, but the martini glass suddenly broke apart in his hand.

He didn't seem to notice.

CHAPTER 39

Jared walked back along the docks towards *Arrow,* cursing under his breath. He'd showered on the run in and put on a sweatshirt and clean shorts and sandals. His eyes were bloodshot and he was gaunt and unshaven, but no longer head-turning scary. His polite inquiries at the marina office were met with polite responses by the woman behind the desk. She was so sorry, but she had no information as to Albright's present whereabouts. Jared had the distinct impression that even had she known something she wouldn't have told him. Albright was something of a celebrity, and he realized the marina staff would consider it part of their job to protect his privacy. He'd wasted the best part of the morning searching for a lead on the *Blue Harp*'s whereabouts and come up with nothing. Absolute zero. The gas attendant remembered the boat but hadn't spoken with any of the crew. She'd left from the gas docks the previous day with topped-up tanks of fuel and water, but nobody knew where the *Blue Harp* was heading.

Jared thought the most likely destination was Desolation Sound, a roughly thousand-square-mile body of water that teemed with boats in the summer months but was still big enough to offer isolation if you stayed clear of the popular anchorages. At this late date there wouldn't be all that many boats still out cruising and a hundred vacant hidey holes would be available. With the bad weather forecast, the *Harp* could be tucked up inside any one of them. It would take days if not weeks to check them all out, and there'd still be a good chance he'd miss her.

The other possibility was that the boat had headed north from Campbell River, past Ripple Rock and up the inside channel. If that was the case, then there was zero chance of locating her. The options in that direction were endless, and the narrow channels meant that *Arrow* would have to motor most of the way and be bucking strong tides a lot of the time. So he'd take his chances on Desolation Sound. At least there would be a chance for some sailing without the endless tooth-grinding motoring that he'd endured since leaving Vancouver.

Jared needed activity, something to keep him involved and awake. Apart from four restless hours of sleep during a brief anchorage in behind Lasqueti Island, he hadn't closed his eyes for more than minutes at a time in the days since the fire. He dreaded the red-rimmed dreams that came in the night and filled *Arrow*'s cabin with smoke and sadness. He couldn't bear Joseph's death; it was why he'd had to leave and why he was carrying out this desolate search. He had to be doing something, apart and away from the numbing collective grief of the family. He didn't know what would happen if he actually managed to find the *Blue Harp*. He supposed it would play out the way it was meant to, and recognized that fatalistic bent he shared with Joseph and the sadness rose up and enveloped him.

He arrived back at *Arrow* and stepped aboard, glancing up at the wind gauge at the top of the mast. The cups were spinning noticeably faster than when he'd arrived, and he flipped the switch on the wind speed display. Seven knots from the northwest. Just about enough. Once he turned the corner past the marina office and moved out into the main channel there would be more. After motoring for nearly eighteen hours, and changing the engine oil earlier that morning — a miserable, blasphemous, knuckle-skinning job in the tight quarters — he was due some quiet time. He raised the main and hardened it off midway on the traveller before jumping back down to the dock and casting off the lines. He kicked *Arrow*'s bow out and climbed back aboard and unfurled the jib and cleated off the sheets. *Arrow* moved sluggishly out into the channel, barely maintaining steerage way in the sheltered marina. He paid out the main and she picked up another knot and now she left a visible wake as she moved past the trollers and seiners tied up to the wharves. A few fishermen working on their nets glanced up at him as he ghosted past and he read the unspoken judgment on their faces as they returned to their labours. Dilettante.

He took *Arrow* slowly up the channel, past the cleaning station where a cloud of screaming gulls fought over offal, and turned her south in a long lazy sweep and loosed the mainsheet and let the sail run forward till it touched the shrouds and then brought it back just clear and cleated it off. He let the jib run right out, and it fluttered and filled, fluttered and filled, and he debated setting it out with the pole, but decided not to and turned *Arrow* a few degrees off the wind until the sail filled. Once he passed Quadra Island, there would be a comfortable run to Cortes with little traffic, and it was easier and more comfortable to make a couple of long jibes rather than run straight downwind.

He took a last look around, clicked on the autopilot, stretched out on the cockpit seat, closed his eyes, and set his internal alarm for thirty minutes. It was a leftover from his time offshore when half an hour was roughly the length of time you had if a container ship or tanker happened to rise up over the horizon on a collision course. He had no illusions about watch-keeping on commercial boats at sea, *Arrow* having had her fair share of close calls over the years. Even a U.S. Navy destroyer with every conceivable navigational bell and whistle and a full complement on watch had managed to run into a freighter on a clear summer night a few years past.

He knew he should check his cell phone but decided to put it off for a while longer. None of the messages would be friendly, and some would be outright savage. He couldn't handle any more bad news right now. He turned on the VHF and set it to scan on the off chance. The *Blue Harp* was a well-known boat and would attract some attention out on the water. Bored boaters gossiped over the airwaves, he might hear something. Stranger things had happened. Jared stretched out on the cockpit seat and in five minutes was fast asleep to a dull background noise of interrupted conversations and idle chatter as the VHF flipped through the channels.

He didn't hear the float plane's call to the *Blue Harp* giving the ETA for a passenger drop-off.

CHAPTER 40

Bill Lacey sat at *Rainbow*'s wheel, the big diesel engine thumping comfortably along at a steady eight knots as the lights of Vancouver gradually faded behind him. The winds were light, the seas calm, and the traffic almost non-existent at this late hour. The sixteen-mile radar was on and showed a tug and barge out near mid-channel. Apart from the freighters anchored up behind him whose blips were now touching the twelve-mile outer ring on his radar screen, that was it. He had the VHF on sixteen and scanning, but it remained silent. He'd listened to the weather channels for the first few minutes, and nothing was expected in the way of extreme weather. The low was coming in with some easterly and possibly some heavy rain squalls later on at the back of it. Then a big high was forecast to come in with clear skies for the foreseeable future. It seemed like nowadays it rained and rained up until mid-spring and then a switch was flipped and it was all sunny and dry for the next few months. Maybe climate change was responsible, he didn't know and cared less. Let the ice melt and the waters rise, not his problem. He was living on a boat.

Lacey didn't really have a specific destination in mind, he was just heading north, leaving behind the city and all his problems there. He felt more relaxed with every mile. Out here away from the pressure cooker that was his life in Vancouver lately, he had time to think and put things into perspective. He realized he had made a serious mistake in his dealings with Albright and Sullivan. He should have kept them separate, strung them all along and let things play out for a while, until he could come up with a foolproof long-term plan. But in an effort to be seen as a team player, he'd casually mentioned Sullivan's nervous, probing phone call to Clint, and the next thing he knew the lawyer was gone. For good, if he had to make a guess. Things were getting desperate and you didn't need to be a genius to know that the next link in the evidential chain that Albright would consider eliminating was his accountant.

He knew now that he would never get his money out of the complex deal that was going to be his last, the one that would have made him rich and let him escape from the web that seemed to be tightening every day now. Things were moving too quickly, spinning out of control. Sullivan had disappeared five days ago, his phone went straight to message, and his office said they had no idea of his whereabouts and had formally reported him as missing to the police. He'd seen a piece on the evening news, and the disappearance was being treated as suspicious. If nothing else they would want to interview him sooner or later, given his close connections with the lawyer. He knew that some of his business deals with Albright and Sullivan would not survive close scrutiny.

After the episode at the bar where the big Indian had gotten into the fight with Clint and Travis, he'd panicked. Headed straight back to *Rainbow*, fired up the engine, cast off the lines, and headed out. He needed space and time to think. He'd suspected for the past two months that this day might come and had made some preparations, prime among them readying *Rainbow* for an ocean passage. She was a seventy-foot ex-Seattle tugboat that he'd bought for a song from an ill-fated kayak expedition company that had just barely been covering expenses when the diesel engine failed and they promptly went bankrupt. He'd changed her name and spent over sixty grand on a refit that included a complete engine rebuild and a month in the yard for replacing half a dozen planks, sandblasting, and new paint.

Lacey felt she was in as trim and seaworthy condition as she'd ever been, and while her frame and bollard rating might not have been quite up to some of the offshore tows she'd undertaken in the past, she was perfectly suited as an offshore cruiser. He had no qualms about taking her on the long run south. With five thousand gallons of fuel in her tanks and a twenty GPH water maker plus a thousand gallons in tankage, she could easily make it all the way down to southern Mexico without having to call in anywhere along the way. He'd wait it out there for a while and see how things progressed back home. If there was a scandal and his name came up, he'd head down to one of the countries in South America with no extradition treaty with Canada. He reminded himself to do some research and find out which were the most suitable for immigrants with questionable pasts.

The previous owners had spent most of their initial budget for the tug on setting up luxurious accommodations, and *Rainbow* was equipped with six big cabins with double beds and separate bathrooms plus a large common room with a commercial espresso machine and a double fridge installed for cold drinks. Hell, he could even run charters down south if he needed. But he didn't think he'd have to. Lacey had been burying money offshore for years, and had more than enough to live in high comfort, if not quite obscene luxury, for the remainder of his life. He was leaving the possibility of luxury behind in the abandoned subdivision deal. On board *Rainbow* he had two passports, one in his own name and the other an excellent forgery in a different name that had cost him fifteen hundred bucks. Behind the false panel in the wheelhouse were ten K in American dollars and five K in Krugerrand.

The more he considered not returning to Vancouver, the more convinced Queer Bill became that it was the smart thing to do, and the more excited he became. Everything of value that he owned was on board *Rainbow*, with the exception of a beater Nissan truck sitting in the Queens Own parking lot. They were more than welcome to that rusty, salt-eroded piece of shit.

He'd foreseen the possibility of a forced departure and taken an eager and ethically challenged junior partner into the firm three years earlier. He had encouraged his associate to assume greater responsibilities and gradually reduced his own role in the business. He wasn't able to completely remove himself from all of the dubious deals he'd been involved in over the years, but he was confident he'd muddied the waters sufficiently to require a committed forensic audit to flush him out. He went back into the galley and poured himself another cup of coffee, added a shot of brandy to it, and took a bracing swig.

He returned to the wheelhouse and sat back in the big leather swivel chair listening to the soft intermittent beep of the autopilot as it made its course corrections, and tried to think of a compelling reason to go back to his berth at the yacht club. He couldn't come up with a single one. He didn't really trust anyone he was involved with at the present time, with the possible exception of his junior partner whom he considered too stupid to be duplicitous. The last time he'd interacted with the brothers — a euphemism, his asshole was still raw — there had been a whole new level of disdain in their attitude and aspect, a smirking secret knowledge that disturbed him. He finished his laced coffee and made his decision. Fuck it. He would head down to Juan de Fuca Strait and go in to Sooke and fuel up. The port tank was over halfway down, and he detected the beginning of a slight list. From there it was just a short run to Cape Flattery and the open Pacific and then, weather permitting, a long gradual turn to port and he'd be off on his long trip south.

He punched in the course change and *Rainbow* swung around and settled onto her new track. Now that he'd made the decision, Lacey was excited about the future and a sense of relief swept over him. He realized he'd been under a heavy strain with the whole business and it was high time for a new life, new scenery, and new young men. He'd heard that in South America they were cheap and plentiful. Maybe he wouldn't even stay in Mexico, just make a brief landfall and then harbour hop down to South America. Better safe than sorry.

He sat there dreaming about young men and boys and sleepy brown eyes. A broadside swell from a distant tug curled under *Rainbow,* and she rolled sluggishly and came back slow and Lacey registered the starboard list again and reached down to the instrument panel and flicked the switch that changed the fuel tanks over.

The explosion was seen twenty miles distant.

CHAPTER 41

"I heard it this morning on the fishing net. Happened late last night around midnight. The tug that called it in reported passing *Rainbow* in the general area of the explosion a few minutes earlier." Jaimie shrugged. "Coast Guard has been calling her all morning, and she's not answering. They have a boat on the scene but unofficial word is there's not much left. No positive identification as yet, but it doesn't look good for her."

The three brothers were sitting bedside in Annie's hospital room talking in hushed voices. Jaimie and Erin had flown in from the West Coast fishing grounds to join Danny in his vigil at the hospital as soon as they heard the news about their mother and grandfather. Annie lay silent in her bed, connected to a hospital monitor and showing little sign of life apart from the slow rising and falling of her chest. Bandages wrapped her head where she had been struck by flying debris, and disfiguring burns on her neck and face were covered with unguent. Other injuries were out of sight beneath the blanket, which was raised in a tent-like structure over her to avoid contact with her body. Danny had spoken to the doctors, and they were cautiously optimistic about a full recovery. There would be some scars, but no long-term disabilities, they said.

"Any news about Jared?" Erin asked. Nobody had mentioned Joseph yet. It was as if talking about his death would make it real.

"No. *Arrow* was spotted heading north. Clarke says there was a report of Jared making inquiries about the *Blue Harp* in Campbell River. They figure he's gone across into Desolation Sound on the chance that Albright is cruising up there somewhere. Chances are slim that he finds her in that maze."

Erin said, "And if he does?"

"Good question. Clarke is hoping they can pick him up before that happens. As for the fire investigation, he says it's unlikely they'll find out much from what's left at the site, although they're not done with it yet. He thinks it will take another week before the different departments finish up."

"What about before the fire?" Erin asked.

Danny shook his head. "They've canvassed the neighbourhood, and no one saw anything suspicious around the time of the fire. Clarke thinks that the arsonists must have come in on foot. They pulled the video from the 7-Eleven down the road and there was only local traffic. They ran all the plates and checked. An old lady three doors down from Annie's says she heard a dog barking just before the explosion, but she's not sure where it was coming from. Let's face it, they don't have a damn thing." The three men sat there in silence.

Jaimie, the eldest, finally spoke. "I'll arrange for contractors to come in and clean up the site as soon as it's available to us. Scrape it right down to fresh soil and truck everything away for disposal. No need for Annie to confront any of that again. Then we'll see what she wants to do with the lot. I won't be surprised if she decides to sell it. She'll get a good price. It would be tough on her to build new and move back there given everything that's happened."

They all nodded in agreement. No one spoke.

The unasked question hung heavy in the air. Erin finally said it. "Do they have a positive ID yet?"

Danny shook his head. "No. They're not sure how long it will take given the condition of the body. They had to send samples away to an outside lab back east that specializes in burn-victim DNA. It will take awhile."

"We need the body back. The Elders are getting impatient. They want to put his spirit to rest. His being a Shaman makes it more urgent."

"I'll talk to Clarke again," Danny said. "I doubt it's his call but maybe he can try and speed the process up."

They sat in silence, trying not to think about it all. Although they were used to death in their community, and it was often early and tragic, they were having a difficult time accepting Joseph's passing. He was the rock of the family, somebody who was always there for them and who had always been there for them as long as they could remember, and perhaps the one person among them whose death was least expected. Danny realized that the thought of Joseph dying had never occurred to him even though he was close to a century old. It was not that he thought Joseph would live forever, just that he had never actually considered the possibility of his death. It still wasn't real to him. He realized he was in denial.

"Well, we're not going to bury him without Annie being there with us, so it's academic in any case," Jaimie said. "She would never forgive us. The Elders will have to bloody well wait, just like the rest of us."

At the mention of her name, Annie stirred. Her eyes fluttered open and she recognized her boys.

"Water," she whispered. The doctors had said the heat and smoke inhalation had damaged her throat and lungs and she would have difficulty speaking for the first while. The three brothers moved to her bedside, and Erin poured a glass from the pitcher and held it to her lips. She gestured and they cranked the bed up and she tilted her head and drank.

She fell back against the pillows and motioned them closer and the three men bent forward and strained to hear.

"Joseph," she murmured. "He sent me a message last night. He said he's not dead."

※

"Well, that's good to know," Clarke said. "What with his mortal remains lying in the morgue and all, I have to admit I was beginning to get a little worried. I don't suppose the fucking raven supplied any details?" He picked up his glass of draught from the table and pounded it down. He'd heard enough about goddamned ravens over the years, starting with the five hundred dollars he'd lost to Joseph playing cards when they'd first met. Jaimie had finally taken pity on him and told him that Joseph cheated. "His Clan is Raven, the trickster," he'd said, as if that somehow made it all right. It still pissed Clarke off every time he thought about it.

"There's no need to get snarky," Merlynn said as she took a cautious first sip of the white house wine they served up in the Lamplight. She winced and picked up a glass of beer and chased it. "I'll be glad when they let us back into the yacht club," she said.

They were waiting for Jaimie and Erin, who had gone down to the marina to meet the nephews who were bringing their trollers in from the fishing grounds. The plan was for Danny to take one of them up into Desolation Sound to try and find Jared. In the meantime, Erin and Jaimie would maintain a twenty-four-hour watch over Annie in the hospital until the situation resolved itself one way or another. The police had posted a guard at the door, but the family was scheduling their own surveillance. The last watch at a hospital, the one involving Bert and Ernie, was still fresh in everyone's mind.

Jaimie and Erin came through the door and joined them and the discussion turned to Danny's projected run north up Georgia Strait the following day and the sectioning of Desolation Sound into manage-able search areas. Then they talked about the Redonda Islands, which were located further north, and the lonely fjords stretching off beyond them. The whole thing sounded hopeless to Clarke and Merlynn and after a few minutes they made their excuses and left. Danny set up a radio sked with his brothers, then went down to the docks and made ready to leave at first light. He phoned Cat on the off chance she had heard from Jared, but her cell phone was shut off. He wasn't concerned until he phoned her office later in the day and the receptionist told him that she hadn't turned up for work or phoned in.

"That's unheard of for her," the woman said. "She always lets us know ahead of time, unlike some of the others."

CHAPTER 42

Ronald Ivery sat in his ten-thousand-dollar wheelchair and watched his TV sets. He had his laptop in front of him and made occasional trades as the New York and Toronto stock exchange numbers flowed across the big screens. He had people employed full-time under his direction in his company office two floors down doing the same thing on a much larger scale, but this was his recreation. Hell, face it, he thought, this was his life. That was not to say he didn't have personal relationships. He loved Thomas like a father, and he had a few friends whom he met up with downtown once in a while, but he didn't have a romantic relationship to speak of. There were the occasional high-end escorts, and he treated them well, but he supposed that didn't really count. He was fond of some of them, Greta in particular, and he thought she liked him, even apart from the money and the occasional stock tip he gave her, but when it came right down to it he didn't even trust her enough to give her his actual name.

"Just call me John," he'd told her the first time they'd met, clearly establishing the boundaries for their relationship. Given that it had been going on now for almost a year, he suspected that she knew who he was, but he wasn't worried. They were friends now, and he was comfortable with the situation. He didn't harbour any Julia Roberts *Pretty Woman* illusions.

There'd been a woman he'd met by chance a year back whom he'd gone out with a few times, and who had meant something to him, and he thought she might have felt the same way about him. But something must have happened, he didn't know what, and she had stopped returning his calls. Thomas had made some discreet inquiries and learned nothing apart from an unconfirmed rumour that she'd been assaulted and robbed. Her roommate said she'd given short notice and left immediately, forfeiting her deposit. Ratchett, the detective on Ivery's payroll, said the department had received no incident complaints involving her, and that was an end to it. He just accepted that some things weren't meant to be. Ronald had a lot of practice at that kind of thing in his life.

He still thought about her occasionally: Rita Allen, a musician and member of the Vancouver Symphony Orchestra where she played the harp. Ronald supposed there was a subtle irony in that given his past derelictions, but the affair terminated, and he moved on from philosophical dissection. He was a donor to the symphony, and had gone to several concerts since they'd broken up, but she hadn't been performing at any of them. When he asked around, the director said she was away on a six-month leave of absence, and he had let it go.

The TV tuned to the local channel flashed *Breaking News* across the screen and a chyron rolled across the bottom. Something about a missing boat called *Rainbow*. The name seemed vaguely familiar to Ivery, and a minute later the accountant's face popped up on the screen under the headline "Missing at Sea."

"I'll be damned. Bill Lacey. What are the odds?" Thomas said as he came in from the kitchen and turned up the volume. The story spilled out in the overheated tones of a small-town broadcaster getting her big break. They listened in silence.

"So he was heading south at the time?" Thomas mused.

"Yes. Well past Vancouver on a course towards the Juan de Fuca Strait."

"Seems damned odd at that time of night."

They sat and thought about it.

Ronald said, "Remember John Newcombe? The organizer who did some work for the party during the last campaign?"

Thomas shrugged. "Not really."

"Not surprising. He was a quiet, low-profile guy who kept in the background. Ratchett tells me he's disappeared and they're treating it as suspicious. And the lawyer Richard Sullivan has been missing for going on a week now. Also being treated as suspicious. And now there's Bill Lacey. What these three men have in common is that they all worked for Albright and now they're all missing or dead. That explosion was not an accident."

"Albright doesn't strike me as a careful long-term-plan kind of guy," Thomas said. "He seems more the full-on in-your-face type. Acts as if he knows something you don't and is looking to take advantage of it. I knew people like that in the ring. Guys who might have had a chance for a win if they'd laid back, played it safe, and waited for an opening. But they never did."

"So what are you saying?" Ivery asked.

"The first two, Newcombe and Sullivan, maybe. They just disappeared, could have been taken right off the street far as we know. But Bill Lacey? This one seems different. Blowing the boat up when it's out in the middle of the Strait with nobody around for miles seems too well planned for Albright. I see him as more of a 'go with your first impulse' kind of guy."

"I take your point," Ivery said. "But what about those two security people who are always around him? I'm sure they are capable of something like that. They always struck me as a cold-blooded pair. Lizard eyes always watching you. Why in God's name did I ever charter my boat out to Albright? I must have been crazy. As if there weren't already enough connections between us."

"You haven't done anything wrong," Thomas said.

"Well, maybe not lately," Ivery said. "But the past has a nasty habit of coming back around and biting you in the ass sometimes. The visit from Detective Clarke is only the beginning. I don't think we can just sit here and wait for something bad to happen. Set up a meeting with Albright. I need to talk with him, see if I can get a handle on things. Just the two of us. Tell him to leave his cowboys at home."

They ate their poached salmon and salad and watched the news but there were no new updates, and after dinner Thomas went into his office to make his phone calls. Ivery went back to his play trades, but his mind wasn't into it. He closed the computer and wheeled himself into the hidden elevator and ascended to the loft. He thought about taking a pill but decided against it. The pain wasn't too bad today. He'd save it for later or maybe even pass on it altogether if things didn't get any worse. Every one skipped was a personal victory. He removed his clothes and lowered the harness down from the gantry and strapped himself in. He rose up and swung out over the pool and lowered himself down. A flick of the switch and the jets started up and music washed over him. He closed his eyes and let his mind escape his damaged body and float free.

CHAPTER 43

Cat was having some serious second thoughts. What had seemed like a great idea when she was back in the flat sipping her second glass of Chablis and contemplating her powers over men seemed much less so when she was strapped into a mini plane with her elbows practically touching both sides of the fuselage with a spotted juvenile delinquent yelling and chortling in the pilot's seat just forward of her. He looked about eighteen and seemed determined to scare the living bejesus out of her. So far he'd been doing a good job. He alternated between turning around and yelling descriptions unintelligible over the roar of the engine — *Keep your eyes on the fucking road*, she wanted to scream back — diving down and banking sharply so she'd have a better view of whatever he wanted to impress her with at the moment (although her eyes were closed tight shut), and intervals of roaring along so close above the water she reckoned she could crank down the window, reach out, and feel the spray if she so wished. She did not so wish. What she dearly wished was that she had never started on this mad journey in the first place. Not that she'd really had much of a choice, she realized in retrospect.

Less than an hour after she'd spoken on the phone with Albright, there was a knock at her door and two men were standing there. Tall, rangy men with jagged toothed smiles, they seemed vaguely familiar.

"Hi, Cat," they chorused in perfect accord. "Good to see you." They extended their hands and she shook them politely in turn. They seemed to think she knew who they were. She hadn't a clue.

"Clint. And this is my brother, Travis," the squinty-eyed one said. "We ran you across to Nanaimo in the Ribby a couple of weeks ago."

"Of course," Cat said. "I wasn't expecting anyone so soon."

"Well, you know Mr. Albright," he said. (She realized now, sitting in the airplane, a bit too late, that she didn't, not really.) "Once he makes up his mind about something he wants to get it done ASAP. He thought your pictures about the East End arson were outstanding."

Cat had got the call from Danny, happened to have her camera with her from an assignment, and, almost by reflex, shot some pictures at the scene of the fire. In a half daze afterwards, she'd let Reese talk her into shopping them to a news organization, something she'd regretted almost immediately.

The brothers told her that Mr. Albright was flying to Ottawa to attend a conference early the following day, but could squeeze her in later that evening. It would be her only chance to meet with him over the next couple of weeks. They knew it was an inconvenience, but if she was serious about enlisting his help regarding the police inquiry, she would have to leave within the next hour. Before she'd really even thought about it, Cat was overnight packed and being herded onto the little floatplane that was booked and waiting in the inner harbour.

She started to make a phone call to tell Danny where she was headed, and then the pilot fired up the engine and the deafening noise ruled out any conversation. She would have texted, but the pilot went immediately into takeoff across the chop of the inlet, and with the shuddering and vibrations of the little plane she couldn't bring herself to release her two-handed death grip from the steel handrail bolted to the back of the pilot's seat. She would have to wait until she boarded the *Blue Harp*. She was torn from her meditations a few minutes later by a shout and a gesturing hand from the crazed teenager at the controls who dropped the port wing ninety degrees and went into a racketing, nausea-inducing dive, shaving past a sailboat. Cat closed her eyes to block out her approaching death and clung to the handrail and alternately prayed for deliverance and cursed the pilot, Albright, and Jared in random order.

❀

Jared started up from his recurring nightmare of sirens and red flames into the dislocation that now accompanied his every awakening. This time the visions were more real, and as the sirens raged over him he looked up and saw a yellow floatplane, its port wing surely no more than ten feet above the water, barreling past. In that wide-eyed split second, he saw sunglasses, the flash of teeth, and a cheery wave; he blinked and envisioned Cat, eyes shut and white-faced in the seat behind the pilot, and he blinked again and scrubbed his eyes and she vanished as the plane tilted up and away from him and screamed off into the distance. Jared stared after it and shook his head to clear it. He went below and threw water on his face and poured himself a large coffee and returned to the cockpit and vowed to drink and sleep no more.

The dreams were becoming too real.

He pulled out his phone on a sudden urge to call Cat but watched as the phone failed to connect. Out here in the middle of the Strait there was no signal. He'd try again later. The sky darkened and *Arrow* bent to a sudden gust then regained her footing and sailed on into the early evening. *Sooner than forecast*, Jared thought, and took a long look around, then went below and turned on the VHF and checked the weather channels. There was mention of the low that had been predicted coming in with some southeast wind increases, and Jared reached across and tapped the glass on the barometer and the needle dropped. Maybe the start of something bigger.

He pulled on a hooded rain jacket and long-billed cap and went back out on deck and sheltered under the dodger where he sipped his coffee and pondered his dream. He'd never paid much attention to dreams before Joseph came into his life, partly because he didn't believe in their relevance and partly because, if they were in some way indicators of the inner self, he wasn't sure he really wanted to know what they revealed about him. Joseph had changed him, and now he looked upon dreams as some combination of things past and a foreshadowing of things to come. It was something he had come to believe reluctantly and would never attempt to explain to anyone. Maybe not even to himself.

A flash of lightning lit up the sky followed almost immediately by a clap of thunder and the sound of something striking the mainsail directly above where Jared sheltered under the dodger. A moment later a large raven fell onto the cabin top in front of him and lay without moving. Jared stared at it, astonished, and it raised its head and croaked angrily at him and hopped a few steps then flew away. It turned back and circled the boat at mast height, once, and then again, its head tilted down, the guttural croaking unceasing before it finally headed off in the direction of Desolation Sound.

Jared watched after it, his heart hammering, eyes half shut as he stared out through the rain-streaked isinglass of the dodger, and without conscious thought he swung the tiller to follow the bird. And then he saw a flash out of the corner of his eye, right at the dark heart of the storm cell that had moved past and was now miles ahead. *Lightning*, he thought, and went to turn away when it flashed again. He picked up the binoculars and focused. It was a hand-held flare, and much closer than he'd first thought. He took a quick bearing from the compass and went to the tiller and clicked the autopilot onto the new course. It brought the wind more on the beam and *Arrow* picked up speed and Jared decided not to bother with the engine.

Twenty minutes later he could make out the Zodiac dead in the water with two men in wet gear and Sou'westers inside waving frantically. He brought *Arrow* past them and rounded up into the wind and ran back alongside and signalled they should tie on and come aboard via the stern ladder. The wind had died back down as the cell moved through, and it wasn't difficult.

"Thanks, partner," one of them said. "The damned engines quit dead on us. Just like that. Barely a splutter. Must have been water in the gas, a fuel blockage, something like that." The man grinned at him, but something was off.

Jared looked at the twin 200 Yamahas bolted on the stern of the Ribby and the hairs on the back of his neck stood up and he remembered Cat's trip across to Nanaimo after the race.

❁

Jared took a deep breath and turned back towards the brothers.

"Don't even think about it, partner," Clint said. The gun in his hand was rock steady. Travis stepped behind Jared and cold-cocked him, and he slumped to the deck. Clint leaned over Jared and bent his legs up behind him and zip-tied them to his wrists. The two men pulled the painter on the inflatable and hauled it up tight against the stern rail, then picked Jared up fore and aft and threw him over the lines and into it. His head crashed against the fibreglass seat and blood spurted out.

"Whoops," Travis said.

There was no reply, just a small but growing pool of blood on the dinghy floor. The brothers turned their attention to the depth sounder.

"Sixty-eight feet, that can't be right."

"Must be a bank here."

"Better phone him."

Travis moved around the deck holding his cell phone up in the air and squinting at the screen through the rain, even climbing up onto the cabin top in his search for a signal.

"No reception," he said.

"He told me there was two hundred feet of water out here."

"Maybe the sounder's not working right."

"Seems to be, it's changing all the time, down to seventy-five, up to sixty-four. It's just too shallow."

"What do you think?"

Travis considered the problem. Not nearly deep enough to sink the sailboat out of sight. Christ, the goddam stick alone might be over sixty feet high. Burn it? That would draw attention and someone might get out here in time to put it out. Smoke and fire would show a long way off, and there were some pleasure boats fishing off in the distance, as well as a tug and tow on the horizon that could be heading in their direction. If someone managed to get on board and found *Arrow* deserted, it would raise a lot of questions. The whole point was to make it look like *Arrow* and Jared had vanished. Gone into hiding.

Travis looked at the chart plotter and it showed that the bank ran for another few miles. They just weren't where they needed to be. It would probably take over an hour motoring in this slow-motion piece of shit once he figured out how to get rid of the sails. He knew he could start the sailboat's engine all right, motors were motors, no problem there, but he hadn't a fucking clue how to get the nervously flapping sails down. *It can't be all that hard*, he reasoned, *look at all those dipshits out there sailing, screaming and raising their fists at him as he cut close across their bows.*

Another squall hit and *Arrow* tilted before it and Travis, staring upwards with his brow furrowed in thought, felt the boat take a sudden list and as he turned to grab the cabin rail for balance, the boom swung viciously across and smacked him across the forehead and he dropped like a stone. *Arrow* rotated and swung into the squall and the sails flogged and flapped and the lines jerked and jittered and the noise increased, like, fucking tenfold and the boom crashed back and forth and everything was chaos and Clint thought *Screw this* and dropped to his belly and crawled over to Travis and dragged him to the stern and shoved him over the rail into the dinghy on top of Jared. He jumped in after him and fired up the big Yamahas and took off on a foaming plane. He never looked back once.

Behind him *Arrow*'s boom swung and crashed against the shrouds and her sails backed and filled and emptied as she moved in erratic circling motions seeking equilibrium. High above her a raven circled and one of the threshing main sheets caught and wrapped around a winch and the sail filled and *Arrow* steadied up and moved slowly off before the wind in halting irregular progress, hauling up till the sail shivered, then falling off again, but always returning to her meandering northerly course, moving towards Desolation Sound like an erratic resurrected shade of the *Mary Celeste*.

CHAPTER 44

Clarke glared at the battered handheld VHF radio lying mute on his desk. He'd retrieved it from the lost and found and plugged in the charger that was stowed in the case alongside. He knew it was sending and receiving perfectly; he could hear the traffic on channel sixteen and had talked to his buddy on the harbour patrol boat over an hour ago. The problem was not with the radio, it was with that bloody Jared who had gone silent. He'd phoned Cat and gotten a message. Similarly with Danny. Likewise with texts to all of them. Nobody wanted to communicate with him and Clarke knew from long experience that was a bad sign. He'd caught up with Erin and Jaimie at the hospital, but of course they knew nothing. Or so they claimed. His captain walked past his desk, slowed, cleared his throat, and Clarke snarled, "I'm flummoxed," and his boss moved on repeating Clarke's pending retirement date under his breath like a mantra.

Five days now, five days since the fire and he hadn't turned up one single damn piece of new information. He'd been down to the commercial docks on three separate occasions and asked around and was met with blank stares and head shakes from the fishermen. No one had seen *Arrow* leave or heard any mention of her on the VHF. For all the good he was doing Clarke thought he might as well take more leave and go back and work on *Legalese*. Merlynn had talked about getting away for a long cruise before the fire happened, and he wondered if they should take *Legalese* up to Desolation Sound for a few days. You never know, they might just get lucky. He toyed momentarily with the idea of justifying it as an official search for Jared and *Arrow* and claiming expenses from the department. It was probably a bit much, but the look on the captain's face might be worth it.

He had other cases pending but none that required his presence at the moment. Two were coming up for trial in three weeks, and he'd already reviewed and signed off on his testimony with the prosecutor for both of them. He absentmindedly shuffled papers around on his desk while he considered his options. He came to a decision and went and spoke to the captain who quickly agreed to a two-week leave starting immediately. Clarke wasn't surprised; he thought if he'd asked for three months of leave, the man might have embraced him.

He went over to the filing cabinet and pulled out the arson file and witness statements and made copies for himself. The case would be nagging at the back of his mind anyway, so he might as well bring the files along in the event something new came up that he needed to check. The fire was still classified as an active investigation but he knew that wouldn't last much longer. They were up against dead ends every which way they turned. No leads on the arsonists and no evidence obtained from the scene so far, other than the broken remains of the glass bottles they thought had been used as the firebombs. They had yielded nothing. The perps had used gloves; or maybe fingerprint DNA wouldn't have survived the extreme heat. Clarke didn't know for sure but it seemed likely. All of which immediately reminded him of the grisly spectre of Joseph's curled remains, something he'd tried hard to forget. He'd seen a lot of violent deaths of innocents over the years and had never learned how to put them behind him. This was one he'd carry forever.

Joseph's identification was the last piece of the puzzle they were waiting on. Once they received confirmation on his DNA, the investigation would move on to "the next stage," another euphemism for a "cold case," the "back shelf," or the "back burner." Pick your metaphor. The old saw about a crime and the following twenty-four hours was often correct. The chances of solving it dropped dramatically as the days passed. The thought saddened Clarke, and he took out the last page from the Xerox machine and slammed the lid shut.

He gathered up the copies and stowed them in his briefcase. He'd share them with Merlynn; maybe she would be able to spot something he'd missed. He thought it unlikely, but what did he have to lose? It was all dead against the rules anyway; if the department learned he'd taken copies of active files out of the building without proper authorization, his ass would be hung out to dry. Clarke wasn't worried about any of that. He'd always assumed that given his lifestyle he wouldn't live long enough to collect on his annuity in any case, and the closer his day of retirement approached, the more surprised he became. He'd never given a moment's thought to what he would do when that time arrived. During his compulsory appointment, the department psychiatrist had said Clarke would miss his job when it was over, and he'd laughed in her face. He picked up his briefcase and took a last look around the office. He had a strong premonition that he would never return.

❈

"Are you sure you really want to do this?" Merlynn asked. "Run all the way up there to look for the *Blue Harp*?"

"One hundred percent," Clarke replied. "We'll call it a vacation cruise with a purpose."

They'd been discussing the case for hours, starting at the very beginning with the attacks on the women and then Cat's sister and everything that followed, from the disappearances of Newcombe and

Sullivan and the probable death of Bill Lacey to Annie's kidnapping and the East End arson. They both agreed that someone was cleaning house. Where they disagreed was about who that person or persons might be. It was straightforward as far as Clarke was concerned. While there might not be a clear-cut connection that would stand up to scrutiny in a court of law, there was a lot of evidence that Albright was involved in it right up to his thick neck. Clarke knew it in his gut, one hundred percent.

Merlynn, being an ex-prosecutor, was pickier on the fine points. In her opinion there was nowhere near enough to make a valid case. Only some circumstantial evidence that pointed to Albright but did not prove his guilt beyond a reasonable doubt. "Guilt by association is not a valid argument in a court of law," she said. She did, however, agree with Clarke that someone was cleaning up.

"Cui bono," Merlynn said. "Who benefits? Why not Ronald Ivery? He has all the connections, his name keeps popping up, and you've linked him to the men who kidnapped Annie. Your informant told you he saw him involved in a drug buy along with that giant who ferries him around. Granted that was a few years ago, and maybe just for personal use, but there were rumours. I'm sure you've heard some of the same ones I did."

Clarke nodded in reluctant agreement. He had. That Ivery might have been a player in opioids back at the beginning, beyond the personal use which he admitted to.

Merlynn continued, "And then there was that bar fight between those men we now know were dealers and his man Rodgers. What possible reason could there be for that incident other than some kind of dispute over drugs? It's not as if they ran into each other by accident in the course of their day-to-day social interactions. The place was an absolute dive. Not a place Rodgers would ever have gone to without some compelling reason."

"You make some good points," Clarke admitted. But his conversation with Ivery had led him to believe that the man in the wheelchair was telling the truth. He had no real evidence for his conviction, just his gut instinct. He didn't bother to subject his intuition to Merlynn's scorn.

"I met him not all that long ago, you know," Merlynn said. "At some black-tie benefit or other. Legal Aid, I think. I'd given a short speech of introduction to the main speaker, and he was in the audience and came up and introduced himself afterwards. Said he'd been an acquaintance of my late husband and they'd had some minor business dealings together."

She spread her hands. "That was news to me. He offered his belated condolences and even gave me his card. It's probably still buried somewhere in my purse. We talked for a few minutes; he seemed a bit shy and lacking in confidence for such a successful man. Lonely, I'd guess. Rodgers was there with him. The whole episode seemed a little strange and also a bit sad at the time. I felt sorry for him."

"Did you ever call him?"

"No. I thought about it, but what would we even have talked about? My late husband? No thanks. Not to disrespect Ralph, but that particular part of my life is long dead and buried."

Clarke extended a meaty hand. "The card, please." He waited while she searched and then took it and dialled the number. "It's Detective Clarke. You'll remember I came by last week. My friend Merlynn Saunders gave me your private number."

He waited for the hang-up but it didn't come. So he pressed on. "The thing is, Mr. Ivery, I'm trying to locate James Albright and I understand you've leased the *Blue Harp* out to him. We think he's cruising somewhere up north at the moment. Desolation Sound was mentioned. Merlynn Saunders and I are thinking of taking her boat up there on an unofficial basis for a look around, and I was hoping you might be able to give us an idea of where we could start looking."

Clarke paused for a moment, trying to think how to frame the next part. Diplomacy was not one of his strong points. "We know of an individual whom some people might consider erratic who holds Albright personally responsible for an injury to a friend of his, and we understand he's gone looking for him. We think the situation could be potentially dangerous."

Clarke listened to Ivery's response, shook his head in bewilderment, said, "Okay, I suppose I could ask her," and ended the call.

"You're not going to believe this," he said to Merlynn. "He and Rodgers want to come along."

CHAPTER 45

Jared woke into darkness. His eyelids were glued shut and he was aware in those first moments of the echoing sound of a big diesel working hard and a faint disagreeable smell. He lay there motionless, fighting off the nausea, and wondered if he was concussed. He remembered the men on the Zodiac signalling him and then the two of them coming aboard *Arrow*. After that, everything was a blank.

His head was pounding and he reached up and felt the dried blood congealed in his hair, then licked his fingertips and gently rubbed them over his eyelids, prising them apart, but it was still black and he still could see nothing. He wondered if his vision had been affected. He rapped his knuckles softly on the floor and realized it was metal. It suddenly seemed to slope and tilt and nausea overcame him and he shut his eyes against the dizziness. The floor abruptly dropped away from under him and then slammed back up and he bounced a little and put it all together.

Good news his vision was probably okay, bad news he was inside a pitch-black room on a big powerboat that was bucking hard into rough seas. The details came flooding back to him then, the big inflatable with the twin Yamahas and Albright's men coming aboard *Arrow* . . . The *Blue Harp* took a hard list into a sharp turn and the diesel slackened off and the motion eased. A short time later he heard chain running out and the boat falling back and coming up tight on the anchor.

He waited silently in the darkness, trying not to think about *Arrow* and what must have happened to her. It was almost quiet now, the engine throttled right down, and just above that distant murmur Jared thought he heard a snuffling sob. He listened intently for several minutes, but it wasn't repeated. He began crawling slowly along the floor with his arms extended out in front of him and came up against a wall. Rising to his feet he flattened his back against it and began to shuffle along in the direction he thought the sound had come from. His eyes were adapting to the darkness now and he could just make out a faint sliver of light coming through the outlines of a heavy steel door set flush into the wall ahead of him.

He felt for the handle and tried to turn it but it was locked. He ran his hands around the wall on both sides of the door searching for a light switch but couldn't locate one. He continued on past the door, sliding his feet carefully along the floor in small, incremental steps, moving even slower now as the smell became stronger. The sharp odour of urine mixed with something faintly sweet and rotten.

His foot came up against something soft and he froze. He heard a thin whistling intake of breath, and then the sobbing sigh he thought he might have imagined earlier. Crouching down he stared into the dark, willing himself to see.

Something reached out and touched him and he jumped back, startled.

"Light." A faint whisper. Jared reached down and felt the hand grasping a stub of candle and box of matches. He struck a match and lit the candle.

The man lying on the stained blanket was shattered, his face puffed and misshapen, one eye half closed, the cheekbones swelling blue lines. His nose was flattened and bent to one side above cut and swollen lips.

He opened his mouth and took a sighing breath and Jared saw the jagged stumps of teeth that framed the gaps. He was wearing an old maroon coloured pair of Everlast boxing trunks, and above them his bare chest and belly were covered in welts and bruises. It would be a miracle if he didn't have broken ribs.

"Water," the man whispered, and Jared saw the water bottles lying alongside him. He picked one up and twisted the cap off and the man reached out for it but couldn't grasp it. His knuckles were swollen and misshapen and his right arm was twisted at a crooked angle and surely sprained or broken. Jared held the bottle to the man's lips and he lifted his head and took a small sip and then fell back again.

"Pissed myself," the man mumbled. "Can't get up." Jared looked down and saw the broken thigh bone jutting through the skin above the knee and the suppurating wound that surrounded it. Up close the smell from it was overpowering. The pain would be intolerable.

"Pills," the man rambled. "Finished. The leg. Two days." The man's voice ran down and he closed his eyes and drifted off. Jared didn't know who the man was or what he might have done, but nobody deserved this. He could have been in a fight, which would account for the bruises and busted knuckles and teeth, but Jesus, the hanging arm and broken leg? What kind of animal does that? He picked up the little pill container lying among the water bottles and held it to the candle to read the label. Painkillers, opioids, a dozen or so left, and if he understood the man correctly there weren't going to be any more. And then the pain would be unbearable and the man on the blanket would be begging for his death. That would make the end result all that much sweeter for a certain kind of person; and from everything Jared knew or suspected about him, Albright was exactly that kind of man.

He lifted the candle high and surveyed the room. Roughly square, maybe twenty by twenty, empty save for a few cases of engine oil and some filters stacked against one wall. He went over and searched through them for something he could use as a weapon, an oil spout used to puncture the cans and pour would have been useful, but he found nothing. Another smaller door was set in the far wall, and he went across and tried the door. It was unlocked and he opened it. A small washroom with a toilet and wall-mounted basin and a pair of towels hanging below a shelf containing matches, candles, and a bottle of hand cleaner. Above it was a small polished metal mirror riveted to the bulkhead. He took one of the towels and wet it under the faucet and went back to the man on the blanket. Setting a case of oil alongside him, he melted some wax and fixed a candle on top of it. He gently sponged the man's burning forehead and battered face, then reached down and removed the stained trunks and washed him from head to foot. When he was done he took the second towel and dried him off and then Jared went into the washroom and cleaned himself up.

He stared into the mirror, running his hands over the lump on his head, assessing the damage. Not too bad. It was tender, but apart from that and a long shallow cut on his forehead he found no other injuries. He had a throbbing headache along with his nausea and for a brief moment he considered taking one of the man's pills but was immediately embarrassed by the thought. Apart from having no idea about their strength and the effect they would have on him, the other guy needed them a hell of a lot more than he did. He went back into the room and squatted down against the wall beside the man, listening to the raspy uneven breathing and waiting for him to wake again. He noticed a lump under the blanket that formed a partial pillow for the man's head and reached underneath and found some clothes. He pulled them out and replaced them with the rolled-up towels.

A dress shirt and tie and a stained navy-blue business suit with a matching vest and expensive labels. Jared went through everything carefully but found nothing. The man had been stripped clean. And then in the bottom of the inside pocket of the vest, an old business card. *Richard Sullivan Q.C.* and a group of initials that was meaningless to Jared. But he didn't need them to realize it was the missing lawyer Cat had read about in the paper. The one who worked for the party.

Shacked up after all, although not in the sense that one of the more lurid newspapers had implied.

"Pill." The man's urgent whisper broke into Jared's thoughts. He passed the man a pill and the water bottle.

"You're Sullivan. The lawyer."

The man nodded. "Richard." His face was greasy with sweat, and Jared handed him the damp towel. He wiped his face and held up two swollen fingers. "Ten minutes."

Jared waited. Sullivan's laboured breathing gradually eased and some of the tension left his body and there was almost the hint of a smile on the battered face. "Whooee," he said. "Much better. How many left?"

Jared counted. "Thirteen."

"Maybe two days then. After that I'm done. I can go almost four hours, I think. Don't have my watch. First hour is good, second is tolerable, then it's all downhill from there. My leg is gangrenous, I know that smell. I volunteered for the Peace Corps in Haiti a long time ago. When I was a better man. He wants me to beg him for my death. Please. I'm begging you. Promise me you'll help me when the time comes."

"We're nowhere near there yet," Jared said.

"Only a matter of time."

They sat there not speaking for a few minutes, and then Sullivan began to talk.

"I'm not sure you could hurt Albright with a ball-peen hammer. I always suspected he was a bit of a masochist, but it's more than just that. I've had some experience, I was decent in the ring once. I dislocated his jaw there, right at the beginning. I was just beginning to realize I was never going to get off the boat anyway and I thought *screw it* and I hit him so hard I broke two of my knuckles. And he just smiled, standing there with his jaw hanging all crooked. It was like he didn't even feel it, like I had feathers on my hands instead of boxing gloves. He tilted his head back, put both hands in his mouth, and twisted and pulled and popped his jaw right back in. It's called congenital analgesia, something like that. You can damage him, but I doubt you can actually hurt him."

Sullivan paused and Jared held the water bottle for him and he drank again, taking in great gasping swallows. "Better," he said. "I was dehydrated. Couldn't manage."

"I've got friends. They'll be looking for me. How many men does Albright have on board?"

"Five or six, including him. I don't know about the captain and the engineer, I think they might have come with the boat. They were never around when Albright's goons set up the ring and we fought. If you could even call what happened in there a fight. Not sure if they don't actually know what's going on or just don't want to know. Either way they're probably not all in. So four of them at least, plus Albright at the moment. Clint and Travis are his main men. Tall, stringy, bad news."

"We've met," Jared said. They talked for a while longer, and then the lawyer began to perspire and his voice faltered and his eyes closed and he drifted off. Jared wiped him down again, this time with cold water, and watched him for a while, thinking it all through. He stood up and did some slow stretching and worked his way through some katas and tried to summon the old skills, but he only felt slow and clumsy. Half an hour in he gave it up and lay back and closed his eyes and concentrated on slowing his pulse and getting some sleep. It didn't come.

His watch had been smashed when he was taken, but he calculated it was three hours later when they finally came for him.

CHAPTER 46

PASSAGES

1
Annie J

The seas were still building. The quick turnaround between fronts had the southeaster blowing against the leftover northwest swell from the high and the result was a choppy, uncomfortable vertical sea that had the little double-ended troller rising up and slamming down with her progress reduced to under two knots an hour. It had been bad enough for the previous six hours but now the tide was beginning to ebb against him as well, and if nothing changed, Danny figured he'd soon be lucky to make one knot an hour in the *Annie J*. He was basically burning fuel to bob up and down in misery in more or less the same place. He cursed and slapped the barometer for the tenth time in the last two hours and it did exactly the same thing it had done the previous nine. It stayed the same, or maybe even dropped another hair.

It was unseasonable and annoying; a complete aberration, and Danny was taking it personally. What should have been a comfortable fifteen-hour run up the coast was well into its second day, and now it looked like he'd have to run in for shelter and tie up behind one of the little islands along the coast for the night. It seemed his voyage was cursed. First a plugged fuel filter that had him drifting and tossing around for two hours and resulted in a savage cut across his forehead as he leaned in to change it, and then a long skein of drifting kelp that wrapped itself around the prop shaft *and would not fucking come off!* And now this sudden shift in the weather. Remaining out here bouncing up and down in the tide rips while taking the occasional green one over the bow was pointless and even a bit risky. With the raised seas and pounding rain the *Annie J*'s radar was having difficulty picking up the logs and debris that were always a hazard out here in the Strait. To make matters worse, there was a lot more clutter than usual strewn about, a result of the high tides and raised swell that had plucked beached and stranded logs off the shore and put them back into play.

The troller was built like a tank, but even so: shit happened. Ever since he'd been a small child fishing alongside Joseph and his brothers, Danny had heard the stories of the "queer ones," rogue waves that suddenly rolled up out of nowhere, compressed and balled like huge green fists and took out windows and cabins, and, sometimes, the men sheltering inside as well.

It just wasn't worth the risk. The weather had to moderate and blow out soon. It was late autumn in the Pacific Northwest for God's sake, not March in the Bering Sea. He looked at the chart plotter and punched in a course on the autopilot that would take him inside Lasqueti Island. There were some good hidey holes from a southeaster in there, two of which he knew well from having sheltered in them previously.

It was annoying, but his search would just have to wait until the weather improved. According to the marine forecast, they were getting the same crappy conditions up north that he was, and if Danny knew

Jared, he would have *Arrow* anchored snug in some sheltered bay by now and be nursing hot rums and waiting for a let-up. Comforting himself with this thought, he ran off towards the islands, a protected anchorage, and a good night's rest. Less than an hour later, Danny was asleep in his bunk with a hot toddy warm in his belly and a childhood dream of Joseph and Annie soothing his mind.

2
Legalese

Clarke hadn't really thought they'd come, him being a cop and all, and them being . . . well, he wasn't really sure to tell the truth. Not innocents, though, that was for damn sure. But the pair of them had showed up shortly after his phone call with their luggage in tow and it was too late to renege. Ivery told Clarke he'd been trying to contact the *Blue Harp* for three days now, without success.

"The terms of the charter specify that they remain in touch, check in regularly, but Albright is not answering his phone or emails. Thomas called the boat on the VHF. Same story. No contact. It's surprising to say the least. Their captain has his hundred-ton ticket, and this is jeopardizing it. There is no way he would not be monitoring the radio channels and responding to our calls. Something has gone badly wrong up there, and it probably has something to do with Albright."

Clarke said, "I have the same problem with the boats I'm trying to contact. It's as if Desolation Sound has suddenly become the Bermuda fucking Triangle. Boats and people are just vanishing into it."

"Which is why we have to go up there and find them," Thomas said. "And the sooner we leave, the better."

Clarke knew they wouldn't tell him the real reasons behind their concern, but it was clear they were worried. The three of them had that much in common anyway.

"Look, I'm not disagreeing with you. It's just that Merlynn had to fly back east to help look after sick grandkids, and she's out of touch for the next little while. It's her boat, and I'm not comfortable taking it out in this weather. It's still way too unsettled. Just take a look at that." Clarke raised his head and pointed up at a particularly dense black cloud passing directly overhead. Spatters of rain fell upon his upturned face. And then a larger, mottled, more solid spatter.

"Fucking seagulls," Clarke raged, pulling out a handkerchief and wiping the shit off his forehead. "I hate those fucking flying rats."

"Actually, I think that one might have been a raven," Thomas said.

Clarke looked up. He opened his mouth as if to speak and then thought better of it and closed it again.

Legalese departed the yacht club twenty minutes later.

3

Arrow

The black clouds rolled in from the southeast in a tumbled mass, piling up layer upon layer before spilling forward as the tops blew off and cascaded down the grey skies like foaming spindrift breakers. Far beneath the leaden skies, a tattered and beaten old wooden sailboat drifted and rolled on the angry seas and bent to the wind. She straightened and tilted, straightened and tilted, the main flapping wildly, the boom slamming from side to side against the shrouds, and the sail dragging down on the deck as it lurched back and forth from port to starboard and back again. The headsail was shredded and in tatters, large strips of it streaming over the bow like giant telltales pointing the way north.

In the cabin below, water coursed from side to side and fore and aft with every sway and roll and splashed up against the cupboards and settees. A shelf had given way and books and magazines floated for a time before they became waterlogged and sank. A galley cupboard sprung its latch and added its contents to the mix. A pulsing red light showed and a high-pitched whine sounded intermittently as the viscous mess found its way into the bilges. And now a sack of flour broke open and disseminated and the bilge water thickened further and the pump faltered then plugged and moaned in protest for a brief moment before it finally stopped altogether. And then there was only the sound of the rain bouncing off the decks and slanting below through the open companionway and the crashing of the boom and the slatting of the sails as *Arrow* writhed and twisted and continued on her tortuous path north.

4

Raven

....

The dugout canoe with the bird painted on the prow had been making good progress until the storm cells suddenly appeared out of nowhere. What had been a comfortable rolling swell that pushed it along and gave them an extra knot of speed quickly transformed into steep four to six footers with the tops blowing off that threatened to swamp their little craft at any moment. For the first minutes after the wind and heavy rain struck, they had attempted to hold their course, but as the waves increased in height and began to break at their crests, it became dangerous and they were flirting with a capsize. Turning back was out of the question; there was only one option left to them and that was a bad one for a fourteen-foot dugout canoe: bear off and run before the storm.

His companion stretched out in the bottom of the canoe to lower the centre of gravity, and the paddler crouched in the stern with the steering paddle and fought the canoe around onto the new course. It lay in the trough between the waves as if resting for a second, and then the first swell overtook her and broke against her stern and then it lifted her up and she began to soar. The rain was coming down so hard now visibility was down to less than fifty feet. They had passed increasing numbers of logs in the last few miles, some of them sun-blackened old derelicts lying nearly submerged in the water while numerous others were fresh with new cuts and rode higher. Under these conditions there was little chance of spotting any that lay in their path in time to avoid them. If they hit one, they were finished. It would be a matter of luck and the gods' will.

The wind slacked off briefly, and the paddler took the opportunity to bail. He could keep up with the water in the lulls when the wind and the rain died down for a few beats, but when the full force of the storm returned it took all his strength and concentration to keep the dugout's stern to the waves, and the water slopping about inside rose to dangerous levels. The canoe was teetering on the edge of control now, down in the water and beginning to surf as some of the bigger waves overtook them and cascaded through, the bow hanging suspended in space for long seconds and the waters hissing up alongside the gunwales in rainbow spray before the wave charged past and the canoe dropped back into the trough briefly, as if catching its breath before rising up again on another mad career. If the canoe turned broadside to the waves, they would broach and overturn and die. Hypothermia followed by drowning in minutes.

Six inches of water sloshed back and forth inside the canoe now, and it was increasingly sluggish and slow to respond to his efforts. It would soon be impossible to keep her stern true to the seas, and the paddler thought a mortal broach was only minutes away. He'd known there was risk in heading this far out into the Strait, but time was short, and they couldn't afford to jink their way along the coast skirting the headlands and navigating through the clusters of islands. While they offered shelter, it would have taken twice as long. He didn't second-guess his decision, he was a fatalist, and if the spirits meant for them to survive, then they would. He knew that most people drowned within a stone's throw of land.

He heard a big one hissing as it curled up and broke behind him and he braced his knees against the gunwales and took a firmer grip on the paddle. The canoe rode it for the first seconds and then the bow dug in and slewed and he heaved on the paddle with all his strength and it flexed in his grasp like a living thing and he thought it would break under the stress but the hand-carved spruce held and he managed to fight the stern back before the wind. He didn't know how many more times he could do it. His shoulders ached from the strain and it was just a question of what gave out first: him or the paddle.

He heard another one coming, louder than any of its predecessors, and he took a deep breath and buried the paddle and twisted it and fought to keep the canoe from slewing and as they slanted up on the wave he glimpsed through the spindrift and rain the lethal dark shapes spread out low in the water dead ahead, a half dozen half seen, and he knew it was the end and his strength deserted him and he bowed his head and accepted his fate. As the wave crested and carried the canoe forward and drove it down, there was a sudden scattering, an upwelling waterspout, and then the rank, oily scent of fish carried on warm vaporous breath.

The paddler bowed his head in greeting.

"Hello, my brothers and sisters," Joseph said. "I am glad to see you."

The pod ranged alongside, a scarred old female in the lead, all of their heads turned towards him and those wise and animate eyes settled upon him and he felt their strength flowing into him like an electric current and he sat up straight and struck his paddle into the roiled waters with renewed energy.

The orcas stayed with him for an hour, never further than fifty feet distant and sometimes so close alongside Joseph could reach out and touch them with his hand. Once they moved in line off the bow, leading the dugout canoe through an enmeshed patch of drifting kelp and logs before resuming their formation around him; rising and falling with the waves in synchronicity; *of* the sea rather than *in it*. They left him when the wind began to slacken, peeling off in a line northwards in the direction of the Robson Bight, their ancient rubbing grounds.

When he lost them to sight, Joseph turned and glanced over his shoulder between the surges and saw the sky brightening behind him and sensed a break between fronts was coming. He locked the steering paddle under his arm and picked up the bailer and renewed his efforts. As the water inside lowered, the canoe became more responsive and easier to steer. The wind dropped and the waves flattened out into the previous long billowing swells and they once again hurried north.

The sun suddenly broke out from the clouds, and Joseph stretched and smiled as the warmth and light flooded over him and his old flannel jacket began to steam. He leaned forward and dug his paddle into the water and raised his head and began to chant. The sodden dog stretched out along the bottom of the dugout canoe pricked its ears, sat up, raised its head, and howled in accompaniment.

CHAPTER 47

A light came on in the darkened storage room, dazzling Jared with its brightness. He blinked as his eyes adjusted, and saw the two men from the dinghy. Clint and Travis, as he now knew them to be. The brothers.

"We going to have a problem?" the squinty-eyed one with the bandage wrapped around his head inquired. He carried a large wrench in his hand and sounded hopeful. His brother stood by the door, his hand resting on the butt of the gun tucked in his belt.

"No."

"Sorry to hear you're showing some sense. This way." They ushered him out through the door. As they turned into the narrow passageway, Jared glanced back at Sullivan who hadn't stirred.

"Don't worry about him, he's not going anywhere. He's done. Finished. Kaput. You give him some pills?"

Jared didn't reply. The man shrugged. "Makes no matter. They'll be gone soon enough. He won't last long after that — he'll be begging for an end to it. You'll see."

"You talk too much, Travis," his brother snapped.

Travis rolled his eyes at Jared and grinned, exposing tobacco-stained teeth. "Just sayin'," he said with a shrug.

A flight of steep steel stairs with a handrail led upwards at the end of the passageway. It might have offered an opportunity, but the brothers were taking no chances. They stood well off to the side and motioned Jared up ahead of them. He went through the door at the top and came out into a corridor that led past a compact galley outfitted in gleaming stainless with a man working at a chopping block who glanced up without expression as the procession passed by. Twenty feet further on, the corridor opened out into a large saloon. A bar was located at one end with a mirror and railed shelves holding glassware displayed behind a long slab of granite. A man in a dinner jacket and slacks was seated on one of the raised-back bar stools with a bottle and three glasses set out before him. As the door closed behind Jared and his escorts, the man turned and waved and Jared had his first look at James Albright.

His first impression was one of thickness. Everything about him suggested strength, from the wide shoulders and barrel chest down to the muscular thighs. His forearms were half as big around again as Jared's, and thick wrists connected to large-knuckled hands. One of his fingers was crooked and judging from the swelling had been recently sprained or broken. There were no other visible signs of damage. Jared figured he must weigh at least two hundred and forty pounds, and then Albright swivelled sideways on the barstool and Jared got a clear look at the depth of the man and revised his estimate up another twenty. The word *mesomorph* flashed into Jared's mind from a picture in an old high school textbook. He thought Sullivan would have had small chance against this man in a boxing match with proper rules, let alone in whatever passed for a contest here.

Albright waved him to a seat and poured out a drink from the bottle in front of him. "Forty-year-old scotch, the very best," he said. "Although, I hear you're not particular." He slid the glass across and lifted his own in a mocking toast. "To new friends," he said. His voice slurred on some of the words and Jared first thought the man drunk, but then he saw the faint bruising around Albright's lower face and realized the impediment was caused by the dislocated jaw Sullivan had mentioned. Even in repose the man had a strutting animal confidence, the primitive alpha attitude enhanced by the large powerful body. "I've been looking forward to meeting you. I believe we have some things in common."

Jared said, "I doubt that. From everything I've heard, you're as crazy as a shithouse rat."

He knew Albright had no intention of letting him leave the boat in any case and saw no point in making nice. If he'd had any hopes about his future prospects, the fact that they'd put him in with Sullivan had removed them. The lawyer was a dead man walking, and Albright wouldn't let anyone familiar with those circumstances loose to speak of it.

"Now, now, Jared, don't be so hasty. You haven't heard me out yet. I guarantee that what I have to say will be of interest to you." Albright took the extra glass that sat before him and poured a shot into it and set it in front of the empty stool between Jared and him.

"We have a guest coming to join us for drinks before dinner," he said. "She should have been here by now, but you know what women are like. They like to make us wait, don't they? You'd better see what's keeping her, Travis. Now, where was I? Oh yes, things we have in common."

Jared stared at Albright and felt a cold paralyzing chill settle over him. Surely the man was bluffing. Cat had more sense than to come on board with him. She'd turned down the position, and there was no way in hell she could be out here. Albright was watching him, the trace of a smile on his face as the silence stretched.

Jared was damned if he'd be the one to break it. He picked up his drink and swung round on his stool and checked out the room. It seemed strangely bare, only a single dining table surrounded by several chairs, a lone couch in front of a big-screen TV, and a roped boxing ring in the corner where Albright must have played out his sick games with the lawyer. It contained none of the trappings you would expect to find on a boat purposely designed for combining business with pleasure. There were no pictures on the wall, no occasional tables to hold lamps or drinks or snacks, no cozy corners for private meetings or trysts. Patches of darker coloured wood on the floor indicated where rugs and furniture had been removed. Ripped panelling in two of the corners showed where fitted shelves had been torn out. Jared thought it resembled a spartan army barracks more than a luxury yacht.

"As you can see, I've done a little redecorating," Albright said with a sweeping gesture that encompassed the room. "I found it a bit cluttered in here for my liking. I'm going with the minimalist look, stripping down to the bare essentials. It's my newfound philosophy in life. No more keeping up appearances. It's all about what really matters from here on."

"I would have thought Ivery might have had something to say about that," Jared said.

"Not going to be a problem, I can assure you. But enough about me." He slid off the bar stool and bowed towards the end door. "Our guest has arrived."

It was Cat. Shoulders back and smiling as she entered the room flanked by Clint and Travis, but Jared knew her well enough to see how shaken she was. She walked towards them and slid onto the bar stool Albright held for her and turned towards him.

"Hi, Jared. This is a nice surprise. I didn't realize you were joining us." Cat was putting up a brave front and he would follow her lead, but he heard the slight tremor in her voice that she couldn't quite hide.

To his relief she appeared uninjured. Jared suspected Albright craved an audience for his actions, someone who cared for Cat present when harm arrived for her. Or maybe it was the other way around, as the lawyer had inferred. Having no real feelings of his own, the man needed to experience vicariously what normal people felt. The psychological equivalent of the physical lack of pain receptors Sullivan had talked about. What was it he'd said? Congenital analgesia? So emotional analgesia then, and he needed to see someone else experience what he couldn't. Or, to put it more succinctly, the man was a raving fucking sociopath.

If it had been within his power to destroy Albright at that moment, Jared would have done so with no more remorse than that incurred from swatting a fly. He didn't know how much Albright knew about their personal relationship and tried to match Cat's cool, impersonal tone.

"It was a spur of the moment thing. How are you?" Jared's palms were sweating and he set down his glass on the bar top for fear it would slip from his hand.

"I'm fine. A little bored at the moment to tell the truth. Mr. Albright says the weather precludes my leaving at present. I'm hoping things will clear up soon."

Jared nodded. "I certainly hope so." What the hell could he say with Albright sitting there? For a wild moment he considered taking the bottle of Scotch and cold-cocking Albright and making a run for it with Cat. But it would be suicide. It was a long way to the door out onto the deck, and the brothers with their guns were directly in the way. He had no idea where they were anchored or how far they were from shore. Cat was a decent swimmer, better than him, but the water was cold and he didn't fancy their chances even if they did manage to get over the side. No, better to wait and hope an opening presented itself, however unlikely that seemed at the moment.

Albright regarded the two of them with raised eyebrows and an expectant smile, like a kid waiting for his favourite cartoon show to start. When they remained silent, he shrugged and picked up a remote lying on the bar before him and pointed it at the big-screen TV hanging on the wall.

"I think we have time for a little entertainment before dinner," he said. The set switched on, and a grainy picture of the room they were in came up and then the shot moved jerkily towards one of the saloon entrances.

"I apologize for the quality. I used my steward as the cameraman that first time and I think he might have been a little nervous there at the beginning. But it gets better as it goes along. Should have had sound. The 'Ride of the Valkyries' would have been outstanding when I made my entrance."

Jared looked at him to see if he was joking. He wasn't.

The camera steadied and framed the door and suddenly Albright appeared clad in tight black trunks, his boxing gloves clasped above his head in a gesture of triumph and salutation. He stood there for a moment and then bowed left and right to the empty room as if acknowledging the applause of a crowd before straightening up and heading towards the ring. The camera tracked him on his prancing way down the empty saloon, bobbing and weaving as he threw punches at an imaginary opponent before climbing through the ropes into the ring. He turned his back to the camera and went to a corner and pulled on the ropes on either side of the post and did a few squats and then turned and faced the camera again and sat down on the little stool and rested his hands on his knees and bowed his head, waiting.

There was a pause and then the camera tracked jerkily back to the door and Richard Sullivan stumbled through, as if pushed from behind, and gazed warily about. He was wearing only boxing gloves and a pair of trunks and was barefoot. You could see him register the ring and Albright waiting for him inside it. Travis appeared from the doorway behind him and spoke to him and took him by the arm. Sullivan shook him off and strode confidently towards the ring. He stepped through the ropes and, ignoring Albright, did some stretching and neck rolls. He finished up with some light sparring and shadow boxing, dancing and weaving in place.

Jared thought Sullivan looked pretty good. He was quick and light on his feet for his size. Although he was probably outweighed by close to fifty pounds and was a decade or two older than his opponent, he looked to be in decent shape. He finished his warm-up and stood waiting, a light sheen of sweat on his face reflecting in the lights. Albright suddenly stood up and walked to the centre of the ring and Clint, who had been standing outside the ring behind him, took the little hammer hanging from the bell and struck it and the match was on.

Sullivan danced out into the centre of the ring, bobbing his head, taking small balanced steps as he advanced on Albright. He looked calm and professional, a man who knew what he was about. He moved in and flicked out a left jab and it caught Albright on the chin and he danced back again. Albright merely stood there waiting, turning slowly as Sullivan circled him. He hadn't brought his gloves up to protect himself and appeared lost in thought. Sullivan came in again with a combination that landed on Albright's upper abdomen and left red marks and still he didn't respond, just that same curious watchfulness.

Sullivan moved back and glanced uncertainly about. Nobody moved. Albright stood motionless in the same spot, studying him, and then waved him forward once more, this time raising his gloves. As Sullivan moved in on him, he crouched and raised his forearms, taking the blows and slowly backpedalling. And still he didn't throw a punch. He moved his forearms apart and Sullivan broke through with a hard right cross squarely on his chin and Albright blinked and grinned and nodded in appreciation to the other man and waved him onwards.

Sullivan stopped his bobbing and weaving and moved more slowly around the ring, clearly saving his wind. If he had ever thought it was going to be a proper boxing match, you could see the notion abandoning him. He spoke briefly to Albright and turned to climb back out through the ropes. Albright grabbed him by the shoulder, spun him around, and hit him so hard that a halo of sweat flew off Sullivan's face before he went down and hit the mat. He lay there for long moments, then began to crawl towards the ropes. Albright bent down and raised him up as if he were a child and said something to him, and then went back to the centre of the ring and beckoned him forward once more.

"I had to explain the rules to him there," Albright said.

Jared couldn't stop himself. "And what were they?"

"There were none," Albright said with a smile.

And so it went. Sullivan tried hard and he fought well but you could see the hopelessness creeping in as the fight wore on. It was never an even contest. It was overpowering brute strength against cautious skill, and the final result was never in doubt. As Sullivan tired and slowed, Albright bulled him into a corner and began to punish him. One of his eyes half closed under the onslaught and his nose was clearly broken but he didn't go down. Finally Albright uppercut him and Sullivan crumpled and remained motionless on the canvas and it was finished. Albright took off his boxing gloves and threw them on the prostrate figure and climbed out of the ring. Clint and Travis stepped onto the canvas and bent down to Sullivan and then the picture faded. Cat had turned away and stared down at the bar after the first moments, refusing to watch any of it.

"Very disappointing," Albright said. "There are two more videos after this one, but you get the general idea. I thought he was supposed to be good at one time and could show me something — give me a chance to get the feel of the real thing — but it quickly became obvious that was never going to happen. Although he did get me a few good ones at the beginning before he lost heart." He rubbed his chin and shrugged. "Ah well. Life is filled with small disappointments. Moving on, I understand the two of you do martial arts."

"I do," Jared said quickly. "She just plays at it."

"Still. The two of you up against me? Or Clint and Travis in a tag team match maybe? It's a thought. Could be fun."

Jared tried to keep his face expressionless, but he realized the crazy bastard just might do it. One more line had been crossed with Sullivan, and Albright could never go back from any of this now. He and Cat would not leave the *Blue Harp* alive. Cat was a weapon for Albright to use against him, and Jared knew that was the sole reason she was on board. Because of him. He had to get her away, no matter what. Easy enough to say, but how? Even if by some miracle he managed to take Albright out, there were still the rest of them. Clint and Travis and at least three others that he knew of for starters. The captain and the engineer might be neutral, but he doubted they were going to jump in and give him a hand as long as the others were around.

Albright said, "The owner's suite for the two of you, then, I've had it made up for guests. Some suits hanging up in the closet, one of them should fit you, Jared. On the *Blue Harp* there is a tradition of dressing up for dinner. The door will be locked with two men standing guard outside with orders to shoot if you attempt to leave." He winked. "But if you are reasonable and behave yourselves, you'll always have tonight."

He turned away, dismissing them, and the brothers stepped forward and escorted Jared and Cat out of the saloon and up to the master cabin. They entered and the door was slammed shut and locked behind them. Jared threw his arms around Cat and hugged her.

"I'm so sorry about all of this," she whispered into his shoulder. "I should never have had anything to do with that maniac. It's him, isn't it? The assaults?"

"Yes. Listen to me. None of this is your fault. This was always about Danny and me. We've been circling around him for a while, and then we came too close and he looked for levers to use against us. He went after Annie and Joseph first, and then he collected you. People he knew we cared about. He'll pay for that, but for now we've got to keep our spirits up and watch for an opening. We will get out of this." Jared tried to sound positive. "There will be a lot of people looking for *Arrow* by now, Clarke will have organized an all-out search."

Jared hoped this was true, but was by no means certain. Albright was a powerful man with influential friends, and it was going to take something more than the word of an unruly detective with enemies in the department and some unexplained coincidences to tip the scales against him at this stage. By the time someone did take Clarke's suspicions seriously, it would be far too late for him and Cat. They would be lying under the deep waters wrapped in a length of rusty chain.

Jared looked around for something he could use as a weapon. But there was no furniture in the room apart from the bed and closet. Like the saloon, the room had been stripped, even the shelves and drawers from the built-in closet were missing. They might be able to barricade themselves in and delay things for a time, but they would inevitably be driven out by smoke or fire or something even worse, Christ only knew what with that lunatic, and end up damaged in the process. Why bother. Better to go out and face things straight on with your head up and in shape to take advantage of any breaks that came your way. Jared had no illusions about what was lying in wait for the two of them. Albright might be crazy, but he wasn't stupid, and if he did make a mistake, Clint and Travis were ready and waiting to clean up after him.

A rap at the door and the steward entered bearing a tray with a bottle of Champagne and two glasses. He announced dinner would be served in an hour and left, locking the door behind him. Jared glanced over at Cat.

Cat shrugged. "Well, why not?" she said. "I'm sure it's the very best."

Jared poured drinks for them both and then they showered and changed for dinner.

CHAPTER 48

It was just past noon when Danny saw the blip come up on his radar six miles out from the entrance to Desolation Sound. At first he thought it was a ghost image as it immediately disappeared again. Then it came back a minute later and stayed for a couple more sweeps before vanishing once more. But now he knew it was something. Not giving off a strong signal so probably not a fishing boat or any type of commercial vessel. But something for sure. Probably just another tangled mass of logs, kelp, and deadheads that had been gathered up by the high tides and driven before the storms the last two days. White-flecked tidal currents and eddies whirled and spun and herded the refuse together like border collies working sheep. The blip was only a couple of points off his course, and Danny decided to go over and have a closer look.

He picked up the binoculars and scanned as he approached and confirmed it was just another confused jumble of logs and kelp, this one close to twice the size of the other ones he'd seen. And then, oddly, at the very centre of it, something higher was profiled above the tangled mess. Danny had seen it before, jammed logs pushed up by the pressure or, sometimes, even whole trees, roots, trunk, branches, and all, washed off a slope by heavy rain, caught up and floating. Sometimes they stood almost vertical so that it appeared they were growing straight out of the ocean.

Only this time it wasn't an upright tree or some pressured logs jammed up tall. It was *Arrow*. Even from a distance it was evident that she was derelict. Her mizzenmast was gone and her main mast broken off halfway up with the top section lying on deck among the tattered remnants of her sails. She was listing badly, and Danny wondered if *Arrow* was trapped by the logs or held up and kept from sinking by them. He held the glasses on her as he approached and saw no signs of life on board.

For a moment he considered tying the *Annie J* off on the edge of the mess and crossing the logs on foot to reach *Arrow* but decided against it. It would be risky bordering on foolhardy. Everything was in constant motion, rising and falling, the logs rubbing and chafing and groaning and gaps opening and closing as they flexed to the impetus of wind and waves. If he lost his footing and fell between them, he was dead. Crushed or drowned and probably both. Whatever had happened to *Arrow* had occurred much earlier, and an hour or two either way wasn't going to change anything.

He circled the cluttered tangle and found a narrow channel that started in towards the centre and nudged the bow of the troller into the opening, shut off the engine, and went to the bow with a pike pole. By alternately pushing logs aside and pulling the troller forward with the hooked pole, it took Danny three long hours of hard labour to clear a path to the boat, and for part of that time he was working down among the logs, forcing their ends off to the side so he could get the *Annie J*'s bow worked in another few feet before she was blocked once more. During that time he came across two sections of wooden dock with blue styrene floats, three faded red buoys lashed together, an inverted aluminum rowboat, two broken teak chairs along with a teak table and bookcase, a drowned cat, and a three-hole outhouse with its door missing piloted by rats.

As he worked his way closer to *Arrow,* more damage was visible. A log had ridden up on the aft railing and taken out the wind vane and remained wedged there, protruding ten feet out beyond her stern. Her bow pulpit was hanging loose over the side and tangled up in the remnants of her forestay and bowsprit. When the mizzenmast went, its shrouds had pulled out along with chunks of the teak decking they had been fastened to. Three of the portlights were smashed, the cabin doors were gone, and the handrails either broken or missing altogether. Judging by how low *Arrow* sat, her pronounced list, and the sluggish way she slow-rolled to the waves and wind, she was taking on water and her engine would be submerged and a total loss. Any insurance company would write off the shattered hulk that had once been *Arrow* in a heartbeat, the cost of her repairs far more than she had been worth in her best days. It was a moot question, as *Arrow* had no insurance coverage apart from the two million in third-party liability that was a necessary requirement for moorage.

Danny pushed a final log and a beat-up old dugout canoe out of his path and brought the *Annie J* alongside *Arrow.* The canoe slid away and then slowly drifted back and he saw that she was tied off with a line to one of the few remaining stanchions. He took down the shotgun fastened over the chart table in the troller and stepped down over the rail onto *Arrow.* At that moment a large wet dog leaped out from behind the house at him, its forepaws on his chest shoving him sideways just in time for Danny to be doused by a bucket of greasy water thrown out the companionway. He fell back in shock as a ghost emerged from the saloon after it.

Joseph nodded to Danny and went back inside, this time returning with a half-filled bottle of rum. He offered it to Danny who could only stare at him, dumbfounded. Joseph shrugged and took a drink from the bottle and asked Danny if the two-inch trash pump was still on board the troller. Danny, still incapable of speech as his mind grappled with the impossible, nodded. *Yes.* Joseph told him to go and fetch it then.

Joseph had been lying awake and heard Sinbad's low growl as the gate latch clicked. He had gone to the open window and saw two men coming into the yard. He quieted the dog and waited. They were each holding something but he couldn't make out what it was. They split up and the small one approached his window. An arm came through and Joseph saw the glass bottle and then the lighter flared as Sinbad bit down hard and jerked the man inside. He fell onto the bed, the lit bomb beside him, his terrified scream drowned out by an explosion from the rear of the house. Joseph went through the window into the yard followed by Sinbad just as the propane tank went up and the force of the blast knocked him through the fence into the neighbour's yard. When he regained consciousness some minutes later with Sinbad licking his face, the fire trucks had already arrived. Joseph saw them loading Annie into the ambulance. He decided there was nothing for him to do there, so he and Sinbad left.

"You could have told somebody," Danny said.

Joseph spoke.

"Apart from Annie," Danny said.

They sat and talked as the trash pump banged away on the foredeck, a flexing hose leading from it down through the hatch where they'd fastened the end inside a crab pot to serve as a rough primary filter. They'd thrown all the cushions overboard along with much of the debris that was loose and floating around inside the cabin, but there were still jams that required clearing every few minutes. Judging from the tide lines on the cabin walls, there had been over four feet of water inside the boat, and with all the rolling and pitching it had splashed all the way up to the cabin roof. The water was black and rancid and everything inside the boat was coated with grease and oil. It was a complete and total write-off; even the interior wall panelling was broken in spots and stained. *Better if* Arrow *had sunk and spared Jared the wretched sight of her*, Danny thought. He refused to consider the possibility that his friend was dead.

Jared wasn't on board when Joseph had arrived at *Arrow* eight hours earlier. There were no indications as to whether he had left voluntarily or been taken, and no clues to his present whereabouts. Joseph did, however, have a good notion of where the *Blue Harp* was. He pointed out the pieces of broken teak furniture caught up in the debris that surrounded them and explained.

The Polynesians on their long ocean passages could detect the presence of an island a thousand miles away by a change in the patterns of waves breaking upon their canoes in open water. Determining the point of origin of broken and drifting pieces of teak furniture in tidal waters with defined currents seemed much more possible. Danny had seen Joseph locate an underwater shelf of rock invisible in storm and spray when all their lives depended upon finding that one precise place in impossible conditions, and he had no problem believing that Joseph could locate the *Blue Harp*.

His problem lay with Joseph's unshakeable resolve that they must park the *Annie J* and take Jared's crippled sailboat on the hunt. He knew better than to argue though.

CHAPTER 49

Legalese moved through the water at a leisurely seven-and-a-half knots, the twin Detroit diesels ticking over at the sedate 1600 RPM that Clarke refused to exceed in spite of the complaints of his two passengers. He couldn't argue excessive fuel costs at the higher speeds, as Ivery's first action upon leaving the yacht club was to direct him to the fuel docks where they filled the tanks. The bill came to just under five figures, and Thomas paid with one of those black credit cards Clarke had previously assumed were urban legend. Clarke could argue caution, though, and had rattled on about the potential hazards involved in cranking up long-neglected engines to continuous high rates of speed, overheating transmissions, worn shafts, and leaking stern glands, etcetera, etcetera, etcetera. As Ivery and Rodgers were even less knowledgeable about matters mechanical they deferred to him, with grumblings.

Clarke didn't know if his arguments for restraint were completely valid (he'd overheard the stern gland thing at the Queens Own bar), he just needed to slow things down and give himself some time and space to consider the situation. Basically he wanted to feel that he was driving events and not the other way around. Despite his sometimes go-to-hell manner, he was not an impulsive man and was already regretting his decision to start out on this mad venture. The plan — if heading off into the wilderness clueless even deserved that designation — was ridiculous and fraught with uncertainty on its own merits, as well as being filled with personal and professional danger. And that was without considering the dubious pair alongside him. Once he'd allowed those two on board, he might just as well have quit the force and ripped up his pension fund papers.

He didn't know what had come over him back at the yacht club. In hindsight, he had been unnerved by the incident with the raven and it had clouded his judgment. He was not normally a superstitious man; and while he had a lot of respect for Joseph, the old man was dead, and Clarke seriously doubted his reincarnation as a large black bird. Yet even as he was framing these thoughts, Clarke could not refrain from a surreptitious glance at the black sky overhead.

No birds.

He reached for the chart plotter and extended the range to get an idea of what lay ahead. It had pretty much been a straight shot down the channel so far, but the complexities of Desolation Sound lay just eight miles ahead now. The summer rush of cruisers was over and there weren't many pleasure boats around, only the occasional fishing boat and commercial vessel. The lack of boat traffic was a relief, but Clarke was well aware of his limitations and knew he was poorly qualified for taking on a trip like this. He regretted not paying attention on his occasional cruises aboard *Arrow*, but at that time he was just a passenger with no responsibilities other than conviviality. Who knew he'd end up captaining a boat and heading off into the unknown like Ahab chasing after the fucking white whale?

The Nanaimo junket aboard *Legalese* had been a straight shot across the Straits with Merlynn, who had made the trip numerous times, standing right alongside giving encouragement and advice. But he was glad she was out of harm's way and would have found another excuse if the sick grandkids hadn't cropped up. Now he was the one who had to make all the decisions. He had taken the B.C. boat licence exam and was peripherally aware of rules of the road, port and starboard, and tides and currents and such like, only now they weren't mere abstractions on a computer screen, but real things that impacted *Legalese* and her crew. He took some small comfort in knowing that if he did somehow manage to sink the old Monk powerboat over the course of the next few days, he might actually be doing Merlynn a favour. He was pretty sure that her boat was worth more as an insurance claim than it was on the open market. So there was that. In the meantime he'd press on and hope for the best.

Ivery and Rodgers wouldn't be much help. Ronald said he never bothered about the actual operation of the boat, it was awkward for him to get around and what was he paying his captain and engineer for anyway? As for Thomas, he'd never bothered about boats after the time a prankish senior exhorted him to try out for the rowing eights in his freshman year at Oxford. His innocent trip down to the docks that first day of open trials had ended in public humiliation and sneering jests about his size. When Thomas was done with the boat crews, he became semi-famous and was offered a place on the local wrestling team. He told Clarke that as far as he was concerned, *Blue Harp* was just the floating equivalent of the penthouse and his duties remained the same in both locations. So no nautical assistance there either.

Clarke realized he was pretty much on his own commanding a very big boat heading into a complex, hazard-filled wilderness area he knew nothing about, in pursuit of people who wished him harm. What could possibly go wrong?

"I think it's time we talked," Ivery said. Clarke switched on the autopilot and watched it for a while. It beeped and whined and made some minor adjustments to the course and Clarke thought that it seemed to have a good idea of what it was about. He gave it an affectionate pat, handed Rodgers a set of binoculars and told him to keep a lookout and call him if anything unusual came up, then turned and followed the slight man in the wheelchair onto the aft deck.

"Do you want a drink? Coffee or anything? Water?"

"I'm fine, thanks." Ivery set his wheelchair brake and stared out at *Legalese*'s wake. Clarke dropped down onto the couch alongside him, leaned back against the cushions, and waited. The silence stretched out, and Clarke was perfectly content to remain quiet. He'd spent a lot of hours in interrogation rooms over the years and knew there were times to push and times to sit back and wait for the other person to begin. Ivery was accustomed to being in charge and answering to no one apart from, perhaps, his doctors. Thomas might have nagged him on occasion, but Clarke was pretty sure that it had been a very long time since anyone had forced the man in the wheelchair to do anything he didn't want to. So he waited.

"When the accident happened, everything changed," Ivery began. "Not just the immobility and the wheelchair, in some ways that almost made everything easier. I felt I deserved what had happened to me, it was my just punishment. My parents were taking me home on summer break, so in that sense it was my fault they were where they were at that particular moment in time." He held up his hand to forestall Clarke's objection.

"Of course, I know that's not literally true, and I've spent a small fortune on psychiatrists who have all expounded on that, but guilt is emotional, not rational, and I doubt it ever truly goes away. I've been in grief groups with parents who've lost children, sometimes crib deaths, sometimes just random occurrences, none of which could possibly be considered to be the fault of the parents by any person's rational measure." He paused for a moment. "And yet there we all sat, caught in the same sad circle. People came and people went, but I don't think anybody ever really escaped the guilt and the grief. Some covered it up better than others, and I was one of those."

Roland shrugged. "So none of that worked and the next step seemed obvious to me. I was taking drugs to relieve my physical pain, and my life would have been intolerable without them. So why not take something for my mental problems as well? I couldn't get legal prescriptions for what I felt I needed, so Thomas went out and acquired the pills under the table. I didn't waste a second considering the morality of any of it. I still don't believe I did anything wrong."

"According to your lights," Clarke said.

"Yes. According to my lights. If I was harming anyone it was only me, and given the circumstances at the time I believed I had the absolute right to do that. Whether it's alcohol, smoking a giant doobie, or popping a pill, whose business is it but mine? Screw the tax collectors." Ivery leaned back in his chair and closed his eyes. "I think I'll have that drink now. Scotch, please."

Clarke poured three Glenlivets, took one up to Thomas at the wheel, and resumed his position on the couch beside Ivery. He handed him his drink. "And then what happened?"

"I was photographed making a fairly large buy, and the silly buggers tried to blackmail me. Thomas had to go and sort that out."

Clarke said, "The brawl in the East End bar."

"Yes. That was part of it. As a result of all of that, I decided to bypass the small-time street sellers and move up the chain. Less risk involved, fewer buys from smarter people for the most part. And I can't deny that I got a little kick out of breaking the norms. That was when I first met Albright."

"Albright is involved in drugs?" Clarke asked.

"No. Not to my knowledge, anyway. I was at a motorcycle club with Thomas picking up some pills when he showed up with some of his guys. You've probably seen those PR pictures of him on his bike surrounded by his security team in their outfits. Almost like a uniform. In fact, a reporter wrote a story about the group around Albright and broadly hinted at the similarities to the ss brownshirts. The family name was Albrecht, they changed it after the First World War. Can't say I really blame them. I'm sure you've seen his team doing security at his rallies and leading the chants. 'James Albright, he's all right.'"

"Not very subtle," Clarke said.

"But his base loves it. Of course his critics say it should be 'He's alt-right.' He showed up with some of his men at a 'Bikers for Trump' rally in Seattle and it caused a stir back home. There were even some questions in the House. He said his presence there was unplanned, they were just passing through and happened to stop."

Ivery shrugged. "Anyway, he knew who I was — the wheelchair is usually the giveaway — and we had a drink together. He can be quite charming. We kept in contact, one thing led to another, and we did an occasional small business deal together over the years. Pretty routine stuff, he'd hear of an individual or group looking for an investor and put me in touch with them, I'd sometimes bring him in with me on something for a small percentage."

"So you were occasional partners in business?"

"Yes, but we never became friends. I ran across him on occasion at private parties or charity events, and there's a hard, unpleasant edge under the veneer that sometimes comes out when he's around women and drinking. Thomas told me recently he'd heard from an old friend of his in the game that Albright was involved at one time with some of the underground fight clubs. Vicious stuff by all accounts. Last man standing kind of thing." Ivery paused and took a drink.

"Then, a while back, Albright contacted me about going in with him on a real estate development. It was a very good deal, and I didn't learn until much later that he'd pressured the sellers with visits from some of his men. Perhaps even threatened them, and they ended up selling the property below market value. I didn't know about any of it at the time, but in retrospect I should have. I was going through a bad patch and didn't do my due diligence. The pills had hold of me then, and there was a woman . . ." He shook his head and set his empty glass on the table.

"Shabby excuses, I know. Two years ago, before I knew or suspected any of this, he inquired about renting my boat, and I thought, *Why not?* I don't use it all that much anyway. The party leases a slip at the yacht club, and he parks it in there now and again. He always calls in every couple of days but he's been out of touch for going on a week now. I think something bad is happening."

Clarke had no more questions and sat with Ivery for a while before he went forward and took the wheel back from Thomas. The weather remained unsettled, low grey clouds followed by short periods of blue sky, the wind up and down, the big boat rocking in the short, steep following seas. Clarke pulled out a cigar and settled back in the big upholstered seat, making himself comfortable, and took a long look around. A couple of boats on the water, nothing within a two-mile radius, and no traffic heading towards them. He sat there, half listening as the radio scanned the stations, picking up intermittent conversations, and then he heard the static-filled words *Blue Harp* and keyed in the channel. A tugboat towing a log boom bitching about assholes in pleasure boats steaming down mid-channel. Clarke held his breath and waited. And then he heard it. Toba Inlet. He looked at the chart plotter. Another thirty-eight miles to the entrance. He yelled for Thomas then reached forward and shoved the throttles ahead.

Legalese puffed out blue smoke, settled her stern deeper as the bow wave rose up, and forged ahead.

"Five hours, give or take," Clarke said.

CHAPTER 50

Albright sat in the chair in front of his dressing table in the owner's suite and stared into the mirror and reflected upon how he had ended up here. It wasn't how he'd planned it, although, if he was being perfectly honest, he would have to admit there hadn't been a great deal of planning in his life overall. It was more a case of bulling ahead and overcoming obstacles in his path regardless, and then seeing what followed on from the wreckage. But now this. Who could have predicted it? About one in fifty thousand people, they said. Up until this happened, he had considered himself one of the favoured in life. Bad shit happened to other people.

He brought his hands up in front of his face and inspected them closely. They looked perfectly normal, apart from the fact that they were no longer reliable and subject to failure at delicate tasks. Case in point, trying to fasten the bloody tie he planned on wearing to dinner. What should have taken less than a minute had taken five times as long and almost required another shower on completion.

ALS. Lou Gehrig's disease. Average lifespan after diagnosis three years, prognosis fatal. Wham, bam, thank you, ma'am! He was fucked.

That was one short year ago, and now here he was. Up shit creek, or, to be more specific, Toba Inlet. But same difference. He could still appreciate irony.

He reached over and cranked up the stereo and Wagner pounded out into the room. It was all he listened to since he'd embarked on his own personal Götterdämerung three months earlier. He'd read the story, apocryphal no doubt, but it should have been true, about Hitler in his bunker at the end lying motionless on his cot for hours while the stirring triumphal music blared from speakers around him.

Albright suddenly swept his hair down over his brow, put his finger crosswise under his nose, screamed "*Sieg Heil,*" and shot his clenched fist out at the image before him, and the mirror cracked and shattered. The off-kilter man in the shards grinned back at him in bits and pieces, some eyes lower than others, the teeth scattered every which way, and he wondered if he was going insane. The thought didn't disturb him as under the circumstances it might be argued it would have been mad not to, at least a little bit once in a while. The man in the mirror agreed with him, nodding brokenly along with his logic. Everything was relative, now more than ever.

He almost felt bad about Clint and Travis, who had always stood by him and served him so well for such a long time and were now caught up in his end-of-life maelstrom. But needs must when the devil drives, as his daddy, that hypocritical old bastard, used to tell him. He needed them, so they got to share in his final act. All in all he felt that he'd done reasonably well so far in settling scores and evening things up before his departure from the world. Newcombe, the accountant, and then the lawyer, not quite done yet, but ready and waiting down below for the last round. That part was disappointing, he'd hoped for a grander finale from Sullivan. After listening to the lawyer's boasts for all those years, you'd have thought he would have performed better. Oh well, he'd given him a few chuckles with his fancy footwork and bobbing and weaving. What was it Tyson had said? Something about everybody has a plan until they get punched in the face. Now there was a man he would have loved to go up against. Could have learned a few things there for sure. And maybe he could have taught Tyson a few things too.

Albright grinned at the thought. Speaking of women, that skinny bitch Cat who'd snubbed him, and her weedy boyfriend were all that remained to him now, and that was certainly disappointing. He'd hoped for so much more. But he was sure that if he thought about it long enough, he could still make it interesting. Some combination in the ring perhaps, he was still up to that. He hadn't lost much strength yet, his workouts had helped there for sure, regardless of what the doctors had told him. They knew nothing about him, he wasn't like the rest of them. But his coordination was beginning to go. He had tripped on the stairs going down to the engine room on his last visit to check up on Sullivan before managing to catch himself on the handrail. Clint had given him a sharp look but hadn't said anything. He wondered if the brothers suspected anything. He thought they might. They had been a little chirpier than usual with him during the last few weeks, and dead set against this current junket involving Jared and Cat.

It wasn't what he had hoped for. His preferred exit plan would have been to hold a splashy party conference on board the *Harp* complete with special guests, reporters, and TV cameras and then just blow up everything in a spectacular *Endkampf Blitzkrieg*. Unfortunately, since his diagnosis and his sometimes erratic behaviour in the months that followed, he no longer had the clout to get the bigwigs aboard. The fuckers all had that acute political knack of sniffing out the first drops of blood in the water (to be fair, he had thrown a few buckets overboard with some of his recent actions), and they were quickly peeling away from him. Although the hypocrites were still more than happy for him to go out on the money trail and earn some dollars for the party with his spellbinders.

It was annoying, but he supposed you couldn't really blame them. In their place he probably would have done the same. So he'd taken what he could get. Sullivan, and Cat and her boyfriend. He would have loved to have gotten hold of that superior little shit Ivery as well, but that hadn't worked out. To think that at one time he'd almost felt sorry for him, stuck in his wheelchair with the ape-man pushing him around. And now look where the two of them had ended up. Ivery would carry on and maybe even improve his life a smidge, whereas he — superior in every respect by any measure — was toast. Well, at least he'd gotten one in on that harp player — the one the little bastard had been romancing until Clint and Travis visited her. The last he'd heard, she was in a Swiss asylum. He wondered if Ivery knew what had happened to her. He doubted she'd contacted him; romantic relationships were the last things she'd be considering for a while. For a pleasant few moments Albright daydreamed a fantasy wherein he and Ivery were ranged side by side in their wheelchairs on the afterdeck and he was telling him about harp lady and then he reached across and grabbed Ivery and his wheelchair and raised them high over his head and —

The intercom rang and Albright picked it up and listened.

"Right," he said. "I'll be down in five."

CHAPTER 51

The wind had settled into the southeast and was holding around fifteen knots. The glass was low but relatively steady and hadn't moved the last time Danny had given it a rap on the way by in one of his endless trips with the bucket of water. They had run out of gas for the trash pump sometime during the night, and the manual bilge pump by the tiller that Joseph worked while he steered had finally died. A broken piece of glass had miraculously climbed up inside the hose and slashed its membrane, rendering it useless.

It was fitting, Danny thought bitterly. The last remaining thing on board *Arrow* that bore any relationship to modern technology was dead and gone. Now they had no engine, no depth sounder, no GPS, no radar, no radio, no lights, no pumps, no galley stove — the lids had popped off and it had filled with rainwater blown through the open companionway — and no head, although now the whole bloody saloon could be called that — and no rest. It had been twenty hours now since they had anchored the *Annie J* in a sheltered cove in behind Lasher Island and started out on their miserable journey. The beautiful, warm, dry, homey *Annie J,* in which they would have been making their comfortable way north at a relaxing five knots, eating hot meals and sipping on whisky as they adjudicated the weather forecasts from their comfortable seats and let the GPS and the autopilot do their work. But no, that would have been too fucking easy. They had to take the cold, dark, wet, miserable, leaking and possibly sinking, creature-comfortless, bloody old sailboat. But with Joseph, protest was useless. Danny couldn't recall ever winning a point.

There was a muffled thump against the hull and a loud crack from topside and then a sudden lurch and *Arrow* tilted under Danny's feet and he lost his footing in the gloom and measured his length in the filthy water once more. The bilge floorboards were loose and floating, and the ones that remained in place were grease-covered skids. Danny stepped into the deepest part of the bilge, where the useless pump lay, and painfully barked his shins against it. Crossing the saloon was like trying to navigate an ice rink with your eyes shut. A constantly moving and tilting ice rink. But *Arrow* was down by the bow and the water pooled the deepest and had to be collected there, and the hazardous trip back and forth was a necessity. If she had been down by the stern, which would have made sense as that was where her weight and breadth were greatest, he could have bailed from the cockpit with the bucket on a rope. But that would have been too easy, and nothing about *Arrow* was easy at the moment.

But he was gaining. A lot of the original water inside *Arrow* was fresh water that had entered from the holes in the deck during the rainstorms that had occurred before they found *Arrow*. The first thing Joseph had done after finding her was shut off all the thru-hulls. When Danny arrived, the two of them had tacked sailcloth over the holes on the deck and the forward hatch, and rain was no longer a problem. Although she was still taking on some water, the rate had slowed enough that Danny could keep up now and even take the occasional break.

Danny regained his footing, refilled the bucket, and lurched towards the companionway stairs. He was too exhausted to even curse. He threw the water out into the cockpit, then climbed out on deck for a break. The first thing he saw was the jury-rigged sail billowing forward from the stump of remaining mast. They were running almost straight downwind — although running was a misnomer in this case, crawling would be a more appropriate word. Danny thought they might just be making two knots in the gusts. He doubted they'd make a knot if they had to beat to weather, that is, if sailing upwind was even possible.

He'd been slammed up against the mast support on a sudden list and had felt it give a fraction. Reaching up to the through bolts on the top plate, he'd found water squirting through. Something had changed in the mast connection, and it was impossible to do anything about it at the moment. Tacking could shift everything loose those final few degrees to the point where the mast ripped right out of the deck and toppled over the side. They were already pretty much a raft, albeit one with a scrap of sail and some steerage. Any kind of a headwind would finish the job and they'd become just another drifting piece of flotsam. Or jetsam. Whatever. Was there even a difference?

Danny took a long look around. The rain had almost stopped now, but at midday it was still almost dark, the visibility shut down so much by the low clouds it was like sailing in a flooded crypt. Joseph sat by the tiller, his arm moving occasionally under the blanket as he steered, an unlit pipe clamped between his lips. A half-filled bottle of rum, some wrapped sandwiches, and Sinbad rested on the seat beside him. Danny slumped down beside the dog and took a long warming swig straight from the bottle before biting into a sandwich. He wasn't hungry, and the cold, damp food didn't taste particularly good, but he knew he would need the energy. It was going to be a long hard night. He didn't know exactly where they were at the moment but they had to be getting close to the Redonda Islands. They'd plotted them on the GPS when they took their last fix from the *Annie J* before they left it behind on its anchor. The warm, dry, comfortable *Annie J,* with the enclosed wheelhouse and cook stove and hot meals and dry bunks and navigation aids and . . .

Joseph spoke.

Danny said, "I don't know for sure. Maybe. I think I'm holding my own for now anyway. Do you know where we are?"

Joseph pulled a chart out from under the blanket and looked at it for a long time before he pulled a stub of pencil from his pocket and marked a spot three quarters of the way down the channel that passed between the Redonda Islands. Danny stared landwards and thought he could make out a thickening in the gloom that could be shore. If Joseph was right, they had managed twenty-six miles in fourteen hours. About what he'd figured. The beacons were few and far between this far north, but Joseph would have a good idea of where he was. He'd been navigating the waters along this coast in canoes and fishing boats since he was a young man. Annie had an old framed black-and-white picture of Joseph in a Shaman headdress at the bow of a war canoe taken when she was a young child, and you'd swear to God it had been shot by Edward Curtis. So he was probably damned close to right about where he was. Danny was less certain that Joseph knew exactly where he was going.

So he asked him. Joseph looked at the chart for a long time without replying, his eyes half closed, the pipe forgotten in his mouth. Danny thought he'd drifted off to sleep and was about to prod him when Joseph opened his eyes, reached down, and put his finger on a spot on the chart north of Desolation Sound at the intersection of two meandering, hazard-filled inlets. He tapped one and then the other and shrugged.

A lot of options, Danny thought. Albright could be twenty miles up inside any one of three inlets with dozens of anchorages, although Joseph had already indicated how they would determine exactly which one. One of the longest afternoons of Danny's life had been spent wandering Gastown as his mid-century modern obsessed girlfriend searched for furnishings for their projected communal flat. That hadn't ended well, and now it seemed he was on the hunt for teak furniture once again. What goes around comes around. He finished his sandwich and stretched for a minute and then picked up the bucket and headed back down below.

CHAPTER 52

Cat and Jared followed the two men into the saloon and seated themselves at the dining room table where Albright sat waiting for them. The ship's clock centred over the bar showed 1930. The place settings were formal, three forks, two knives, and two spoons. Three glasses, one for water and one each for the red and white bottles of wine that sat near Albright at the far end of the table, Jared assumed. He didn't really know for sure, and had even less notion about the tableware. Cat would know, although he wasn't about to ask her. Choosing the wrong piece of cutlery was the least of his concerns. He waited to see how the mad bastard wanted to play it.

"I've given a lot of thought to this meal," Albright said. He popped the cork on the white wine and smelled it before pouring some in a glass and swirling it around for a bit. He sniffed and then sampled it and smiled.

"Excellent," he said, and the steward went around the table and filled their glasses.

Jared thought about asking for a beer but decided against it. Keep the man mellow as long as possible. He sampled the wine. It *was* good.

"How do you like it, my dear?" Albright asked.

"It's really very nice," Cat replied. "A rich, crisp taste with just the slightest note of raspberry." Albright smiled and nodded in satisfaction.

Jared wished he had asked for beer.

Albright pressed a buzzer and a minute later a small Asian man in a chef's hat emerged from the galley and served them each a tiny dish of seared scallops.

Jared waited to see which fork Cat used before he started on the scallops.

"Maybe a hint more garlic," Albright said, his face screwed up in consideration.

"No, they're absolutely perfect," Cat replied.

Jared took the pepper mill and grated until the shellfish had disappeared under a black cloud and took a forkful. "Absolutely wonderful," he said. Albright frowned and Cat kicked him under the table.

And so it went, one tiny course after another, braised snapper with fresh asparagus, a single lamb chop with mint jelly, a thick slice of roast beef au jus dabbed with horseradish followed by the desserts, and then a plate of assorted fruits and cheeses served with port to finish up with. What little appetite Jared had vanished after the third course when Clint and Travis appeared and began setting up the boxing ring in the far corner of the saloon. They were wearing tight T-shirts, white duck pants, and runners without socks. Stripped for action. Travis caught Jared's eye and winked at him.

And still Albright prattled on about the food and the preparation of it, the difficulty of obtaining fresh supplies and finding and keeping good kitchen staff and on and on. The surprising thing was that none of it seemed forced to Jared, he seemed genuine, and it would have been perfectly palatable conversation under normal circumstances.

But this was a million miles from normal, and it was getting on Jared's tits big time. But he'd promised Cat. She'd insisted their best chance of surviving was to avoid confrontation, try to stay out of trouble, and hope their friends found them. The longer they played nice and stayed non-confrontational, she said, the better their chances were. It would be suicidal to attempt to break out on their own. He'd agreed with her at the time, but the problem facing Jared now was that as the evening wore on and the charade progressed, he became more and more convinced that it was not only he and Cat who were programmed for exit, but Albright as well. The man chatted animatedly with Cat as the courses came and went, flushed and smiling and even charming under different circumstances, but there was a *fin de siècle* tone about the whole evening, a sense of savouring things for the last time that surrounded and enveloped Albright. Although not in the least bit drunk to Jared's practised eye, Albright dropped his wineglass once, spilling red wine on the white tablecloth, and merely shrugged and carried on. Throughout the course of the evening, his voice would slur for a time and then all of a sudden be clear again. Something more than a dislocated jaw at work.

Albright caught Jared studying him and smiled and said, "Not there yet," and picked up a fork and bent it in half until the ends touched and winked at him.

What the hell? Jared thought.

But Cat suddenly caught on. A favourite aunt of hers had died from the disease, and she'd seen the overtaking paralysis, the frightened eyes as the hands curved slowly into claws, and now it all made sense to her. "How long?" she asked.

"Not long, I'm afraid." Albright wiped his lips with his napkin, rose from the table, and shoved in his chair with a nod towards the ring. "And I'm sorry to tell you that you've got even less time."

Before Jared could make a move, Clint was behind him with a gun pressed to his back.

"Do your men know you have ALS?" Cat said.

"I doubt they would even know what it is, so I haven't troubled them with it."

Cat said, "It's a fatal disease, Clint, it means he's dying and—"

Albright back-handed her and she flew across the table, dragging the tablecloth, glasses, dishes, and all with her as she went over the edge. Jared lunged at Albright and all the lights went out.

❀

When the lights came back on, he was lying face up in the middle of the ring in a puddle of water. He looked down and saw that he was barefoot and wearing a stained pair of Everlast boxing shorts. He was pretty sure that the last time he'd seen them, the lawyer Sullivan was wearing them. He blinked and saw Travis standing a few feet away with an empty bucket.

"Wakey, wakey," Travis said as he stepped forward and kicked Jared in the side of the head. "The man says it's time to play."

"Give him a minute," Cat yelled.

It's going to take a lot more than a minute, Jared thought. His head was splitting and his vision was blurred. He shook his head to clear it, and the sudden pain immobilized him. He wiped his eyes and his hand came away bloody and he wiped again and his vision cleared and he struggled to his feet and looked for Cat and found her sitting alongside Albright at the bar, her eyes blazing into his. It took a moment for him to realize she was tied to the stool, her hands bound behind her.

"To give credit where credit is due, she wanted to get right in there alongside you," Albright said. "Couldn't have that. Damaged goods."

Cat turned her head and spat at him and he laughed and drew back.

"A firecracker," he said. "My favourite kind. Well, Jared, it's finally come down to showtime. Let's see what you've got. And don't forget the rules now . . ." He paused for effect, and in that waiting second Jared took a quick step forward and kicked Travis so hard in the balls he lifted him six inches off the floor.

"There are none," Jared said before the lights went out for the second time.

CHAPTER 53

The big grizzly with the scarred muzzle and the limp moved along the mountainside on his slow, meandering way down to the beach for food. He stopped to sample some late season berries and mixed them with a decaying insect-ridden log that he cuffed open. The mixture was tasty but did nothing to satisfy his hunger, it was just an appetizer for the feast that awaited him down by the water's edge. Mussels and clams in abundance and perhaps still some of the late-run Chinook with their juicy fat-filled heads and bellies heading upriver through the shallows. It was getting late, the frost was spreading down the mountain now, a little lower every week, but there might still be some stragglers. He'd been in the area for a long time now and knew that he didn't have to rush. There was always food enough for him. He was the dominant male and didn't have to worry about being driven off just yet. The biggest of the young males had growled at him the last time he'd been on the beach a week earlier but had backed off and moved away in the end. It would be awhile yet before he faced a serious challenge. He was still a fierce fighter in spite of his damaged leg.

He raised his head and sniffed the wind. It was blowing down the inlet towards him and he filtered the individual smells out, searching for anything unusual or out of place. In the summer, man was often around on the water, sometimes even on his beach, but rarely at this time of year. He was wary of them since he'd been hurt in the time before he came over the mountain and into this place, but here it was safe. There were many of his kind on the mountain, and all of them foraged on the beaches and mud flats that bordered the end of the inlet where the river came in, and they were never bothered by man. Sometimes he'd see them watching, or smell them at a distance, but they never disturbed him, and over the years he'd grown accustomed to them and no longer considered them a danger.

He moved into a small area of brush and paused to grub up some bulbs under a spruce tree and open a ground squirrel burrow with the swipe of his paw. It was empty, only the debris of a nest and the faint scent of the litter remaining. It didn't matter, it wasn't far to the beach now, and there he would gorge himself before going back up the mountain to sleep. He heard a far-off engine echoing across the water, but he paid it no mind. He stopped to rest his aching leg and growled softly at the pain, biting at the place where the bullet had entered. It was always worse at this time of year when the cold came down the mountain, and sometimes he almost wished one of the young males would challenge him so he could take his rage out on him. After a few minutes his pain eased and he continued on his way down to the water.

❀

"It has to be them," Clarke said. "Nobody else would be anchored out here this late in the year." The blip on the radar was six miles further down the inlet, tucked in a quarter mile offshore behind a long curving outcrop of rock that gradually tailed off as it entered the water. The chart showed a shell beach that extended to the river mouth another mile further on and merged with a large expanse of mud flats. Clarke had *Legalese* doing her flat-out top speed of twelve knots, and the whole boat was shaking and vibrating nervously under the strain, as if in protest after her long rest. One of the engines had developed a slight knock, and on the other one the needle on the temperature gauge was hovering just below the red line. Clarke patted the instrument console and muttered words of encouragement. "Just another fifteen minutes," he said. "You can do it, I know you can." The port engine responded with a sudden increased clattering and then a loud bang and *Legalese's* speed dropped.

"Fuuuck!" Clarke screamed in frustration, as he pulled the locked throttles back to idle. He waited for the next shoe to drop and tried to assess the damage, but knew he didn't really have a clue. The oil pressure was abnormally low and the engine temperature dangerously high on both engines now, but at least they hadn't shut down. Not yet anyway. The gauges seemed locked in, neither rising nor falling, and after a minute he gingerly put the engines back in gear and *Legalese* moved slowly forward once more.

There was a good chance she might make it yet, but now they would definitely have to go with their second option. The three of them had been discussing plans for the last two hours, although arguing might have been a better description. Clarke had been drinking heavily, his normal reaction to stress, and the effects of this combined with his recent nautical reading had led him to the conclusion that they should "just go at them." Steam *Legalese* along the channel as if heading past the *Blue Harp* a couple of boat lengths off, and then, at the very last possible second, swing her hard over and pull up alongside and board them. Clarke's befuddled mind stumbled over concepts like grapnels and boarding ladders to go along with his plan, but he wasn't up to expressing them in credible terms.

Ivery and Thomas were for a casual idling-in-alongside approach, just another friendly voyager bumbling up to engage in harmless conversation, seeking local knowledge perhaps, and a shared drink and anchorage. They saw no reason why anyone on the *Blue Harp* would recognize *Legalese,* even if they had glimpsed her at her berth in the yacht club. Her name was on the stern and couldn't be seen from a frontal approach, it was dark and raining, and the visibility was poor. Clarke had his revolver, Ivery had brought along a pair of shotguns he used for trap shooting (a sport well suited for a man in a wheelchair, and one at which he excelled), and there was Thomas the Slab, the great equalizer. Once he was landed amongst the *Blue Harp* crew, things would even out in a hurry, regardless of any manpower advantage they might have.

Clarke thought his plan was much the better one, but under the circumstances there was no longer a choice. He was down to under three knots now, one engine clattering loudly even at this low speed, while both were redlining. Only another mile left to go, but it seemed to take forever.

Ignoring the frowns, Clarke poured himself another drink.

❀

Arrow was sinking and Danny could no longer pretend otherwise. When the water inside started to rise again, he picked up his pace, taking quick strides forward and back, hurling the water out through the companionway door, and then doing it over and over again. But the water kept rising and forced him to move further and further aft. Minutes after he'd first noticed the increase, Danny was backed up and perched on the companionway steps reaching down inside and scooping up full buckets. And still the water rose, and still he bailed faster, the sweat running off him, his arms aching. Finally Joseph reached in and touched him on the shoulder and shook his head. Danny took one last look around *Arrow's* cabin and joined Joseph on deck. He thought that they'd be lucky if *Arrow* floated for another twenty minutes.

They were well past all the spots where they might have been able to run *Arrow* up onto shore and strand her above high water. They had been heading her down the middle of the channel, intending to drive her onto the mud flats at the top end of the inlet where it might be possible to salvage her later on. Joseph tapped a finger on their current position on the chart, and Danny knew that option was long gone. *Arrow* wouldn't even make it halfway. They were currently in over a thousand feet of water in the middle of a steep-sided fjord where the depths carried right up to the steep bluffs that framed the inlet. In some places you could step off the bow of your boat straight onto shore without getting your feet wet and have a hundred feet of water under the keel.

But there were no other choices left now. They had run out of time. Joseph swung the tiller and *Arrow* made a slow, laborious waterlogged turn and ploughed towards the towering side of the inlet. Danny reached over the stern and grabbed the rope tied to the dugout canoe and pulled the little craft up onto the deck. It was a short lift now. When it floated free they would step into it and leave.

It took twenty minutes and they were still three hundred yards from shore when *Arrow* went. A long sighing exhalation as the displaced air rushed out past them and then the sound of bubbling waters flooding her as they stepped into the canoe and the boat dropped slowly out from under them. First the bow tilting down and then the stern sloping away and disappearing in eerie silence, the last thing seen her broken masts slanting forward and following *Arrow* out of sight as she slipped silently to her final resting place beneath the waters with the same grace she'd shown when she sailed above them. One last swirling circular eddy marking the spot, and then it was as though she'd never been.

When she'd disappeared for good, Danny turned away and picked up the crude paddle Joseph had fashioned from the split bowsprit and set to work with a vengeance. He thought it couldn't be much over six miles, and the wind and tide were still with them. A half hour earlier he was on his last legs, exhausted and spent, but the sinking of *Arrow* had fuelled a residue of energy and rage that lifted him up and drove him onwards. He bent his head and flexed the paddle and thought of nothing but revenge. Joseph sat in the bow, setting the cadence and keeping the craft straight while Danny supplied the power in long curving strokes, his paddle tracing swirling curlicues in the water as he drove them on.

A half mile across and ahead of them towards the centre of the inlet, running lights showed through the darkness from a big pleasure boat labouring slowly up the inlet on a course parallel to theirs, the engines erratic, the RPMs rising up and falling down, the soft knocking apparent as the sound amplified and came across the water. Engine trouble, Danny guessed, and they were trying to make it to the head of the inlet where the water was shoal enough to drop anchor. He thought they would be lucky to get there, they were barely keeping pace with the canoe.

The dog lay between the two men, his head raised and nose up as he searched the wind for scent. He caught one coming down off the mountain in a katabatic puff of wind and the hairs rose on his back and he growled softly and switched his tail.

Bears, Danny thought as they flew up the inlet.

❀

"Look at the dumb fucks pottering along," Clint said. "What do they think, they're invisible?"

"They don't know we're expecting them," Albright said, taking a slug of his whisky and espresso. Mixed together, they wired him like nothing else. Fuck Red Bull. He rolled his neck and flexed his shoulders in anticipation as he loosened up, his eyes bright, a grin stapled to his face.

"They think they're going to take us by surprise."

Albright had known about *Legalese* and the extra crew she'd taken on board since the moment she'd left the dock. He'd never underestimated Clarke and had given one of the dock boys at the club a retainer to keep an eye on *Legalese* and let him know the minute she left her berth. When the man phoned and told him about Ivery and Rodgers, Albright promised him a bonus. He never doubted for a second that they were coming for him or that they would find him. He was ecstatic. This was Albright's final gift from the gods, and it was more than he could ever have imagined. A fight to the death in the northern fjord with the snow-capped mountains witnessing the epic final battle? It was Götterdämmerung and he was Siegfried.

It was perfect that he would have a chance to defeat Rodgers, what more could he ask for? The man was a giant, one of Nietzsche's supermen, and it was Albright's manifest destiny to destroy him. He knew he could take the big man if his body didn't let him down. Albright realized now it was everything he had trained for all those hours. He could hardly wait. He was fairly bouncing with anticipation and took another long drink. A tremor shook his hand as he set the glass down and he clamped it tight with the other until it faded. The sooner the better now.

"It's the fat cop at the wheel," Travis said. "With this set-up, I think I could take him out from here. No sign of the other two. Must be back in the main cabin." When he looked through the night scope on the .308 rifle, it made the inside of the wheelhouse as bright as day. Green sunlight, it was magic.

Albright said, "Wait till he gets closer. Until he idles down and takes the boat out of gear to come alongside. He'll do it when he's within three or four boat lengths. When you take him out, she'll glide right up to us and we'll have the other two cold."

Clint rested his rifle on the cushion he'd set on the aft deck locker and knelt down and refocused it. Perfect. Steady as a rock. Christ, it was like shooting fish in a barrel.

"Ready now," Albright whispered.

The boat was four lengths away, the cop's fat face wreathed in smoke from the cigar between his teeth, his eyes squinted in concentration as he peered ahead, the stupid hat jammed down low on his forehead.

Clint began taking up the trigger slack, the cop's head as big as a pumpkin now as he saw the hand pulling back the throttles and he squeezed and—

"Now!" Albright said, and then a big brown man flew across the deck and body-slammed Clint as the world exploded in a whirl of wet fur and shining teeth and a giant wolf seized Albright's leg in his jaws. He stumbled back into the lifelines and then the man — *Loki?* — shambled forward with a shimmering knife extended before him and Albright thought he must be losing his mind just as the knife slashed across his face and the blood covered his eyes and he threw his hands up to protect himself and the wolf — *Fenrir?* — heaved back on his leg and he lost his balance and fell backwards over the rail twenty feet down into the cold black water and disappeared from sight.

❁

Clarke screamed as the wheelhouse window shattered in front of him and hornets stung his neck, pieces of glass flying everywhere, his cheek burning as he stumbled and fell, his hands jamming the throttles ahead.

Legalese's stern sank as the twin screws bit and then her bow was up and rising over the *Blue Harp's* boarding transom and her engines screamed in protest as she climbed up the long slope of the aft deck with her nose rising higher and higher as clouds of thick blue smoke rose up from the engine room. And then *Legalese* slowed and stopped and her stern sank and the water poured into her and she hung there balanced for long seconds as her engines steamed and died and she settled, slowly grinding her way back down into the water. Clarke rose to his knees, stupefied as Rodgers appeared beside him, carrying Ivery with his shotguns as lightly as a child.

"Time to go," the big man said and opened the wheelhouse door and took Clarke's arm and propelled him out onto the deck. They went to the rail and stepped down to the deck of the *Blue Harp* seconds before *Legalese's* bow tilted up a final few degrees and she slid back all the way off the rear deck and disappeared under the water below, a bubbling, oily circle that spread slowly outwards.

CHAPTER 54

Jared raised his head from the mat and looked around. He'd lain there playing dead for long minutes trying to recover and maybe get a chance to do something. But he wasn't sure if he could even stand up. When he went to take a deep breath, he almost screamed. Ribs. His whole body was one giant ache and he knew he must have taken further punishment while he was unconscious. Travis no doubt, who had left the ring and was now limping towards Cat. The brother approached her and said something and reached out to touch her and Cat flinched away as Jared managed a feeble shout and rolled over and up onto his knees and almost blacked out from the pain.

For the life of him he couldn't stand. He could barely even keep his head up. Travis turned and regarded him, shook his head, and went behind the bar and came out with a pistol. As he started back towards Jared, there was a shot from out on deck, a shriek of pain and a loud crash, the sounds of screaming engines that stopped abruptly, and then a loud splintering grinding that slowly subsided. And then silence.

Travis turned and ran towards the door when it suddenly banged open and Clint came through with his hands held high in the air. If

Travis had any thoughts of putting up a fight, the sight of Thomas Rodgers with two shotguns and Clarke beside him with a pistol pointed directly at him put them to rest. Travis dropped his pistol and put his hands up.

Jared stood amazed at the sight of the two men and knew he must be hallucinating as Joseph and Sinbad came through the door behind them. Jared dropped to his knees and held his head and then a rough tongue on his cheek, a hand on his shoulder, and the familiar scent of smoke and cedar, and he knew it was real. He started shaking and then Cat was there.

The rest of it was easy. They rounded up the remainder of the crew, all of them loudly protesting their innocence, and locked them and the brothers down below in the room where Sullivan had been confined. "Guilty until proven innocent," Clarke said. "We can sort it all out later." Thomas carried Richard Sullivan upstairs and set him on a couch in the saloon, and he and Cat worked to make him comfortable. The lawyer was in bad shape, running a high fever, his broken leg swollen and purple, and passing in and out of consciousness. His pills were finished, and Ivery pulled out a container and gave him some of his. Rodgers strapped Jared's ribs, and Ivery gave him half a pill as well, and he joined the others at the big table in a benign daze. Ivery sat in an armchair at the head of the table, and it seemed natural that he should lead the discussion.

"I'll go first," he said. "Can we assume that Albright is dead?" They'd put the big searchlight on the area where he went over and swept back and forth for half an hour after he hit the water and seen no sign of him.

"Yes. He took a twenty-foot fall, the water is cold with strong currents, and it's over half a mile to land," Danny said, shrugging. "Plus, he was badly injured. Sinbad tore a good chunk out of his leg and Joseph got him with the knife. He's done."

Joseph reached over and tapped him. Danny listened, nodding his head in agreement.

"What does Joseph think?" Ivery asked. He'd gone from an unbeliever to a disciple when Danny explained how they had found the *Harp.* "Followed the teak," Ivery had murmured, his eyes wide.

"My grandfather just wanted to apologize. He went for the neck, should have had him, but Albright's arm went up when Sinbad hit him and the knife just took a slice off his forehead."

Silence.

"Yes, well," Ivery finally said, "I don't think the statement to the police needs to be quite that specific. So we all agree that Albright is dead?"

Nods all around. Joseph shrugged and stared off into space.

Cat turned to Clarke. "What will happen with the rest of them?"

"I think the crew will probably get off, depending. If Sullivan makes it, he might be able to testify about the extent of individual involvement. Who among the crew knew that he was kidnapped and what was going on with him. That sort of thing. But it's hazy with Albright out of the picture. There's a lot of wiggle room. My guess is they get away intact save maybe for their reputations if the story gets out."

"If the story gets out? How the hell can they hush up something like this?" Cat was incredulous.

"Politics, lack of solid evidence, it's how these things sometimes go. And if we're being honest, whose interest is it really in for the full story to come out?" Clarke pointed to Ivery. "Not yours. Certainly not mine. And do you really want this story out there?" he asked Cat.

She shook her head in disbelief, but remained silent.

Danny said, "So what about the brothers? Clint and Travis. Surely they don't get to just walk away from all of this?"

"The two of them will probably do some hard time, although I wouldn't bet on it. With Albright gone, they can claim they didn't know what was really going on. They were innocent dupes, just victims like the rest of the crew. My guess is the party gets them a firm of top-notch lawyers and makes some kind of a deal with the prosecution in return for their silence about Albright."

"And what about the women?" Cat said. "My sister and all the others. Where's the justice for them? Albright is dead, but those two bastards collected them for that predator. They are accomplices in his crimes and are equally as guilty. It's not right that they just get to walk."

Clarke remained silent. He could have gone on at length about similar cases involving people in high places going unpunished, the Mueller thing south of the border being a prime example, but what was the point? Sometimes the boundaries shifted.

Joseph leaned across and spoke to Danny who interpreted for the rest of the gathering. "Joseph says he'll cut their throats and throw them over the side after Albright."

Ivery cleared his throat. "I think perhaps that might be a little drastic," he said.

"Overkill you think?" Jared said. The pill was working and he felt better than fine.

Thomas had been sitting on the couch sponging the lawyer down and now he got up and approached the table and loomed over them.

"I understand the brothers were planning on going a round or two with Jared," he said. "It seems a shame to deprive them of their fun. Seeing as he's under the weather at the moment, perhaps I might fill in for him."

Danny leaped to his feet. "I'll go and get them right this second," he said.

Five minutes later the brothers were standing together in the ring, looking nervously at Sinbad who was crouched tight up against the ropes and growling softly. Clint licked his lips and slowly reached for the bottle of water by the stool and then changed his mind as the animal's neck stretched out towards him and the growl rose a couple of notes. He was still frozen in position when Thomas appeared, bare-foot and wearing only his trousers with the legs rolled up. He was that kind of man who looked bigger with his clothes off. He walked across the room, ducked through the ropes, and faced the two men huddled together in the opposite corner of the ring.

"You might not want to see this," Jared told Cat. "It won't be pretty."

"I wouldn't miss it for the world," Cat said. She finished her drink, poured herself another even larger one, and settled in.

Thomas reached behind him and struck the bell, signalling the first round. Which, it turned out, was also the last.

CHAPTER 55

Albright staggered along the edge of the inlet, his vision blurred from blood, his damaged leg switching between fire and ice, his mind a broken shambles. When he'd dragged himself out of the water, he was so numb and stiff from the cold that for the first while he felt nothing. Only relief that he'd survived. If he hadn't come across the cluster of floats tied to the crab pots, he would never have made it to shore. He'd floundered the last hundred yards, trying to keep his head from dropping, swallowing water and then coughing and puking it out. But he'd made it. Most men wouldn't have, but he was Übermensch, a chosen of the gods.

Now, six hours later, his body was like ice, and he knew he needed warm clothing soon to survive. He'd torn off his jacket in those first frantic minutes in the water and was left with a ruffled dress shirt and thin slacks. The strip of skin sliced by the old man's knife had peeled down across his forehead baring the bone beneath and he pushed it back up and tightened the cummerbund around it again. It wouldn't stay in place and the skin fell back once more and he left it as it lay, peering out from under it, and tied the cummerbund around his neck.

His shoes had disappeared somewhere along the way and his feet were bleeding through the thin silk ankle socks.

Albright was bone-weary from his long ordeal but dared not rest. If he fell asleep, he would not wake. He had no matches to start a fire with and knew he would die from cold and exposure before the night was over. He tripped and fell in the dark and hauled himself up again. His leg was swollen and purple where the wolf had bitten him and taken out a chunk of meat the size of a quarter pounder. He'd wrapped the wound in moss and tied his suspenders around it as tight as he could. It stopped the bleeding, but now the leg was numb and unreliable and without the rude crutch he'd fashioned from a branch he would have been helpless. If only the eternal night would end. He knew he must be heading north towards the base of the mountain; the inlet was on his left, revealed by an occasional gleam through the trees. Once, he'd tumbled down the low bank and fallen into the water before he managed to crawl back out again.

He sensed the sky was beginning to lighten and daybreak was not far distant, although he had no idea of the time or how long he'd been in the water. His biggest regret was being denied the battle with the giant Englishman. To have that epic dish set out in front of him and then taken away again was heartbreaking. It was so close he could almost taste it, the man was just a few feet off and then he was snatched away at the last second and his destiny denied. Could the giant wolf have been a signal from the gods? Was it Fenrir driving him over the side and into the water towards a greater battle, a more glorious destiny? It must be. He felt it in his marrow and it comforted him.

He began to sing, roaring out Wagnerian rhythms as he limped along. It was astounding, magnificent, primeval; the original force of nature. And he was the gods' chosen one. He broke into the final glorious verse, his injuries forgotten, limping forward with his chest thrust out and shoulders thrown back, blood streaming down his brow as he stepped over and around the logs strewn on the beach in scattered jumbles.

Several of them were stacked up high across his path and he used the crutch to lever himself up and over them, his face incarnadine, his voice roaring out the paean to wild nature and primitive man. Suddenly a big-breasted flaxen-haired woman jumped up in front of him at the same moment his makeshift crutch slipped and he tumbled headlong down inside the blind. He looked up in awe at the magnificent fashioning of the gods. His eyes teared. It was Brunhilde. A true big-breasted blue-eyed Aryan blonde with long braided pigtails streaming down her back.

"Shhh, be quiet, you idiot, you'll scare them," she hissed, and Albright reached up and squeezed her breasts and screamed "Yes" as his manifest destiny enfolded him. He had reached his final destination here in the valley of the gods, and Brunhilde was waiting for him. How could he have ever doubted? He was Siegfried, and he was the chosen one. Chords from "Ride of the Valkyries" crashed through his mind.

And then a small person in a fur-trimmed leather coat and lederhosen and an alpine hat with a feather in it sprang up from beside her. One of the hammering dwarves. He saw the brow flap fallen, the bare bone and mad eyes beneath, the blood streaming down the crazy man's face.

"*Mein Gott,*" the dwarf said.

"*Jawohl,*" Albright said, and struck him senseless with the crutch. He took the man's coat from him, he was shaking from excitement and the cold now. It was barely half his size and he threw it aside in disgust. His golden-tressed woman stared at him, open mouthed. Albright grinned at her and rolled his eyes. They would mate now and she would warm him. He took a step towards her but suddenly he heard the magic ravens of Odin croaking and scolding in the distance. Huginn and Muninn were summoning him. He turned towards the noise and squinted under the fallen flap of skin. The blood was running freely from his last fall and blurred his vision but he could see now that there were more dwarves spread out along the beach. At least a half dozen and none of them much over four feet tall. And the gods be praised. All of them were wearing fur coats. Perfect. Brunhilde would sew them together for him.

Albright tried to sneak up on them but his damaged leg betrayed him and he stumbled over the logs and crashed down once again. He cursed under his breath, but the nearest dwarf didn't move, he hadn't heard him fall. He pushed himself to his feet again and limped forward, holding his breath in anticipation, concentrating on moving silently as he closed the distance. He couldn't run with his bad leg and would have to creep up to get close enough to finish him. The dwarves were dim-witted, but they were fast. This one was hunched over and poking at something now, grunting like an animal. He was short, all right, but damned broad in the beam and Albright thought his fur coat would fit him just fine. He was warmer already with just the thought of it. And then the dwarf stood up and moved away a few paces and Albright thought, *My god, he's not one of the dwarves, he's a giant, he's even bigger than the Englishman. And look! He has the same limp as me! The gods are fair and just!*

He lurched into a shambling run towards his glorious destiny, a broad smile on his face now, and as he got close the fur coat turned and faced him and Albright's smile turned into a toothy grin as the grizzly ripped off the remainder of his face with a swipe of his claw. Then he bit off Albright's head.

The German tourist who had been recording it all on her iPhone fainted.

CHAPTER 56

The day started miserably with the loading of a delirious Richard Sullivan onto a chartered floatplane with a medic on board that flew in at first light. The lawyer had a high fever and his leg was black and swollen and the unspoken consensus was that he would lose it. The medic gave him a massive dose of antibiotics and shook his head with a grave look.

The trip back down Toba Inlet to the site of *Arrow*'s sinking was equally miserable. The southeast wind had picked up and brought a soaking slanting rain along with it and they were bucking tide as well. Jared stood alone at the *Blue Harp*'s rail regardless of the weather. He'd barely spoken since Joseph showed him the cross he'd marked on the chart of Toba Inlet. When they reached the site of the sinking, Clarke ran the boat in and stopped directly above *Arrow*. The screen showed they were in two hundred and sixty feet of water. With the state-of-the-art sonar and the thirty-two-inch display, they could see *Arrow*'s outline clearly. She was sitting almost upright on the bottom, facing towards the side of the inlet.

Jared came into the wheelhouse and looked at *Arrow*'s profile on the screen for a few minutes as if memorizing it and then went back out on deck and leaned against the rail and stared down at the water once more. After he left the wheelhouse, Cat took some pictures of the screen.

"Could she be raised?" she asked Danny.

"Probably, all it would take is money. The Brits got that old warship up in the eighties, and she had been sitting underwater for over four hundred years. But what would be the point? You'd be salvaging a worthless hulk. And if you were rich enough and insane enough to raise and rebuild *Arrow* to her original standards, what you would end up with is the marine version of the hundred-year-old axe. You know, the one that's had four new handles and two new heads replaced over the years. I don't know what the actual cost would be, but it wouldn't be cheap. Not at that depth. Insurance companies pay out rather than repair in cases like this, it ends up costing them less. Not that *Arrow* was insured anyway," Danny said.

Cat nodded and went down and joined Jared at the rail. She put her arm around him and raised her umbrella so it sheltered them both. She wasn't sure he even noticed. After waiting for a few minutes, Clarke realized that no one was going to come and suggest it was time to leave so he took matters into his own hands. He put the boat into gear and moved slowly out from the shore and down the inlet, just idling along as he thought things through. He was in no rush to get back to Vancouver where he knew things were going to quickly get complicated for him on both a personal and professional level.

He dreaded telling Merlynn about what had happened to *Legalese* and his part in it. Beyond that, Clarke knew that collecting on *Legalese*'s insurance was going to be a nightmare when they learned who was driving the boat when it ploughed into the *Blue Harp* and sank. The mere thought of sitting in the witness box under questioning about his nautical expertise had him in a cold sweat. Court martial scenes from old naval movies rolled in an endless loop through his mind. He realized he was driving everyone nuts with his constant questions when Danny handed him a pair of ball bearings from the engine room.

Clarke dialled Merlynn's number, hoping that he wouldn't get through. No such luck. She was happy to hear from him and said that her grandkids were on the mend and she'd be flying back in a day or two. She loved the twins dearly but they were a trial at times and she looked forward to returning home. Merlynn said she'd promised them a week on *Legalese* next summer now that the old girl was whipped back into decent shape. Maybe a trip back to Desolation Sound?

Clarke took a deep breath and plunged in. To his surprise Merlynn was amazingly nonchalant about the loss of her old boat. She told him that she or one of her daughters would have copies of most of the photos in the boat, and there was nothing on board her that couldn't be replaced. Furthermore, *Legalese* had been a constant expense and worry for her since Ralph died and it was almost a relief to see her gone. As for the insurance claim, she was up for a good court battle and didn't need the money in any case. (Clarke didn't know whether or not to believe the latter, but it became moot that evening when Ivery asked him to obtain the name of *Legalese*'s insurer and assured him there would be no problems with the claim. Clarke, who suspected that all the people in the top one percent were somehow connected, and often in league against the rest of them, was relieved but not surprised.)

After swearing Merlynn to secrecy he briefed her on the fate of Albright and his crew.

"I wish I'd been there to see the fight," Merlynn said wistfully.

"You'd probably have been disappointed. It was more like an exhibition, didn't last very long." Clarke figured about three minutes. Put another way, two forearm shivers, two body slams, and a helicopter and a double slab to end it. The latter was a career first for Thomas, he had told them afterwards. The only other highlight was when Clint flew out of the ring and Sinbad got him by the ear. By the time Joseph could intervene the ear was off, but he managed to retrieve it before the beast could swallow.

"It's mainly cartilage you know," Thomas had said as he sewed it back on. "Chances are it's as good as new in a fortnight."

Clarke said goodbye to Merlynn and peered out the pilothouse window as he jogged the *Harp* around a drifting log and considered his next move. Everyone had been too excited, too drunk, or too depressed to coordinate an account for the police the previous evening, and they'd decided to wait until the next day to get their stories aligned. That was the easy part and Clarke foresaw no difficulties there. Neither was he concerned about the testimony of Clint and Travis. It would be several days before they were in any shape to be interviewed, and by then the party would have their team of defence lawyers arrayed around them with wet fingers in the air testing for the political winds. The brothers would be . . . encouraged, for lack of a better word, to go along with the plot line that caused the least amount of turmoil for the party. What did trouble Clarke was the regular crew of the *Blue Harp* presently under lock and key. How much did they really know about what had transpired with the lawyer Patrick Sullivan? He would have to interview each of them individually and make a decision about how to proceed from there. He knew it was tip-toeing along a thin ethical line, but landing in Vancouver with the situation unresolved was not an option. The ensuing shitstorm of publicity would ruin them all. The problem was taken out of his hands when Ivery casually informed him over lunch that he and Thomas had met with the captain and crew while Clarke was putting in his long shift at the wheel. He said that none of them had known anything about a kidnapping, and they had all signed statements to that effect.

It had been further agreed they would be signed off in Vancouver with handsome down payments on their severance packages, with the balance of the money to be paid out over the following two years. Clarke thought some people might consider that arrangement a bribe. Ivery said that the exit interviews had been conducted by Thomas in one-on-one meetings where he took down everyone's personal information including next of kin and wished them all happy lives. Clarke was secretly impressed that Ivery managed to relate all of this with a straight face.

None of it troubled him overmuch. Albright was dead and the brothers would do some time. How much was questionable given the leverage they had, but a few years at minimum, so that was some justice. One of them would have a limp for the rest of his life and the other a crooked arm barring extensive reconstructive surgery. You won some and you lost some.

One last thing. Clarke called the police chief on his private number and reported in. The conversation was short, and the early retirement buyout offer was thin, but Clarke was all over it. He didn't have that long to go anyway, and it beat the hell out of all the other alternatives that were presented to him.

CHAPTER 57

Jared had just turned eighteen the last time he'd seen the old house from the back seat of the police car taking him to serve his two-year sentence. It was smaller and shabbier than he remembered, with gravel along one side where his grandfather parked the Sunday-go-to-church car and the old work-truck that leaked oil. The big red Dutch barn sat wide hipped two hundred yards further on; a long and scary walk for a young boy on a dark winter's night. Jared gripped the worn skeleton key in his hand. Silly to think inanimate objects could contain emotions like fear and dread.

He pulled out the papers with the official stamps and witnessed signatures. On top was a note scrawled in shaky handwriting.

Jared. I'm so sorry. Forgive me. Be happy.

A signature scrawled underneath. *Betty?*

He still found it hard to believe. He'd been told a hundred times that he would never inherit, that the property would pass on to the commune, just one more lash in the old man's whippings. But his grandmother had defied her late husband when she called the lawyers near the end of her long illness. She had given instructions that Jared not be told about her decision until she'd passed. The lawyer raised his eyebrows in judgment when he told him this, but Jared remained silent. He'd think about it all later.

A car came over the crest of the hill and the real estate agent pulled up and slid gracefully out of the German luxury sedan that defined her success. A tall good-looking redhead in her forties with a warm smile and a strong handshake.

"The old homestead, huh? I'm Sally Trenton. Pleased to meet you. Sure you want to sell? Seems like a pretty nice spot. I'm told it has good grazing and an excellent well."

"I'm sure."

They went down the slope to the house, and she told him about comparables that had sold within the last year. When her firm got the listing from the lawyers, they told her that the neighbouring farmer had made an offer to the widow when her husband passed. Sally said she'd contacted him and it was low, he was only interested in the property for its acreage. She told Jared the number and said he would do quite a bit better if he waited for a buyer who intended to live on the property.

Jared unlocked the door and stood aside for her. He took a deep breath and followed Sally in and everything was just like he remembered. He went past the living room with the two stuffed chairs facing the TV, one of them deeply pocketed where the old man had sat and watched the church channel, and continued on upstairs to his room. They had taken down the pictures, the bed and desk were gone, and the old chest of drawers in the corner was empty. It was like he'd never lived there.

He went back downstairs and found Sally standing in the middle of the kitchen alongside the ash table with the high-back chairs.

"Some nice old furniture," she said. "My partner has an antiques business. She'll make you a good offer for some of this if you're not planning on keeping it."

"She'll need to pick it up today," Jared said. "It will all be gone by tomorrow."

Sally made the call and they walked over to the barn. The value of the listing was mainly in the land, she said, but the old barn was a plus for the hobby farmer types who would be attracted to the offering. The house needed a lot of upgrading but could be a candidate for renovation for some buyers. After a walk around the property Sally suggested an asking price a hundred and twenty K above the farmer's offer. Jared said he'd think about it.

When they arrived back at the house, Sally's partner was waiting. They settled on a lot price and Jared helped the women load up their van and trailer with some of the old dressers and the harvest table and chairs. It was getting dark when they finished. The McClary kitchen stove was nickel plated and charming but burned out inside and not worth the trouble.

He watched them drive away, then climbed into his rental and headed for the motel he'd checked in to after he left the lawyer's office. The one with the bar three doors down.

❀

Jared had set the alarm early so he'd have plenty of time. He popped a couple of ibuprofen and washed them down with the remainder of a can of warm beer sitting beside the bed. After a quick shower he packed his knapsack and checked out. He stopped at a co-op station and bought gas and a large can of Clamato juice to go with the beer from his motel fridge. When he reached the farm, he parked at the top of the slope and looked down at the old house and thought about the ten years he'd spent there with his grandparents after his mother and father died. He sat in the car for an hour, drinking beer. After his third he called Sally and told her he would take the neighbour's offer for the property.

Then he opened the trunk of his rental and took out the gas cans and walked down the slope to the house.

CHAPTER 58

"That much?" Danny was incredulous. In all the years he'd known Jared he might have heard him mention his grandparents half a dozen times. And now all this money.

"Yep. Less a few thousand for cleanup at the site. The realtor is arranging for a bulldozer to come in and do some grading and levelling where the old house stood. There was a fire."

Danny regarded Jared thoughtfully but let it go. "So what are your plans?"

"I thought I'd like to take Cat on a trip later on. We're thinking about flying to French Polynesia and chartering something to cruise around in for a few weeks. She's never been to the South Pacific. Maybe you and Jordana could come out and join us for a while, and we'd get to try out one of the French Cats. See how fast we could get her going. Twenty plus knots is not unheard of in the right conditions."

Jordana was the high-flying real estate agent Danny had originally contacted to discuss some of the options at Annie and Joseph's old address. Since her release from hospital, their mother was uncertain about returning to the old property with all its recent bad memories and her sons were considering building a spec house on the lot that she and Joseph could sell. One thing had led to another.

"She's always busy, but I could check when you firm up your plans and give me some dates. I'd have to drop her phone overboard within the first hour, of course. Her monthly data bill is higher than my monthly rent; I think she must have her ear buds plugged in fourteen hours a day. I keep waiting for her to ask if she can leave them in when we have sex."

They were sitting around the *Annie J*'s table, sipping hot rum on the coldest day of the year to date, with snow in the forecast. Sailing in the South Pacific sounded like a hell of a fine idea.

"You said later on for the trip. I guess you'll be having too much fun looking around for a new sailboat to leave town just now, huh? I want to come along and check out some of the eye candy with you. I'm really excited for you," Danny said.

Jared smiled weakly.

"A brand-new Beneteau or Hanse or even a lightly used Catana is well within your reach now," Danny said. "Or a Wauquiez Pilot. Something around fifty feet. Just think, laminated go-fast sails, big self-tailers, electric furling, a cockpit enclosure, a beautiful smooth-handling leather-wrapped wheel instead of a clunky old wooden tiller; hell, two leather-wrapped wheels, one on each side for opposing tacks. Why not? They're common now on the big cruisers. Instrument pods, an open transom, electric dinghy mounts, a remote-controlled anchor winch." He paused for breath.

Jared fiddled with his watch, stared out the window, sipped his coffee.

Danny was relentless. "And never mind all that sweet sailing stuff. Can you just imagine living aboard on something like that? It would be a palace in comparison to what you had before. En suite staterooms with giant double beds, leather upholstery in the saloon, a big fridge and freezer with an ice cube maker, AC for warm days, hot water heating for cold ones, Bluetooth sound in every stateroom, and in the cockpit, a great big beautiful—"

"I'm flying up to Desolation Sound next week and meeting a guy there," Jared blurted out. "He's a salvage expert and we're going to look at raising *Arrow*. I've sent him all the info along with the screenshots Cat took of her lying on the bottom. He says given the depth it will be tricky, but she's sitting well and it should be doable with a good weather window. Deep sea divers, air bags, we'll lift her and get enough pumps going to make the tow across the inlet to the logging camp on a flat day. Maybe need a sling under her tied off to a companion boat on each side. Then we crane *Arrow* onto a barge, block her up and chain her down, and move her to a boat yard. Maybe Port Townsend. Lots of wooden boat people there."

"That sounds stupid expensive."

"It's not cheap, but I'm playing with house money here." Jared intended to use the windfall exclusively on *Arrow*. If there was anything left after all the work was completed, he'd donate it to a charity; the sooner he was rid of the money, the better. It had felt wrong taking it, but the thought of his grandfather rolling over in his grave about the spending of it made it seem almost okay. "I got hold of that East Coast shipwright who did the repairs on *Arrow* in Papeete. He's back home now and I think I can talk him into coming out here to supervise the work."

Danny sighed and shook his head. "And then, Jared, when all is said and done, what you'll end up with is an insanely expensive old-fashioned, outdated marine version of a hundred—"

"And if I hear any more talk about old axes from anyone," Jared broke in, "I'll take that red one hanging up over there by the engine room door and bury it in that person's skull."

CHAPTER 59

Clarke lounged in teak on the canvassed-in afterdeck of the brand-new forty-two-foot Ranger tug, adjusted the visor of his brand-new captain's hat, and took a sip of his martini. It was, as always, perfect. He reached across and touched glasses with Merlynn and looked around the anchorage. Not many boats this time of year.

"I suppose we should get going soon," he said with little conviction.

"Why?" Merlynn queried.

Clarke had no answer. Why indeed? He supposed his mild guilt was the residue from thirty-four-and-a-half years of punching the clock and showing up for work, day after day, week after week, and year after year. It was hard to get used to the idea that that part of his life was now over and he was completely free to do with each day whatever he chose. Putter off to the next anchorage, lay in bed, fool around, any combination of the above. Even after three months, it still seemed a bit sinful to him.

His friends on the force whom he saw at his weekly poker sessions were full of gloomy predictions: "The novelty will wear off and he'll miss the excitement of the old days" — that one was a non-starter, most of Clarke's days had been as dull as dogshit. "He'll end up drinking himself to death" — oh well. Etcetera, etcetera. Clarke suspected most of the doomsayers were married men who would no longer have a valid reason to leave the house. He glanced over at Merlynn who now had her hat tilted down over her eyes and the ever-present book dropped onto the table beside her. In another five minutes she'd be asleep.

He had never been able to nap during the day and read little apart from the occasional bestseller. He could list a dozen other ways in which they differed, diet and lifestyle for starters. Perhaps the difference between them was the magic ingredient in their relationship. That, coupled with the fact that neither of them were zealots. She didn't try and get him on the early morning treadmill, and he didn't press her to join him in cholesterol breakfasts. In three months together on and off the boat they hadn't had one real argument. Not since she'd bought the Ranger with the insurance settlement, registered it in both their names, and presented him with a *fait accompli*. Clarke, after a long losing battle, drew up a will for the first time in his life and bequeathed his share back to her. He watched Merlynn for a while, a smile on his face. Maybe he should try and get into the nap thing. He leaned back and closed his eyes.

EPILOGUE

Some of the buses were old and travel worn, but Joseph didn't mind the rattles. They'd all been warm and comfortable and he'd loaded his tablet with movies for the trip. And he liked old. It had been fifteen years since he'd visited his relatives on the prairies and they'd been badgering him to make the trip. They'd all journeyed out to the coast, they nagged, and it was past time he came out east to them. Joseph thought it was like the people in hell wanting the people in heaven to come and stay with them, rather than the other way round, but it had been good to travel through the high mountains and across the prairies one more time. It might be his last chance.

It had been a fine journey, five weeks of travel and visiting with his people, some of whom were old and he might not see again, but he was looking forward to returning home. Just one final visit to make and one last thing to do. He turned away from the window, leaned back in his seat, closed his eyes, and half dozed while disjointed memories of the last months sparked and flashed through his mind. Sometimes the present interwove with the past into one long tapestry winding all the way back to his childhood in Haida Gwaii, and sometimes even further, all the way back to the Creation, when he dreamed he was Raven Child and put the stones in the water. When that happened, it was better than the movies he downloaded from the Pirate Bay.

He woke up when the bus stopped at a small town for supper. Joseph was disappointed that there had been no dreams this time. Although maybe there were and he didn't remember them. He thought that happened sometimes, and it was too bad. He picked up his knapsack and went into the diner with the other passengers. While he waited for his meal, he pulled up the map and notes on his phone. Annie was out of hospital and staying with Jaimie while she recovered, and she had coordinated the different routes and lay-overs with the friends and family he visited. His daughter was always looking for things she could do from her bed, and organizing Joseph's itinerary had occupied her for days. If it had been left to him, he would have just showed up. He hadn't told Annie about his last stop. She would worry.

He finished his supper, meat loaf, one of his favourites. This one was on the bland side, but that was why they invented hot sauce. He paid his bill and left a five-dollar tip for the waitress, whom he didn't blame for the meal's shortcomings. It was a block to the Seven Eleven Motel he'd looked up online, and he took a ground floor room and paid for it in cash using a dead cousin's name on the sign-in sheet. He napped and watched TV until nine o'clock when he slipped out of the motel and walked a mile back down the road to the lay-by where the crew cab waited.

"Welcome back," Erin said. He reached across the seat and hugged his grandfather. "You sure you have to do this?"

Joseph said that he was. He lit his pipe one last time as the truck carried him down the road back towards where it all began and thought about what lay ahead. He didn't relish any of it, but debts were owed. It needed to be finished.

A half hour down the road, Erin looked at the odometer and slowed.

"Should be getting close," he said. It was another quarter mile before their headlights lit up the hand-lettered sign in front of the gravel road leading off into the bushes.

Welcome to God's country
PLENTIFUL
6 miles
Jeremiah Albright Prophet

Joseph got out of the truck, swung his knapsack up onto his back, and opened the rear door. Sinbad jumped lightly down beside him, and the two of them moved off into the darkness.